I0670479

BEAUTIFUL
DANGER

BEAUTIFUL DANGER

GABRIELLE DELACOURT

Beautiful Danger Book One of The Crimson Crows Series
Copyright © 2021 by Gabrielle Delacourt
First Edition | Paperback Publication Date: February 22, 2022
ISBN: 979-8-9856984-1-1

All rights reserved. No part of this book may be reproduced, distributed or transmitted in any form or by any means, including information storage and retrieval systems, without written permission from the author except for the use of brief quotations in a review. This is a work of fiction. All characters, names, and events in this book are products of the author's imagination. Any resemblance to any place or person is simply coincidental.

Copy Editing by: Jessica Schmit @readsbyjessica and Alexa Thomas @thefictionfix
Paperback formatting by: Books & Moods Internal
Page Design by Lexi @readsbylexi
Cover design by: Emily Wittig Designs©
Published by Gabrielle Delacourt

READ THIS FIRST!

This book contains elements of intense grief and loss, mentions of sex trafficking, graphic violence, panic attacks, endometriosis and talks of reproductive issues, verbal, parental and physical abuse, explicit sexual content and lots of swearing. We are each in control of our own content consumption, so please, if any of these things make you feel uncomfortable, do not continue.

In addition to these things, I want to note that my editors are I only human. Mistakes will happen. Please, if you find any mistakes, don't report them to amazon as it will remove my book. Instead, email all errors to gabrielledelacourtauthor@gmail.com.

To stay in the know on all things bookish, release dates, giveaways and more follow me on social media @Gabbiesshelf on Instagram and TikTok.

Lastly, I want to thank you for being here. Thank you for taking a chance on me and my beloved characters. I hope you enjoy.

xx Gabbie D.

To the two most important men in my life: Stone, Look!
I fucking did it!
Dad, you're my hero.
You loved me first, and I'll never
thank you enough for that.

Playlist

Bitter (feat. Trevor Daniel) – FLETCHER & Kito

Tennessee – Allen Rayman

Hurt Like __ – OSTON

Present – Khalid

this is how i learn to say no – EMELINE

Demons – Alec Benjamin

what it means to be a girl – EMELINE

Love Is a Bitch – Two Feet

Fall In line (feat Demi Lovato) – Christina Aguilera

Beautiful – Viigo

The Devil is a Gentleman – Merci Raines

High Heels – JoJo

Drunk (And I Don't Wanna Go Home) – Elle King, Miranda Lambert

Main Attraction – Jeremy Renner

Belladonna – Ava Max

Call Out My Name – The Weekend

12 Rounds – Bohnes

Ipo Lei Momi – Keali'i Reichel

So Pissed – Bohnes

In Your Arms – ILLENIUM, X Ambassadors

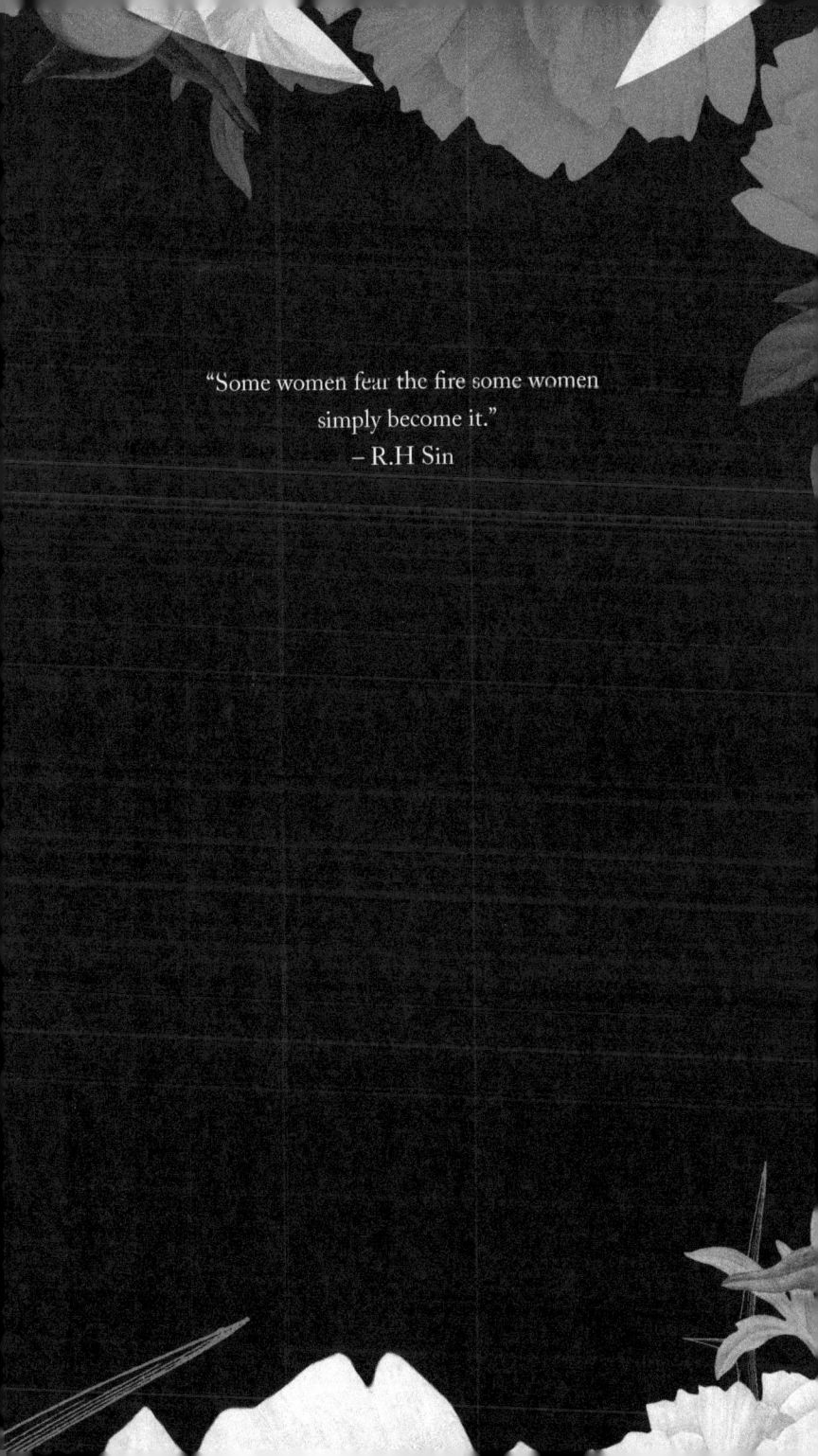

"Some women fear the fire some women
simply become it."
– R.H Sin

PROLOGUE

Briar

Hushed voices fill the small space of our tiny apartment. Knowing my mom, she probably has one of her shitty boyfriends over for an afternoon fuck.

"Hey, mom! I'm home! Did grandma call yet?" I feel better announcing my presence. That way I can avoid as many awkward encounters as possible.

Tossing my bag onto the kitchen table, I make my way to the small cabinets to grab a glass of water. When I turn, glass of water in hand, a stack of papers catches my eye. An official copy of a will rests on top. Leaning in, my hand grazes the top of the stack, trying to see what's underneath. I set my water down on the table, rifling through the papers. A knot forms in the back of my throat. This is my grandmother's will.

Why would she have my grandmother's will? They haven't spoken in two years.

I didn't understand for a long time, but my grandfather was what one would call "old money". He was born into a family of early industrialists who saved and invested their money and built a substantial amount of wealth for themselves. No one would have known by looking at him. He was one of the humblest men I ever met.

I shuffle through the papers again, trying to figure out if what I'm seeing is true. An old will, a new will, and various official forms and letters are all there. *What the hell?*

A codicil is attached to the old will.

"As of January 20th, 2021, Mrs. Wilhelmina DuPree hereby strips Ms. Iris DuPree of all inheritance and rights granted under this will and testament. In the presence of the necessary and appropriate witness and official persons, Mrs. DuPree has named Ms. Briar DuPree sole heir of all inheritance and rights granted under this will and testament."

Excuse me, what?

Did I just read that correctly? She removed my mother and named me the sole heir. Fear washes through my body. If these papers are here, that means that my mom knows and has hidden it, or… My stomach drops, leaving behind rolling nausea.

Soft moans come from the bedroom down the hall. *Disgusting.*

I reach into my bag and pull out my phone. Scrolling through the contacts, I find who I'm looking for and push the phone icon with my thumb. The phone rings for a moment and then almost simultaneously a soft ringing comes from my mom's room.

It's just a coincidence.

The ringing continues until it sends me to voicemail.

"Sup. You've reached River. Leave me a message. Or not." *Beep.*

The sound of the headboard making contact with the wall grows louder. Moans waft through the small apartment. *Gag.*

I end the call and decide to try again. Mom's sex life is the last thing I care about right now.

A dial tone and then ringing from the room once more.

Heat spreads through my body like wildfire. I push the feeling down, taking deep breaths, keeping my face stoic and calm.

My feet carry me through the kitchen, and down the short hallway to the bedrooms. The closer I get, the louder and more intense the moans become.

"Yes!" a female voice screams. "Like that! Yes!" Her breath comes out in harsh pants.

The door is cracked open. The most sickening and malicious part of this all is that they know I'm home. This feels like it's all part of some sick plan. I creep to the door, feeling the fire in my blood, growing hotter with each step. My hand grips the cool metal of the doorknob. With minimal effort, I push it open further and fix my eyes on the sight before me.

Bare ass is the first thing I see. The muscles of the naked man flex as he thrusts. His hand rests against the wall, the other is gripped around a leg resting on his shoulder.

I stand in the doorway, staring slack-jawed for a moment. The words are caught in my throat, unable to claw their way out.

My mother's eyes meet mine, her gaze full of hate. She holds my stare as he pumps into her fast and hard. A wicked smile spreads across her face a moment before she throws her head back, releasing an ear-piercing scream. The man grunts a few times, making rather unpleasant noises as he comes. His body collapses on top of her in a sweaty heap. *Fucking disgusting.*

I clear my throat, finding that it's the closest thing I can get to talking at the moment.

Blue eyes drift across the room, eventually meeting mine. *River fucking Nolan.*

"Hey, babe," he says, his tone sarcastic. Who is this River? This is not the man I thought I knew.

"You fucked my mom," I say, my voice quiet and surprisingly steady as the rush of emotions roil in my stomach. "You—What kind of boyfriend does that?"

"Oh honey, he was never yours to begin with." My mother lies on the bed, not bothering to cover up. My body instinctively turns away from her brazen nudity. I muster as much anger into my voice as possible when I turn my head back to look at them.

"Why?"

"To see the look on your face when I took what was yours." She sits up, wrapping a sheet around her body. Her legs swing from the bed and she stands. "Call it a parting gift."

My mother saunters to her closet to dress. River moves to the edge of the bed, pulling his pants on. I move my head back toward my mom—watching her every movement closely. It's likely they see nothing wrong with what they just did. The jingle of River's belt draws my attention back. There is absolutely no shame on his fucking face. Not a trace.

"Parting gift?" I choke out. My hands clench at my sides. Sweat pools in my palms, my fingers numb from clenching so tightly. I force myself to swallow the knot in my throat.

"A goodbye—of sorts," she clarifies, without actually clarifying anything.

"What do you mean goodbye?" My body begins to shake as

adrenaline courses through me. Every cell in my body is screaming at me to run. To get away from this place and never come back.

"Well, if things don't go the way I want them to tonight, I have no other option but to choose the best route for me. It was always going to be me in the end, darling. You were never important and anyone who tells you otherwise is lying." She deadpans, lifting her arms above her head and tying her bleached blond hair into a bun.

Run.

"What do you want?"

"I want what's rightfully mine." She spits at me, the hot liquid splattering my face. It stings my skin where it lands—the DNA of utter betrayal. I lift my hand to my face and wipe away the sticky saliva. "I had a contract drawn up. A will. When you die—which you will—everything becomes mine. But I would rather we come to a more *peaceful* conclusion."

The bed creaks as River stands to his full height. Together, they begin to close in, coming at me from both sides. Why did I stand here so long?

Run.

Instinctually, I take a step back, my body connecting with the wall.

My mother sneers. "All you have to do is sign over everything to me. That shouldn't be a problem."

I shake my head a few times. The will is ironclad. How could she pull something like this off? "No?" Her face draws up into a pout, eyebrows meeting. Her head cocks, taunting me. "Well, maybe you need the proper motivation."

The breath is knocked out of me as River's hand slams against my throat and I feel the smooth metal of a gun against my temple.

Hot tears stream down my face as I strain against his iron grip, trying to move my head away from the gun. I whimper a pitiful noise. *You are a fighter.*

"Are you going to sign the papers?" River's hot breath on my cheek burns my skin. I shake my head, the tears flowing more freely now.

"Please, just let me go." My body shakes beneath his touch, the lack of air beginning to fog my head. Gripping my neck, he yanks my body from the wall, shoving me toward the kitchen. With the gun now pressed into my back, he leads me to the table and shoves me into the seat.

"Sign it," my mom spits, moving a paper in front of me and slapping a pen on the table. River moves the gun to the back of my head. The click of the safety being released sends a shudder of fear through me. I pick up the pen and sign quickly.

Run.

"There. Can I please go? I swear I'll leave and never come back. Just please let me go."

My mother takes the paper from me, nodding to River. "Sorry, babe. You're a liability now."

Bang.

A loud scream tears from my lips as the gun goes off into my back.

Pain bolts through my body. Hot liquid pours down my back—I know it's blood without even looking. My body aches for me to move. To get away. My face, wet from tears, meets the hardwood of the table. It's as if my body is giving me one last push because one moment I'm slumped in the chair and the next I'm launching myself at River. My nails tear into his skin as I scream, before River's fist connects with my face. In one violent hit, I feel the bones in my face breaking.

You will fight. You will survive. You will not die.

I dig my nails into his flesh harder, more violently, sending as much force into my hands as possible. He screams, trying to rip my hands from his mangled face. If I survive this, my bones will mend, but he will be left with the scars of this day forever. Blood drips down my arms as my nails maul and slice.

Pulling myself from him, I try to sprint to the door but I'm too slow. River's arms wrap around my middle, sending burning pain through me as his body slams against my wound. All I can do now is scream. My mind battles for consciousness. The pain radiating through me and the loss of blood is getting to my head. Dizziness overtakes me, my breath slowing. River's hand comes to my mouth to finish the job, but instead, he finds my teeth. I bite him—hard. I fall to the floor, my knees slamming down in a painful crunch.

I'm going to die.

I'm on my stomach, fluttering in and out of consciousness. A bang sounds through the room.

Did River shoot me again? There's no pain. The front door crashes to the ground with a reverberating thud. A larger body in the doorway is blurred by my quickly fading vision. Am I hallucinating now? More figures rush in behind, their voices all muffled.

The large one rushes to me. At least his proximity allows me to establish that he is, indeed, a real-life human. His brawny arms lift my head, holding me to him. He murmurs something, but I can't quite make out what he's saying. I blink, trying to force my eyes to focus. Blinking again, his features become slightly less blurry. Deep green eyes stare back at me. They're the color of jade. The kind of jade my father left behind in the form of a bracelet. My mind wanders, struggling to focus. What was I thinking before? His eyes...

His hand strokes my hair. "Stay with me," he says, his voice a smooth velvet. My body shivers, my breathing slowing. "Stay with me."

My eyelids feel heavy and I swallow around a knot in my throat.

It's hard to breathe now, my body seizing in pain. As my eyelids droop further, the jade eyes stay locked on mine.

"Stay with me." The world goes black, a peaceful calm washing over me as I disappear into the darkness.

There's power in knowing that you're going to die. What is life other than a timeline with an eventual end? Varying in lengths, some are longer or shorter than others. For me, I always expected death at an early age.

Now at twenty-two, I'm staring death in the face. I masked my pain with optimism. As I wane between life and death, I have a decision to make—to stay or to go. There's little holding me here to the world. I've got no friends, no family I care about and no one that cares for me.

Like a movie, I run through the memories of my last moments to distinguish between fact and lie. My ex-boyfriend cheated on me with my mother. Fact. My mother wants me dead so that she can claim my inheritance. Fact. I'm going to die alone. Lie.

Tender eyes gazed into mine a moment before the world faded into a blurry haze. His arms tightened around me, keeping me grounded, and looking at me like I was worth something. The way he pleaded with me to stay with him…it did something to my heart. I don't know him, but now I want to.

I should feel pain, but I don't. I feel almost nothing. I can't move, my body not responding to my pleas. Run. Move. Do anything.

Do I have something to live for—a reason to stay here? This can't be the end of my story—no. It is only the beginning. I'm slipping further, but I refuse to let this be the end. I feel the fire lighting within my soul, my will to fight stirring.

My fight is not over. This story is only just beginning. Death will not be the end of me. Beauty will come from this tragedy.

Everything beautiful has a dangerous side. Animals, flowers, and people can be dangerous and deadly. After the fucked up life I've lived, my goal is to become one of those beautiful but deadly things. My mom used to call me a monster for ruining her body, her life, her relationships, but what she doesn't know is that she's the reason for this monster, now coming to life within me. Takes one to know one, right?

TEAGUE

PROTECTION DUTY. THAT'S all this was supposed to be. I'm a watchdog, a spy for my Don, Killian Ruarc. I have felt *nothing* for years. I am a robot, a slave to my profession. I'm to watch her and report back, never to intervene. What is this feeling, this warmth and madness that my body experienced when I realized she was in danger?

I've always watched from afar. This woman is an anomaly. I don't know much outside of what I've seen and the things within her file, but I've grown to know bits and pieces of her. Despite her circumstances, she is always kind, sometimes to a fault. She goes out of her way to help the old lady cross the street or stops on the side of the road to rescue an abandoned puppy. It's these things that have drawn me to her.

The world is an ugly place. My world is full of darkness and danger. People are evil and cruel without a care for others around them. Maybe it's the way that she seems to love life despite her terrible mother, but maybe it's the sheer draw of her. I'm completely enamored by someone I don't even know. I wonder what it would feel like to be on the receiving end of that kindness and those smiles that light up a room.

Everything inside of me is on high alert as I pace through the hospital lobby. She's alive. That is all that matters. Before I ever had time to know her, she could've been taken away from me. I can only wish I will ever be so lucky to *know* the whirlwind that is Briar DuPree.

Hospitals are the bane of my existence. Killian would have my head if he knew I was wandering the halls like a guard dog watching over *her*. For someone who wanted a security detail for her, he is eerily hands off. Each time something happens, my orders are to withdraw and return to home base, but nothing like this has happened before; this obsession of mine almost slipped through my fingers.

My phone buzzes in my pocket, but I ignore it. My eyes are trained on the door, waiting. In my line of work, hospitals are a no-go. A member of my own team is medically trained which has come in handy more times than I can count. Bullet wounds nearly always lead to the involvement of cops who stick their noses in places they don't belong. Their questions will come back with answers they don't want to hear. Thankfully, I have a contact, Kris, who was able to come to New York. She promised me no questions asked and the best care possible for Briar. We don't need an investigation on our hands, and I still need Briar off the radar. For now, I'm the only one that knows she exists outside of a select few people.

I watch each person who comes and goes from her room. This dark cloud radiates from me and every person who walks by me moves faster to get away from my tangible rage. My fists and jaw are permanently clenched as my mind pictures all the things I wanted to do to Iris and River. How dare they harm her! Although I feel anger towards them, most of my anger is aimed at myself. How could I have missed it? How did I not see the signs?

What angers me most is that they slipped from my grasp. This rage within me has no escape. That is most dangerous. My monster needs release, yet I stay here, against Killian's orders.

Killian.

I whip out my phone, scrolling through the list of notifications I've been silencing. I can only ignore them for so long, so I hit the call button, the line ringing once before a gruff voice answers.

"Teague. Report." Killian's clipped tone sends a fresh wave of irritation through my body.

"She's alive. Not out of surgery yet, but my source says any moment now."

"Good." The line is silent for a moment, and I wonder what is going through his mind. "I want to bring her in, but I need her to come to LA of her own fruition for this to work. She needs to want it, *need* it."

"What are your orders?" I ask.

"Keep watching. Iris has gotten out of control, and I can't afford to risk losing Briar. She's too valuable." He's never said something like this before. I don't understand why suddenly she is valuable to him. It's best not to question him, so I grunt an affirmative. "Once she's healed, I'll arrange for travel to LA. Guide her in that direction, Teague, but remember, it must be of her own choosing."

I nod, although he can't see me. The line clicks off and I hold my phone another moment, thinking. Direction and guidance. How can I even think about guiding her to LA when she's not even out of surgery yet? I decide to put it on the back burner for now. This situation has gotten much more difficult than I had expected. It continues to grow harder and harder not to intervene, to not pull her close to me. That fact alone is dangerous. I must remain in the shadows, silently watching.

A door opens, drawing my attention. I see Kris walking toward me, her face neutral. I rarely see her in a white coat.

"She's out of surgery and waking up now." Her hand grips mine, giving it a tight squeeze. My face remains indifferent, but the relief I feel is instantaneous. She observes me a moment longer before speaking again. "I've never seen you like this," she says. "You care about her."

I say nothing. I don't know Briar well enough to care, but a part of me knows that's not the truth. After so many days of silently watching, guarding, a part of me begs to protect the woman in that room, to lay my life down for her.

"I can see the fight behind your eyes." Kris sighs. "Whatever you need, I'll do it."

"Get her to California," I say. "I'll do the rest."

She nods, taking my hand again. I want to pull away, but she tightens her grip. Her eyes bore into mine. "Do you want to see her?"

"No." *I can't.*

"Teague," she says. "Back when we dated, I could never figure you out, but enough time has passed for me to reflect on those years. I flew here for her because you trust me enough to help her. So trust me enough when I say that I don't know who she is to you, but if you're like this, she must be someone great." She looks down at her badge, adjusting it so that it lays flat against her chest before turning around and walking away.

Is she someone great? Who is Briar DuPree? I'd like to know.

There's darkness within me. I've fought it for a long time until I became one with the darkness. For years my life was littered with violence and death. It's not just a job, but a lifestyle. That all changed the moment she stepped into my life. She doesn't know it yet, but she started a war within me.

My mind and body fight, one begging for violence the other seeking normalcy, balance and light. The closer I get to her, the more terrified I become. *The monster within me reacts, calling to her like a puppy begging to be pet. I am an untamed beast, yet something about her calms that war within me. She is light in the darkness. I fear what I will become without this monster. Am I redeemable? Do I deserve her kindness?*

There's darkness within her, too. I can see it. Maybe, just maybe, our stories will overlap. Only time will tell.

1

Briar

ONE YEAR LATER

T he sound of voices pulls me from my internal spiral of rage and hate.

It's been a year since I moved to Los Angeles from the Bronx. My heart is still healing from the betrayal I experienced. Secrets were tossed around like currency, one of those secrets destroying the life I once had.

I came to California with little more than a small suitcase and a mission to find someone who didn't want to be found.

Little did I know that I'd end up becoming a thief for the rich and powerful. My clients are usually nameless, faceless people who seek power. If I have learned anything in the past year, it's that money and power make people do stupid shit. Like betray their daughter and sleep with her fucking boyfriend.

Feeling for my gun strapped to my thigh, I saunter into the ballroom, melding into the flow of people. My emerald-green gown hugs my body, my red-bottomed stilettos clicking lightly on the floor, creating a calming rhythm. A member of the staff approaches with a tray full of champagne flutes. Grabbing a glass, I bring it to my lips, sipping the bubbly liquid. It sends a flame through my body, warming me from the inside out. Liquid courage—exactly what I need right now.

An uncomfortable shriek spills from the speakers, jarring guests out of their champagne-fueled revelry. A woman standing on the stage shifts awkwardly as she adjusts the microphone, assuring that our eardrums remain intact.

"Uh—hi!" She chuckles uncomfortably. "I mean, welcome, everyone, to the 25th annual Raven Charity Gala."

Her voice is an unpleasant, grating sound that makes me cringe. The guests are becoming increasingly absorbed by her, so I take that as my cue to move.

Swiftly weaving through the crowd, I find the hallway that leads to the back of the stage. Thankfully, my small stature and unthreatening appearance renders me essentially invisible. If someone questions me, I can easily feign being lost.

Unlike my usual jobs, this one requires two parts. My client had an item stolen from them and entered into this auction illegally. In my purse, I hold a replica of the stolen artifact to leave once I take the real one. To justify the switch, my client needs physical documents proving the sale of stolen artifact. When I looked over the building's layout and studied the routine of the museum curator, I noticed an opening to the main office, letting me in and out with the documents without being seen. I knew the museum would station multiple guards at the entrance of the auction displays. What I didn't prepare for was the sheer *number* of guards at this event. My source promised that the guards would move when the auction starts, leaving a small window of opportunity for me to slip into the office, grab the papers, and get the hell out of dodge. Hopefully, my source is right.

Peeking down the dimly lit hallway, I see the path is clear. I rush down the hallway, sneaking through the oak door at the end of the hall and closing it behind me. Leaning against the door, I take in my surroundings. The room is large for an office. The museum curator is certainly a collector, that's for sure. All four walls are decorated with rare artifacts, paintings, and knick-knacks: everything from Van Goh's *Sunflowers* to African tribal masks.

The buzz of music from the ballroom reminds me that I'm on borrowed time. I go to the filing cabinet in the corner, pulling open the first drawer. My fingers graze the files, searching for the one I need. When the first drawer is unsuccessful, I move on to the next and the next. As I'm searching, a file catches my eye. *Ruarc, K.*

This isn't relevant to the job I'm on, but it's important enough to pause my search. I pull out my glasses from my purse and shuffle through the file's papers, the built-in scanner in the frames sending copies straight to my laptop. The top paper has a handwritten address, like an afterthought, or someone's scribbled notes. Folding it up, I decide to stuff it into my bra—for safekeeping, or maybe mischief if I'm feeling up to it.

Finally, I locate the file I need and scan its contents, making sure to double-check the information. I only need one copy to make my client happy, but it doesn't hurt to take precautions.

Stuffing the file back into the cabinet, I close the drawer softly and exit the office. The piercing voice from earlier travels through the hallway, signaling the beginning of the auction. The first item is a handcrafted 400-year-old Lunula necklace replica. I mean, I wouldn't pay $100,000 for a replica, let alone… well, maybe anything. *Rich people.*

Growing up, my mother struggled to feed me. I saw the way that poverty affects a family. I wish I could count on one hand the number of times I went to bed with my stomach panging with hunger. Now I am surrounded by people gathering to flaunt their wealth and fluff their egos as they "donate" to charity. Ironic, isn't it?

My steps are swift as I slip back into the lingering crowd unseen. Making my way through the clusters of people, I sweep my gaze across the room for my client. I really don't understand the need to meet so publicly, but I don't question the choices of those who pay me. Deciding that the nearby balcony is the best option, I waltz up the stairs, attempting to reach higher ground, away from the rich and famous. This pony show of the finest regalia makes me cringe; there are less ostentatious and obnoxious ways to be rich.

The balcony gives me a better view of the room, but looking across the hundreds of faces, it's proving to be more difficult to find Mr. Nolan than I expected. I'm used to the secrecy, particularly in my line of work. But this level of security for a reasonably easy job makes me regret agreeing to it. My usual clients are powerful, yes, but usually harmless. Out of desperation, I accepted this job without looking into it much, but maybe I should have. Why does the name Nolan sound familiar? *Think, Briar.* A creeping feeling sneaks up my spine, my instincts warning me that maybe I've made a mistake taking this job. I fear I am dealing with someone who makes death look like an orgasm on the kitchen table.

Out of the corner of my eye, I see a man round the corner of the staircase. Turning to look at him, my lips part and the thumping of my heart rocks my body. Standing frozen like a deer in headlights, I stare at him. As he makes his way over to me, his face is inscrutable. I lean back into the railing of the balcony, feigning indifference, my face now devoid of emotion. With each step he takes toward me, my heart races faster. The world feels as though it's moving in slow motion.

Three more steps.

Two more steps.

One more step.

I can feel him moving behind me until he positions himself by my side.

"Hello," he says, his voice caressing my ears, sending a pulse of fear through my body. He leans into the balcony railing, his tall frame dwarfing me. What was once a stunning face is now one that haunts my nightmares. His scarred face is a memory of that night. He bends closer to me, and I try my best not to react. "Briar."

The unexpected use of my given name sends a shiver through my body. "Briar is dead. You made sure of that," I say, venomously, trying to mask my fear. I take a deep breath, feeling my body begin to tremble. My mind races, trying to think of an escape route. A deep laugh escapes from my throat. *Fucking nervous laughter.* This job will have to wait. I have to get away. "How did you find me?" I covered my tracks as best I could. Not changing my name may have been a stupid move, but they got what they wanted…at least I thought they did. Why now? Why come looking for me a year later?

I need to get away from him. I need to protect these people from him. "That's not important," he says.

"Briar, darling. I would like to know how you survived."

My guardian angel. I want to say the words, but I can't speak. My body continues to tremble in his presence, and I scold myself for it. *Don't be weak.*

"Why are you here?" I force the words out of my mouth.

"Isn't that obvious? You're here because of me." He leans in closer to me, resting a hand on my waist. His teeth brush the top of my ear. "It was so easy to lure you here. You're predictable, darling. You've gotten sloppy. If you were trying to hide, it's no longer working." His finger trails along my back. "As for how I found you, well darling, I have friends in high places. You're not the only one who can find people who don't want to be found."

It takes every drop of my willpower not to react in the way my body is telling me to. The utter repulsion I feel from his touch causes my stomach to roil. I try to pull away, but my attempt only makes him tighten his grip on my hip. "Now, now, none of that, darling." His hand comes to my chin and yanks my face up to look out at the ballroom. "Do you see that podium?" I whimper, feeling his grip tighten when I don't answer. "The stage is rigged with a bomb. You don't want all these poor, innocent people to get hurt, do you?"

I shake my head, feeling a tear slide down my cheek. "What do you want?" I breathe, my voice barely a whisper.

His nails drag across the skin of my arm. A sharp pain suggests he's cut me somewhere, but his hold on my face restricts me from looking.

A wicked grin spreads across his face, his head tilting as he speaks. "You're wasting time asking stupid questions, darling. You know the answer to that already. Your mother and I... Well, we want you dead. You have something that belongs to us, and the only way we can take it is if you're…"

I shudder at his intentionally drawn-out pause.

He slides a finger down the side of my neck. "Dead."

"I signed over everything to her." My breaths are coming in quick gasps now and my vision is starting to waver. *No. NO. Now is not the time for this.*

"It's all hers now," I whimper in his grasp.

"See, that's where you're wrong. Your darling grandmother was a smart woman. And seeing as you have no other living relatives, the only way for the inheritance to pass to her is if you're..." He waves a hand toward me, prompting me to finish his sentence.

"Dead," I say through my teeth.

He nods, smiling coldly. "Now you're getting it."

Before I have time to react, the sound of fist meeting flesh reverberates through my head. I feel someone's firm grip on my arm pulling me to the side. My body crumples from the anxiety coursing through me. I wait for the impact of my body hitting the floor, but the feeling never comes. Powerful arms hold me up, keeping my body from falling into a heap on the floor.

The edges of my vision start to darken. That fucker knew this would happen to me—he knew how much I fear him, and he used it to his advantage. Sucking in sharp breaths, I try to regain control of my body, but I can already feel that I'm fighting a losing battle. A soothing voice invades my racing thoughts.

"Briar," he says. I move my head to find the source of the voice. Quickly, I find the eyes of my savior.

Feeling myself slip further into my darkness, I manage to get out one word before the world disappears around me.

"You."

2

Briar

Thrashing screams wake me from my nightmare. It takes me a moment to realize the screams are coming from me. I'm tangled in soft sheets, my body clammy. As I suck in sharp breaths, I use my arm to wipe away the night's sweat. The room is shrouded in darkness, requiring more time for my eyes to adjust. Feeling smooth fabric on my arm, I glance at the bandages wrapped around my bicep.

Sitting up, I take in my surroundings. I'm in a hotel room. My hotel room? How did I get here? This all feels too familiar. I rub my eyes as I think. When I was shot a year ago, I was deposited in a hotel similar to this, except this time, I'm actually living out of a *name.* I swing my legs off the bed and pad to the bathroom. My body feels weak and heavy. The effects of a post-anxiety hangover, no doubt. My eyes gaze around the room and zero in on my belongings in the corner, meaning the person who rescued me knew where I was staying.

Catching a glimpse of myself in the mirror, my fingers trail over the bruising on my neck from River's grip. My eyes fall to the large white shirt that drapes over my body, erasing any trace of the curves that lie beneath.

He dressed me.

The caramel strands of my hair hang loosely over my shoulder. The golden color is accentuated through the twists of waves and curls. Yesterday's curls still hold and I stare at them. All that work, just for them to disappear under the warm streams of water. The long strands of dead cells remind me of my mother and her ultimate betrayal. Grabbing the bottom of my shirt, I pull it up and over my head, leaving my naked body exposed. I grimace, feeling the ache in my bones. When I reach the tub, I turn the water to scalding hot, waiting as the water heats. Stepping under the falling streams of hot water, I let it wash away the revolting memory of River's hands on my body. I watch as the touch of him and every other disgusting feeling on my skin spirals down the drain. The light scent of lavender fills the bathroom. My muscles relax, tensions leaving my body. Sometimes a shower is like magic.

When I am certain I'm clean, I turn off the water and step out onto the cool tile floor. The skin of my bare feet sticks to the floor, making a sucking noise with each step. I run through the steps of my routine: brush my teeth, brush and dry my hair, then braid it over my shoulder, and apply a small amount of makeup. Each simple, mundane task clears the fog from my head.

Making my way to the dresser, I spy a bottle of aspirin resting on a folded piece of paper that I didn't notice before. Oh no.

I dress quickly in black ripped jeans, an emerald green shirt, and a leather jacket. I pull socks over my feet and slip on my leather boots. When I am fully dressed, hair dried, and makeup on, I reach for the bottle, opening the cap and dropping a pill into my hand. I swallow the pill and grab the note.

2707 W 48th Street.

The note is handwritten. *So what... he rescues me, drops me off, and leaves me a note? For what?* I chuckle to myself.

Suddenly, something clicks in my head. I groan. *I'm fucked.* I rush from where I'm standing and rummage through the pile of clothing on the ground. My breath quickens, the panic setting in. I reach for my purse and dump its contents onto the bed.

FUCK!

The paper I shoved into my bra last night is gone. I rush to the side table and pull out my laptop from the drawer. I lightly tap the keys with my password and groan. They deleted every scanned file from last night. I release a sound of frustration.

Are you freaking kidding me?

In the top right corner, a notification slides into view. I see red. *Disk Not Ejected Properly.*

That fucker took my shit.

Fine. If he wants to play this game, let's play. Strapping my holster to my back and sliding into my jeans, I shove my gun into the holster and push my jacket over it. I grab my wallet and slip it into my jacket pocket, my keys jingling in my hand. Grabbing my black motorcycle helmet, I rush out the door, slamming it angrily behind me.

The motorcycle roars to life under me, sending a thrill through my body. I've always wanted to ride a motorcycle. One of the first things

I did when I moved out west was to learn to ride. When I finally got my official license, I took my savings to the Harley Davidson dealership and purchased the bike that I had been ogling for weeks. My girl, Darcy, has taken good care of me since. I stroke a hand over the black matte finish of the body before pushing up and riding out of the hotel parking lot.

My GPS GUIDES me to a large cement building on an empty street. Of course, the area is a dead zone. The street is home to ample warehouses and empty, unregistered buildings. I glance around, looking for any cameras or security precautions. No doubt there are some, somewhere, but none are catching my eye. I shove the kickstand of my bike down, balancing so that I can dismount. The building spans the length of most of the street, interconnected like a strip mall. The middle building is decorated with a cement arch, painted with the words Ruarc & Co. Well, at least I know why I'm here. Maybe they'll give me my shit back, too.

Taking a deep breath, I stride to the double doors marking the front of the building.

Um... should I knock?

Deciding not to knock and risk looking like an idiot, I push forward, revealing the dark building entrance. A gust of wind pushes my hair right into my face, obstructing my vision for a moment. When I clear the hair from my face, I pick a random direction and start walking.

The heels of my boots click on the cement flooring, echoing to the point of it being eerie. I have a feeling I just walked straight into the lion's den—or the Crow's nest. I'm sure they'd quite appreciate that.

Someone deeply clearing their throat draws my attention.

"Ya lost, little girl?" The man's gravelly voice taunts, his brown eyes narrowing as he takes me in. I'm in a mood. And not the good kind. It's time to play.

I plaster the sweetest smile I can muster across my face. I bat my eyelashes a few times before flipping my hair over my shoulder.

"Terribly," I say, raising my voice an octave or two. "Can you tell me how to find," I bring the piece of paper to my face, looking at the address again, "2707 W 48th Street?" Smiling at him again, I bring my hand to my hip. The corners of his mouth turn down and his eyebrows scrunch together.

"Can I see that?"

I extend an arm to him, allowing him to take the paper. He unfolds it rather aggressively and reads the words with a scowl.

A loud chuckle bursts from his lips. "Is this a joke?"

The corners of my mouth turn down at his question. "No?" I shift on my feet, gazing at him sweetly.

"You need to leave. Right now." He reaches for my arm, and I flinch, taking a step back. I shriek in response, surprising even myself. My eyes go wide and I clap my hand over my mouth, the embarrassment of such a strong reaction seeping in.

"Don't touch me," I hiss through my fingers. My voice is louder than intended.

The man throws his hands up. "I wasn't going to hurt you." He sounds serious.

Loud footsteps reverberate through the halls. Three large men come bounding through the halls, no doubt alerted to my ill-times scream.

"What's going on here?" the first man asks. He brings a hand to his long, full beard, drawing my attention to his face. Grabby Hands turns to the other three, but not before he sends me some angry side eye. All three men are strapped to high hell with weapons. Knowing I have my weapon, hidden from view, brings me comfort.

"She just walked in and had this note with her." I roll my eyes behind Grabby Hands' back. As the four bicker, I spy a familiar face walking up behind them. Grabby Hands extends his hand to the three men, attempting to give them the note, but before they can grab it, a pair of hands shove him aside and rip the note from his fingers. I smirk.

"I should've known," he says. His jade green eyes stare back at me, his face unamused. The men are all tall, but this one has a few inches on them. His dark hair is shaved on the sides and long on the top. Running a tattooed hand through his hair, he locks eyes with me for a moment, not speaking. We stay like that for an uncomfortable amount of time. I refuse to lose this game. Grabby Hands clears his throat, causing us to break eye contact.

Unfolding the note, he takes a moment to read it before releasing a chuckle. "Good one." His tone lacks any conviction in that statement.

"Teague, sir. I apologize for the noise. She just walked in here with the note and I tried to grab her—"

His sentence is cut short as Teague's large hand slams into the man's throat. I flinch, but quickly recover, refusing to let them see my discomfort.

Teague…. Such a sexy, villainous name. Fitting.

I should smack myself for being so immediately turned on.

"Did you touch her, Hal?" Teague's gaze is feral, deadly. Hal, which is apparently Grabby Hands' name, is white as a sheet. He shakes his head furiously.

"No, sir. She moved away before I could."

"You ever touch her, and I'll see to it that every one of your fingers are ripped from your body." His grip tightens on Hal's throat. His head tilts in question. "Got it?"

"Got it," Hal chokes out. Teague holds him there another moment before releasing him and turning to me. Hal is gasping and grabbing at his throat on the floor, but I hardly notice. Teague's eyes are so dark. The jade green that I recognized is overpowered by the darkness lingering there. A shiver runs through my body.

God, that's hot.

Almost as if he can hear my thoughts, Teague's eyes smile, the corners of his mouth turning up so quickly that I would've missed it if I blinked.

I'm going to need a new pair of underwear.

"Come with me." It was an order, one that shot right to my clit.

The men part, leaving a pathway clear for us. I hear their grumbles and whispers as we pass. Feeling their glares pierce my back, I flick my chin up and hold my head high as we walk to see the one person I have been waiting to meet for twenty-three years.

Teague leads me down a series of dimly lit hallways with cement floors. Well, this is eerie as fuck.

Our footsteps echo as we walk in silence. I try not to stare at the plethora of art hanging on the walls as we walk, but it is hard not to when Manets and Rembrandts stare back at you.

I look over at Teague as we walk. He doesn't acknowledge me, but I decide to talk anyway. "Was everyone okay? River said there was a bomb."

Teague continues walking, his only answer in the form of a low guttural grunt.

So that's a yes then?

"Did you dress me? How did you even know I was there?" At this point, I can sense my questions only piss him off. A shrill of excitement runs through me at his side eye. I can't help but smirk. Silence it is.

I don't bother asking where we're going because as soon as we round the last corner, the hallway opens into a wide open space. My eyes lock on a painting decorating the long wall in front of me. My mouth gapes at the—what the fuck would I even call this thing?

The painting—mural—depicts what looks to be a modern version of the last supper. There are several men gathered around a dinner table, but that's where the similarities end. The men are wearing suits in various shades of gray. On the table, there is… I squint as I take a step closer, not bothering to watch where I'm going. Are those guns? Those are definitely guns. I scoff, causing Teague to spin back to glare at me.

"Is that a mob version of the last supper?" I ask. *That's* ironic. He doesn't answer, instead, he just continues walking until he reaches an office door.

The door is nothing spectacular. It doesn't stand out from others in the room, which makes me worry more than I should.

"He's waiting for you." He knocks once, then swings the door open. Dramatic, much?

Taking a deep—very deep—breath, I step inside, accepting what I am about to do.

3

Briar

A pair of golden eyes meet mine through a pair of dark lashes. His face is so familiar, and yet worn from age and stress. No doubt that this job is more taxing than sitting in a cubicle and punching keys.

"Teague." He gestures to the door, "I'll send for you when we are finished. Please make preparations."

Teague nods, then quietly closes the door behind him.

"Sit." Coming from his lips, it sounds more like a command than a suggestion.

I don't make an immediate move to obey, and his impatience with my resistance starts to show, his eyes narrowing at me from across the room. His demeanor grows more impatient, his eyes narrowing at me from across the room. He jerks his chin toward the chair. With a defeated sigh, I take a step forward and plop into the chair rather ungracefully.

"Sup, dude?" I raise my eyebrow, waiting for a reaction. When he doesn't react, I huff. "What do you want?"

He frowns at me.

"Twenty-three years and you say 'Sup, dude.' Briar, I really don't have time for this." He folds his hands on the desk in front of him. "I'm really not a man you want to play games with."

Before I can help myself, sarcastic laughter escapes me. I sit up straighter in my seat, resting my elbows on the desk, and leaning closer to him.

"Oh-kay. What am I supposed to say to you? 'Hi, dad! Thanks for fucking abandoning me with my psychopath mother. Thanks for sticking a guard dog on me and saving my life what—" I look down at my fingers, counting. "—twice now?' Was that what you were expecting? I have a lot more I could say—scratch that—want to say, but what's the point?"

His knuckles turn white as he tightens his folded hands. I can see the muscles in his jaw clench through his graying beard.

That's what I fucking thought, bastard.

"You will address me as Killian. Not... *Dad*," he says with disgust, placing extra emphasis on the word. What? Is he ashamed he has a daughter or is this denial?

"I'm so beyond used to rejection. I have a habit of loving people who will *never* love me back. So I'll do you a favor and walk right back through that door and save you the inconvenience." I bring myself to a stand, ready to rush through the door. Killian sucks in a sharp breath and releases it with a huff.

"Sit the fuck down, Briar Ruarc. Or is it DuPree? Or Griffin? What did you choose?"

My gaze drifts to him. His eyes are teasing, but I'm too wound up to relax. I purse my lips, steeling myself before sitting down again.

"I don't care. Whatever I feel like that day. None of them feel like me, anyway. But my legal name is Briar DuPree since before grandma's death."

Killian's face turns sad a moment. "I'm no father, but I am sorry for your loss. I always liked that old hag. She was almost as crazy as your mom—But in a good way."

I snort. "Ain't that the fucking truth." We just look at each other for a moment in silence. I fidget as the atmosphere grows more uncomfortable with each passing minute. Refusing to let it grow anymore uncomfortable, I break the silence. "So... The Crimson Crows, huh?"

The Crimson Crows is the clan name for my father's crime syndicate, spread across California and Arizona. When I was fifteen, I discovered I had a knack for finding people who didn't want to be found and information that didn't want to be uncovered. I taught myself to code and the inner workings of a computer. Killian would kill me if he ever found out, but I hacked my way into his network and found his files. Interesting way to find out your father is a crime lord.

Of course, my mom would shack up with a crime boss. Totally her speed. I bet she saw a walking dick with money signs and jumped at the chance.

"I don't have time for small talk today. Let's cut to the chase. You and I both need something," he says. Oh, so *that's* how it's going to be.

"Alright then. You stole my files and I want them back. But there's more," I reply. He quirks a brow, looking interested now. "I already know that you have someone watching me, but I came here because

I want your protection." I lean back, crossing my arms. "My gold digging mother tried to have me killed. Twice now. And I really don't feel like dying."

"And in return? What do I get?" His eyes narrow. The time for pleasantries is over.

"Well, I know you need something too, or you wouldn't have stolen my shit and summoned me here." A ghost of a smile crosses his face. I hold my breath, waiting for the proposal.

"Work for me." Unfolding his hands, he brings a hand up to his beard, resting on his chin. My eyebrows shoot sky high.

"W—What?" I gape at him. I really need to get my ears checked. Did he just ask me to work for him?

"I want you to work for me. I don't know if you truly know what we do here, but your talents would be very valuable. I have a couple of conditions, but if you agree, I will provide you protection… and give you back your files."

The slight curve of his lips tells me that he's enjoying this, my vulnerability. He knows I can't refuse, not now. I open and close my mouth a few times, unsure of what to say. I'm sure I closely resemble a fish.

"Why?"

"Briar, I am an art dealer. I've seen some of your work and I need someone who is small and swift enough to get in and out quickly. You would have a team, of course. Teague would be the team leader, so everything passes through him first, which he will have approved by me." He strokes his beard a few times, looking around the room.

"What are your conditions?" I ask, waiting for the other foot to drop. *This is too good to be true.* He sighs. I'm not going to like this part.

"I can't send you out into the field if you don't know how to protect yourself. So you will learn to fight."

"Oh-kay, what else? There has to be more?" I push. He's obviously not telling me everything and it irritates me beyond measure.

"You cannot continue living in that rundown hotel. You will move into our designated living quarters. Everyone on my payroll has their own apartment, and you will be no exception. This also allows me to keep tabs on you at all times, ensuring your safety." Rolling my eyes, I cough into my arm, trying to break the tension I'm feeling in my body. I wave my hand, urging him to go on. He raises an eyebrow, clearly surprised at how agreeable I'm being. Or so he thinks. I know there's a catch; I'm just waiting for him to reveal it.

"I do not take this last part lightly. Once you are in, the only way out is zipped into a body bag. I will not make exceptions just because you are my daughter."

And there it is. Crimson Crows for life. I twist uncomfortably in my seat, crossing and uncrossing my legs.

"Two questions," I start. He nods, urging me to proceed. "Do I get a cool tattoo if I say yes?"

He winces at that one. I couldn't help myself. "And what happens if I say no? Oh, and a third. Do I have time to at least… think about it?" My eyebrows raise, my eyes locked on his. His eyebrows drop, his face scrunching into a scowl.

"If you want a—" he throws up air quotations like someone trying to be a *cool dad,* "—cool tattoo, you can definitely get one. Just know, they're permanent."

I'm not stupid. Of course, they're permanent. That's the whole point of a fucking tattoo.

"To answer your third question, you have until you walk out of this office. As I mentioned earlier, I am short on time today." He folds his hands in front of him again, leaning slightly towards me. "If you don't agree to the conditions, I will keep your files and call off my guard dog. Your call."

What a fucking dick. He's basically leaving me to die, and he knows it. *Real stand-up guy you found, mom.*

"Will everyone know I'm your daughter? I don't want special treatment. I have always been alone, and I prefer to keep it that way." My eyes flit to him, seeing recognition and understanding there.

"Not if you don't want them to."

Our banter back and forth is sending pulses of adrenaline through my body. I didn't come here seeking a father. In actuality, I didn't even find one here—I found something better. I found my next challenge. My next battle and my next hill to climb. *Bring it on, Killian. You want my help, I'll help you, but I won't make it easy for you.*

"I will agree to your terms on one condition."

His eyebrow raises in curiosity. "I will hear it, but no promises."

"I want a cool code name. I want to be called Raven. Not a stupid crow." I'm playing a dangerous game poking the bear. What happens next is the thing I expected the least. He laughs. He actually laughs.

"You're different than I anticipated." Now that shocks me. I am literally speechless. It takes me a moment to recover, but I scrunch my face in confusion, unable to form words. He seems to get it because he responds. "You remind me of myself when I started with the Crows. Maybe you're more like me than I thought."

"What do you mean? I look exactly like you? At least that's what…" I make a disgusted face before saying, "*Mom*, said. All the time." I spit the words out like they're made of acid.

I am what some people would call a mutt. Killian is part Irish, part Puerto Rican, and part Hawaiian. His olive skin is several shades darker than mine, as if he's spent multiple days in the sun. His light eyes are the only thing that reminds me of the Irish swimming through my blood. My mother, on the other hand, is a very fun mix—German, Jewish, and Scottish. My father's genes won out with my exterior in the end though.

Killian rolls his eyes at me, but for a moment, his eyes soften. A spark of hope flares in my chest. I immediately frown, internally scolding myself for being so naïve. I imagine myself taking the small spark of hope and stomping on it like a child throwing a tantrum. *There, I fixed the problem.*

"I have one last question. What happened to River? And what will happen to my mom?" Genuinely, I don't really care after everything. I am more hopeful that this of my life will close. The thing I crave most is to fully become someone else, find a new life and discover who I am without my past holding me back.

"River is in holding. Teague suggested we leave him there until you have a chance to speak with him. His fate is for you to decide. As for your mother, I have never been happier to have a reason to order a hit." A delighted grin spreads across his face, turning him downright diabolical. Trying my hardest to keep my face neutral, I adjust myself in my seat.

"Okay then. What do I need to do to make this official?" I ask, eager to get this done and over with.

"A handshake will do for now. But an initiation will take place once you are fit for the field. Teague will oversee everything. You will respect him like you respect me. Got it?" he replies.

I nod my head a few times. *Respect? Joke's on you, old man.* But there's no reason to vocalize that particular sentiment.

"Okay, then. Welcome to the Crimson Crows, Briar DuPree. You will see and experience some rather unpleasant things. Trust and respect are the building blocks of this clan. Everything that happens with the clan stays with the clan. Clan business is only clan business.

Teague will catch you up and teach you everything you need to know." He pauses a moment before reaching his hand out toward me.

If I shake his hand, I am committing to this life forever. There is no turning back. I have no family, nothing left for me to care about. If I choose this, I become the villain of my own story. Is that what I truly want? Killian winks at me, hand still extended as if he could hear my thoughts warring with each other in my head.

"Okay," I say, taking his hand and shaking it—sealing my fate in a deal with the devil.

4

Briar

Teague escorts me from the office and leads me back out through the narrow hallway. When we eventually make it back outside, he walks me to my bike.

"Go back to your hotel and pack up your things. I'll meet you there," he says gruffly.

I frown at Tall Dark and Handsome standing before me. He truly is a man of few words and not the most personable, either. Great, I'm stuck with a statue for the foreseeable future.

"Then what?" Questioning him is going to bring me so much life. I can already tell by the way his eyes narrow at me in annoyance. At least I can make this entertaining.

He just walks away without answering, leaving me standing alone by my bike.

Well, okay then.

Swinging my leg over my bike, I turn the key, starting the engine. A slight sinking feeling forms in my gut. This uncertainty is terrifying. I've never quite had a plan or a purpose other than to care for myself and my mom. But now... now my life and my purpose are left entirely in the hands of another. A crime boss, for fuck's sake. I sigh. Too late to turn back now.

I let the sound of the wind in my ears carry away my unease. Time for the bitch to come out and play.

When I pull up to the Hideaway Hotel, I see a black F150 Raptor parked in front of the stairwell leading to my room. Teague's long leg exits the truck, making a show of climbing out of the driver's seat. I say climb, but what I really mean is easily step because even though this truck would be considered enormous compared to my size, it looks like a normal sized vehicle next to this monster. I'm going to destroy my neck trying to see his face. It's like the world moves in slow motion as he exits the truck and turns to face me. His dark brown hair flops in front of his face before he gently flicks it away. Those green eyes are piercing, even from a distance.

Fuck.

I let out a shaky breath and dismount my Harley. When I turn back around to face Teague once more, his gaze is stuck on mine.

His eyes squint into a glare.

"Didn't your mother teach you it isn't kind to stare?" He says it like a statement and not a question.

My jaw drops for a moment before I close my gaping mouth and glare daggers. "You tell me. Do you think my mommy dearest would have taught me something like that?"

He shakes his head, then turns away from me. His long legs carry him up the hotel stairs in a matter of seconds.

Sighing, I make my way up the stairs and into my room. I am not even surprised that he had a key to get in. He is unceremoniously shoving things into a bag, clearly not willing to wait for me.

"You know I can do that, right? Also, why do you need a truck? I have literally nothing to move."

He doesn't look up at me as he speaks. "The apartment isn't furnished."

"And? I can sleep on the floor," I say. Rolling my eyes, I snatch the bag from him and haphazardly shove anything around me into it.

"You will not," he huffs. "We're stopping to pick out furniture after this."

"I can't afford that yet. It'll have to wait," I say. The zipper sticks as I try to close my duffle bag. I struggle with it a few times before Teague takes it from me and easily zips up the bag, earning an annoyed eye roll from me.

"Your father is paying. He ordered me to get you settled, and that is what I plan to do."

"Oh, you can help me get settled alright," I mumble under my breath as I walk into the bathroom to gather my things. "Settled on that dick." My voice is barely a whisper as I say it, but I regret it almost instantly.

I'm bent over the tub in an attempt to reach my shampoo and conditioner when I feel Teague's presence behind me. His warm breath caresses my neck.

"Don't say things you don't mean," he breathes into my ear. "You wouldn't be able to walk for a week once I get between those pretty legs." His hand rests on my back, sending an electric pulse up and down my spine. "But by all means, go ahead and settle on *this dick*."

The hand that was braced on the tub slips causing me to fall face first into the tub. The air leaves my lungs in a harsh *whoosh*, leaving me frozen and red in the face. Is it hot in here? I think it's way too hot in this bathroom. *Oh shit. Did I say that out loud?*

I laugh awkwardly. "Ah—oh, my big mouth. I—um. I think that's all of it."

I climb out of the tub, fisting my shampoo and conditioner in both hands. Stepping outside the bathroom door, I shake off the bottles and put them into a plastic bag that Teague handed me earlier. My legs shake as I try to walk, my brain running through every possible scenario of Teague between my legs. He walks past me with ease, carrying my single bag over his shoulder.

"Follow me to the apartment. We'll leave your bike there."

So freaking bossy.

Stomping over to my bike, I mount it—fuck. *Get your head out of the gutter.*

I settle myself onto my bike with a sigh and follow Teague to the apartment complex that will be my new home.

CLIMBING INTO TEAGUE'S truck is a whole new level of sexy. I never knew that a vehicle could turn me on, but here I am, sitting in his F150 and feeling my panties moisten over the feel of the leather seats, the smell of smoke and sea salt, and the pure feeling of power in such a large vehicle.

I could see myself loving someone who drives a big ass truck.

The drive is silent. I can't seem to form coherent sentences when I'm sitting next to Teague. A part of me says I need to be afraid of the big, bad, mafia man, but another part of me is drawn to him. It may be the fact that he's saved my life twice already. Let's not get stuck in the dicksand so fast.

Over the course of our fifteen-minute drive to the furniture department store, I learned a few things about Teague just from observing.

One: Teague drives like a grandpa when other people are with him.

Two: Teague has an obnoxiously extensive collection of CDs. Who still has CD's still?

Three: Teague is a very clean person. His car is pristine. Like, 'I could swipe my finger across the dash and lick my finger' kind of clean. It's a little scary, seeing as I am perhaps one of the least organized people when it comes to my living space. That will have to change now, though, I suppose.

"She'll take this one," Teague says, bringing my mind back to what we're supposed to be doing. He's pointing to an entire bed set sans decorative bedding. The queen-size mattress is set on a steel gray bed frame with a tall matching headboard. I really don't need all of that. The sales associate looks to me for confirmation. I purse my lips, warranting a *look* from Teague.

"What?" I ask.

"What's wrong with it?" he counters, confused and irritated that I'm yet again questioning him. "I haven't had a bed frame before... I just slept on a mattress. Or I frequented the couch when my mom had her frequent fliers over." I whisper it under my breath, with the intention of only Teague hearing. I don't know why I shared all that, but it's too late to take it back now.

The young saleswoman nearby turns to me, placing a hand on my arm in a kind way.

"Oh, honey. Let me help you." She glares at the men and drags me away to show me the store.

After an hour, she's helped me pick out a full bed set and matching furniture for my new apartment. I hate that she's spent all this time fussing over me, but it also feels nice to have this extension of simple kindness.

Teague's lengthy frame sits by the register, scrolling through his phone when we finally make it back to the front of the store. Reva—the kind saleswoman—has written a list of essential 'new apartment things,' She stalks right up to Teague, seemingly immune to his good looks and permanent frown. I've got to hand it to her. She's brave.

"I made this list with everything she still needs. I trust you will help her get all of it." She hastily thrusts the list into Teague's chest, waiting for him to take it.

He stands, towering over her, and yet she still holds her ground. I snicker at the sight of it. He takes the note and looks it over before nodding and shoving the piece of paper into his pocket.

Reva walks back to me and slips me a piece of paper as well.

"You need anything, hun, you call me, okay? No matter the time of day." She smiles warmly then begins yelling commands to the delivery guys on how to load my new furniture into the truck. I stifle a laugh at the entire scene. Two large men bossed around by a five-foot nothing woman. It's comical and yet empowering to see a woman with so much power. One day, that will be me. I'll make sure of it.

On a normal occasion, I hate shopping. And after four hours of this, I hate it even more. Back on the East Coast, I didn't have many friends that stuck around long enough to do the typical girly shopping trips, getting our nails done, and learning how to have healthy relationships with women. Part of that was me closing off the possibility and part of it was not being able to trust anyone further than I can throw them. River once told me that the next person in my life would have to take on all of my baggage. That starting over would be extremely difficult. In hindsight, I realize that fucker manipulated me, but I hate to say that over time, I've begun to believe it. Is my baggage worth the trouble? I doubt it.

Teague huffs loudly in the driver's seat. Turning my head to look at him, I shoot him a glare.

"I'll help you unload and set up. Then take the night off. We start training tomorrow," he says matter-of-factly.

Oh... Right. Training. Well, this is going to be just great. Let's hope that everything I've taught myself comes in handy. I jerk a nod and go back to staring out the window until we pull up to the apartment complex.

We spend the next two hours setting up my apartment. By the end, I am sweaty and exhausted and my arms feel like noodles. I practically crawl over to the new couch in my—*holy shit*. This is *my* apartment. My own place, all to myself. A wave of emotions washes over me. Feelings of relief, fear, anxiety, happiness all crushed into one, invade my body. Feeling my eyelids begin to droop, I wrap myself in a little ball. Sleep overcomes me without warning. The last thing I hear is my front door clicking shut as Teague leaves me to my new normal.

My eyes snap open at the sound of voices outside my door. It sounds like three voices, but I can't quite make out distinct individuals in my sleepy haze. Gazing down at my wrist, I notice it's 11 at night. I groan as I throw the blanket off my body. I freeze; I don't remember pulling a blanket over me before falling asleep. In one swift motion, I sit up and stand, seeing stars from moving too quickly. I make a show of stomping over to my door and yanking it open to see the commotion outside. Teague stands with two other people I don't recognize—a gorgeous auburn-haired man with perfect pale skin, and one of the most beautiful women I've ever seen. She is absolutely glorious. Her long brown hair flows in natural curls at her sides, her brown skin glowing like she's some angel.

Is this place just full of beautiful people?

They all turn to me at once, their eyes raking over me without any shame. No one speaks for a moment, then suddenly a wide smile spreads across the woman's face. She practically bounds toward me and pulls me into a hug.

"Hiya!" she says with a lot of enthusiasm. "I'm Ondina and I am your sort of neighbor." She points down the hall. "Two doors down. Anyway, besides the point. I brought you food because this brute here probably didn't feed you on your first night here." She bends down to pick up a box from the floor and hands it to me. I take it, unsure what to do or say. "This human over here…"

She grabs the other man by the arm and pulls him to stand in front of me. "This is Gabe. He's your other neighbor. And you know Teague is here, so the four of us rule the second floor for now."

I look at Teague now, questioning. "I didn't know Teague was staying here too." His face remains passive, just staring at me. "What are you looking at?" I ask, adding a bite to my voice.

That seems to shake him because he immediately shifts his eyes away from mine.

"Ignore him. He's not much of a talker." Ondina puts a hand on my shoulder. I smile weakly.

"Do y'all want some pizza?" I open my door wide, extending the invitation to everyone to join me. It's Gabe who reacts first. He pushes past me immediately, making his way to the bar in the kitchen.

"Yes, please." Gabe sits in the chair like a toddler waiting for food. Ondina grabs Teague's arm and drags him into the room, apparently ignoring his soured mood. "Let's eat!"

5

TEAGUE

I won't be getting any sleep tonight. I spent way too long watching Briar's lips as she ate her pizza. At one point, she caught me staring, and I just shrugged, which annoyed her more. Maybe the more I annoy her, the less she'll enjoy my company. I can't help but stare at her, though. My fingers ache to run through her golden hair that is always in a braid or wrapped in a bun. Being close to her is harder than I thought it would be. A piece of me hates myself for entertaining the idea of being anything more than her trainer, her team member, her boss. My fucked up life is dangerous. I wish I could go back and tell her to pack up and run away.

Her fucking father owns me. To disobey his order is a death sentence. I'm playing with fire as I continue to stare at her. The way her eyes light up when Gabe and Ondina ask her questions sends sparks straight to my cock. *Down boy, she's off-limits.*

That simple fact doesn't stop the fantasies of having her lips wrapped around my cock, my hands fisted in her hair... *I can't.*

I think back to the first moment I saw her. Killian has had me on her case for years, always watching from afar. Briar has always been the light in the darkness. Her mere presence is magnetic, always drawing me back in. I've wanted to intercept so many times because of that *bitch* who called herself Briar's mother. During my tenure with the Crimson Crows, I've seen some fucked up shit. I've killed more people than I care to count and I've destroyed lives just for the fun of it. Hell, my own father brutally murdered and mutilated my mother, then turned the gun on himself in front of me. Death is nothing new to me.

Gunshots still trigger me in a way that I never thought possible. I think back to the sound and my heart stopping. My body lit on fire, every possible scenario running through my head at lightspeed. I relive the moment I saw this woman that I've never met and may never get the chance to fight for her life. In her last-ditch attempt to survive, she clawed at *his* face. This man who was supposed to love her and protect her. He hurt her. They hurt her. My anger nearly destroyed me. When I saw her lying on the floor, helpless and bleeding out, I saw my future, everything that could be, disappear.

I'm determined to hold her at arm's length now. I am only destined to hurt, to cause pain, and to destroy. No one could love someone like me. But the way she looks at me. It gives me hope. Even now, as she sits listening to the others talk, her eyes flick to me, observing and curious. Those beautiful green eyes have left a brand on my soul.

I glance down at my watch, realizing it's almost two in the morning. I'm due to meet Killian and the leaders of a neighboring gang at the docks. Some unrest between gangs has spiraled into something more. If we don't get it under control now, it could become deadly.

The last thing I need is for Briar to be involved in a war.

I clear my throat and stand, swiping the empty pizza box from the coffee table.

"I have somewhere to be," I say. I run a hand through my hair, suddenly feeling awkward with Briar's doe eyes watching me. At first, I avoid her gaze entirely, but then when my eyes flick to her again, she's watching me, waiting. "You need to go to bed." I direct my statement at her, and she knows it.

She frowns, annoyed by my suggestion.

"Right." Gabe agrees. "Training tomorrow. You best get some rest, girl. You're going to need it. This brute will kick your ass tomorrow."

Gabe claps me on the back, and I frown.

Ondina claps her hands together and stands. "Alright. Let's go then. Let Briar get some sleep in her new home."

She pulls Briar into a hug, whispering something in her ear. Briar laughs and a wash of envy flows through me. I turn and walk out the door with no goodbyes. Footsteps sound behind me, but I don't turn.

"Wait!" Briar calls out to me. I stop, my back still to her. "I just wanted to say thank you for all of your help today. I've never had anything to call my own. So, thank you."

Looking over my shoulder at her, I see her bare feet shift beneath her. Her arms are wrapped around her chest and her face is soft. I jerk a nod before leaving her alone again.

"Teague." Killian's voice is an unwelcome sound to my ears.

"Killian," I say with a nod, addressing my Don. "Have they arrived yet?"

He shakes his head. "I wanted to be here first. It gives us the upper hand."

He's right. Arriving first to these meetings is a way to assert dominance. Usually, the first ones here set the mood for the meeting. We're due to meet with the leader of the Corcoran Roosters and his second. The Roosters have control over the docks, so technically, we're in enemy territory right now. Unlike the Crows who deal mainly in art, the Roosters are known for trafficking drugs in large shipments through cargo. I don't fuck with drugs, and. Killian refuses to deal. That world is nasty and vicious, not to mention extremely risky with the law enforcement. Our gangs can coexist only because we operate in different sectors and our dealings don't overlap.

Killian called this meeting because there's been a sense of unrest among our people. After a sting operation took out dozens of Roosters, recruiting has brought in reckless and ruthless replacements. People unfit and untrained to take part in this business.

Standing on the dock, I look around me, reading the names on the sides of the boats.

Luscious Lexi, Alluring Ash, Bodacious Britt, and *Juicy Jess.*

Killian taught me that boats are often named after women for protection. Much like Mother Nature, the mother of the sea will protect the sailors, watching over the children that visit her.

I can feel the presence of our guests before they speak, their faces still draped in shadow. "Killian," a voice sounds from my right. I mentally scan for guns, feeling the handle press into my back. Another rests against my waist.

"Declan. Gavin," Killian nods to the men. "Where's that son of yours tonight, Dec?"

Declan laughs darkly. "Axel does what he wants."

"So do you and your people," Killian takes a step into the light, leaving me to watch his back. The dock lighting illuminates his dark hair. I see the resemblance between him and Briar now. Although his hair is a few shades darker, the same golden accent is there.

"Tensions are high, my friend," Declan taunts. "My people are angry and ready to riot."

"The drug trade is a messy place to be, Dec. You know that. We don't need more attention on us." Killian points out to the water. "There are other options for you."

Declan scoffs. "Like what, Killian?" He takes a step forward but steps back when I bare my teeth at him. A feral beast. That's what I am and will always be known as. "This is our way. But I am willing to hear you out, peacefully. What would you suggest?"

Declan pulls out a pack of cigarettes, pulling one out and bringing it to his lips. The pungent smell of Declan's body odor makes me nauseous as it hits my nostrils. He reeks of sweat and rotting blood, wearing it proudly like cologne. The click of a lighter brings my attention to Gavin. His hand reaches for Declan's face, lighting the cigarette.

"The casinos I run. I'm willing to offer those up to you… for a price." Declan's second looks at me with curiosity. The world would be a better place without both Declan and Gavin infecting the planet with their sickness. Killian turns a blind eye to their real dealings. Drugs are just a front for the much darker business that Declan partakes in. A majority of his wealth is dirty money. Drugging and trafficking young women is this fuckers' specialty. I have never understood why Killian allows it to happen. This sick and twisted way of acquiring wealth when his own daughter could be one of those poor girls. Once word gets out, Declan will start searching for her, most likely putting a hit out on the head of the heir to the Crows.

"I'm willing to negotiate. What is it you desire, Killian?"

"The Da Vinci and the Kooning."

"Now Killian. Why would I give up my one bargaining chip? I'm not stupid." He takes a drag from the cigarette, blowing the smoke in Killian's direction.

"I'm not the one at a disadvantage here, Dec. Your men step out of line, and it's not my ass taking the fall." He takes another step toward Declan and Gavin. "I'll get what I want, eventually."

I have no doubts about that. Killian is ruthless when he wants something.

"We'll see about that." He takes one last drag from his cigarette, then drops it to the ground, extinguishing it beneath his foot. He spits then smiles, his rotting teeth on full display. He turns away, walking back into the shadows, Gavin close behind. I wait to speak until they're far enough away not to overhear.

"What now?" I ask. Killian faces me fully. His face is annoyed but there's a hint of something else. I question whether to push or not.

"Declan has outlived his usefulness. I only keep him alive because the fucker was once cooperative." His eyes flick toward the water. "I want those paintings and I'll find a way to get them. After that, you can have the honors of turning Declan in yourself."

He turns away from me now, his footsteps light on the wooden dock.

"How's Briar?" He asks noncommittally.

"Fine," I say, my tone casual and uncaring.

He twist so that only his face is towards me, and his body is still poised to leave. "Good," he says. He looks like he wants to say something else.

"Say it," I push. Killian turns his eyes flicking up to mine. He sighs, running a hand through his beard.

"I've kept Briar away from here for as long as I could. I thought that sending her back to her mother was the right thing to do." *Right. Sending her back to her abusive mother was the right thing to do.* "But now that she's here, there have been some developments." His face grows increasingly serious, his posture shifting into a protective stance.

"What?" I ask.

"Declan's moving into our territory, seeking more control than he already has. I've been receiving death threats." Even in the dim light, I can see the muscles in his jaw twitch. "I can handle my own death threats, but when they started threatening Briar's life as well... Do whatever you need to do to protect her." I barely have a moment to process before Killian disappears into the shadows, leaving me alone under the bright lights of the dock. A seed of worry plants itself in my belly, concerned over what Killian has planned. With Briar in the mix, I will do anything to protect her. Whether she likes it or not.

6

Briar

A knock—scratch that, pounding—on my door at promptly 7 am stirs me from the nightmare I was having. My dream was forcing me to replay River's hands around my throat, his gray eyes haunting every corner of my dreams.

Clearing the sleep from my eyes, I grab an oversized shirt off the floor and throw it over my head. I really should be more careful when sleeping naked now. There may come a day when someone busts into my apartment and finds me buck ass naked and tangled in sheets. *Awkward.* Another knock and I swing the door open to find Teague dressed in workout clothing and… is that a smile on his face?

"Why do you look… happy?" I grumble, barely awake. What was

a smile moments ago is quickly replaced by a frown. So much for happy Teague today.

"Get ready. We're training today." He holds up a white pastry bag and hands it to me. I look at his other hands to find two coffee cups. "Ondina made me pick up breakfast for us before training. You're going to need it."

He extends the coffee to me, and I take it, holding it like it's liquid gold. Teague smirks as I snatch it out of his hand.

"You're welcome, gremlin."

I hiss and close the door in his face. A few minutes later, I emerge wearing biker shorts and a sports bra. I really need to go shopping for more clothes.

Teague is leaning against the wall, with both hands in his pockets, looking glorious. When he spots me, he straightens, his eyes raking over me. When he finishes his observation job, his eyes lock with mine. I see darkness lingering there, like there's a war raging within him. My eyebrows scrunch in questioning, but he just turns away and starts walking toward the staircase. *Cool, we're ignoring feelings today.*

"Where are we going?" I run after him, taking two steps at a time. He's outside by the time I catch up to him.

"The gym down the street. Get in," he commands, swinging open the driver's side door.

"You're in a great mood this morning," I mumble to myself as I climb into the truck.

The gym is empty when we get there. Teague pulls a key from his pocket and uses it to open the front door.

"Does my dad own this too?"

Teague shakes his head, walking into the gym. "This is mine."

We walk into the gym, Teague several steps ahead. He flips on the lights, revealing the gym's full glory. In the front is a large boxing ring. Behind the ring are several sets of punching bags, and to the right of that is all the gym equipment. At the very back of the building is what appears to be an office and a private training room. *Oh, how I'd love for Teague to take me into that back room.*

"Why do you own a gym?" Genuinely curious, I turn to face Teague, hoping he'll actually look at me when he talks this time.

"I used to do a lot of illegal fighting. That's how I met Killian." He runs his hands through his dark hair, turning his body to me fully now. "The gym was a passion project for me. We take in a lot of stray kids. We place them in homes and teach them how to take care of themselves. Keeps a lot of kids from joining gangs or getting into trouble like I did."

Well, color me surprised. He does have a heart.

"Okay coach. What are we doing today?"

"Don't call me that." He drops his duffle-bag on the floor and takes a knee to ruffle through its contents. "We start with a warmup." He pulls out his watch and secures it to his wrist. "Today, that means we're running. Timer starts… now." His gaze flicks to me. "That means run, Briar. Or do you need me to chase you?"

I smirk.

"There's only one place and for one reason I want someone to chase me and it is *not* at the gym." At that, I take off running, right out the front door of the gym and around the perimeter of the building.

After twenty minutes, I gallop back into the building and almost collide with Teague's chest. Teague is hunched over with his hands on his knees. Panting, he says, "You have better stamina than I expected." I raise an eyebrow at him and laugh. His eyes darken a moment and then he shakes his head and walks to the private training room. "Others will come soon. I'll train you back there so we can have some privacy."

YIPPEE! Let's not get too excited, Briar.

Shrugging, I toss my bag over my shoulder and follow him.

"I need to get a gauge of what you already know and what you need to learn," he explains as we walk.

"I took some basic self-defense classes in college, and I know how to shoot. That's about it. My strength is lacking, I guess." *Some* self-defense classes… More like I taught myself everything I could, but he doesn't need to know that. I'd rather him think I'm a beginner.

Teague pulls out his phone and types something out. Shifting my weight, I look around awkwardly, waiting for his reply. His voice is husky as he speaks next. "Here's what we're going to do. For the next four weeks, we'll focus on different areas. This week, I want to start with self-defense and strength training." He continues typing on his phone as he talks. "Next week we'll go to the range and work on training you with different guns, mixed in with some strength training. I want to teach you how to fight, not just defend. I may enlist someone I trust to be in the ring with you for a mock fight." He takes a step closer to me and grips my upper arm. "You're weak."

His attention is still not fully on me, so I used this opportunity to show him what I'm made of. I take a step back, pulling his arm with me, then twisting from his grip. I spin into him and flip his body over my shoulder. Half rolling over him, I pin his arms to the ground with my legs and rest on his chest, my arm wrapped around his neck.

Teague releases a gasp—my body weight surely doesn't help him catch his breath.

"Ya know… I think I like the view from up here." I smirk down at him. When I get up to stand, he brings his leg behind me and sweeps my feet out from under me, causing my back to slam into the floor. Groaning, I turn my head to look at him.

"You got cocky. Don't make that mistake again." It was supposed to be a warning, but it sounded more like seduction. I watch Teague stand then extend his hand to me. Glaring at him for a moment, I finally take it, allowing him to pull me up. I mutter my thanks, then shuffle away from him, nursing my pride.

"Alright. Let's get to work," Teague instructs, ensuring my slow demise over the next couple of weeks.

FOUR HOURS. *FOUR fucking hours.* I collapse on the floor, panting from the brutal training session that Teague just put me through. We spent about an hour on regular strength training. Then, from there, he spent some time assessing what I knew. We spent an hour sparring and working through basic footwork, which I had apparently forgotten. If he thought my stamina was good during a run, I really don't think he's impressed now.

Every day for the last two weeks, we have spent *hours* doing strength training and sparring. It feels like I have gotten no better. Teague is terrifyingly intense when it comes to perfection. Everything is repeated, again and again, until I get it right. One wrong move and we start from the beginning. At the beginning of the week, I asked Teague to teach me something cool. I wanted to learn a fighting move that I could actually use. After being a 'good girl' this week, as he made me promise to be, Teague decided to be nice to me and taught me a move called the Flying Triangle Choke. Using your legs and arms to wrap your body around the neck of your opponent, you bring their body down and eventually pin them to the ground using pure body weight and momentum.

Bouncing on the balls of my feet, I celebrate my victory because, after three tries, I mastered the move, even earning something close to a smile from Teague. I throw little air punches at his abs attempting to be cute.

"I'm gonna be a pro in no time," I tease. The soreness in my body is still very present. Another ice bath is definitely in my future. Spinning in a circle, I celebrate some more, letting my excitement overtake me.

Teague reaches over his shoulders and pulls his shirt over his head, revealing a very muscled, very toned set of abs. A large tattoo covers his pectoral muscle and wraps around the entirety of his right arm. Both of his arms are covered in tattoos, but only that small part of his chest is inked. He wipes the sweat from his face with his shirt and tosses it to the floor.

When he turns back to me, I realize I had completely stopped celebrating to stare at him. His sweat moistened hair flops to one side of his face, making his defined jaw stand out even more. He's got a hint of stubble, sending my mind in a million directions. I imagine the feeling of his scratchy stubble between my legs, along my chest, the way it would scratch the sensitive skin of my neck.

Good lord.

My breathing hitches as I look him up and down. His joggers accentuate whatever he's got hidden in his pants. The little bit of hair peaking from his waistband catches my attention and it takes everything in me to lift my eyes away. Sliding my gaze from his waistband up to his face, my eyes catch on his. He's observing me just as much as I am him, his gaze darkening to something almost feral.

A loud throat clearing behind me causes me to jump. "Hey guys," Gabe says. His tone is tentative, like he's feeling out the vibe in the room. I haven't recovered from my stare down with Teague yet, so Teague is first to speak.

"Hey," he says, his voice scratchy and dripping with irritation. Or is that something else?

"Boss needs to see you. I can take Briar back home."

Teague nods, staring at me a moment before turning and picking his shirt up off the floor, swinging his bag over his shoulder. As he walks by me, he stops by my side and leans down to whisper in my ear. "Come find me later."

His breath warms my body and sends a shiver straight to my core. I watch him leave the building, climb into his truck and drive away. Gabe makes a noise, suspiciously like a snicker, drawing my attention back to him.

"What's up with you and Teague?"

I cough in surprise. "U-Uhm. Nothing. There's absolutely nothing going on."

Under my breath, I mumble about wishing there was but walk away before Gabe can interrogate me further.

"Right," he says, walking into the gym.

"Do we just leave the gym open or?" I pull my T-shirt over my head, covering my sweaty sports bra. The worst thing ever is trying to peel a wet sports bra off your body. I'm hoping to cool down enough to ease the problem. Gabe continues watching me.

"What?" I snap at him.

His eyes go wide and then he doubles over, laughing. "Girl. You're pink."

"I am not." I squint at him before stalking to the mirror along the back wall. Looking myself over, I see my reddened cheeks on full display. I groan and roll my eyes. "Can we just go?" I stomp to the door, waiting for Gabe to follow.

"Yes, ma'am." Gabe follows me out the door to his black Ford Mustang.

"Nice car." I swing the passenger door open and plop into the seat before Gabe even opens his door. I'm ready to become one with my bed and ignore the light of day for a week. "So. Can I ask you a question?"

"You already did." I purse my lips and glare at him.

He sighs. "Go ahead."

"Are Ondina and Teague together?" Gabe backs the car out of the parking spot. I see the corners of his mouth turn up as he looks over his shoulder. I catch a glimpse of a shimmering by his nose and when I look at him fully, I see the small, silver ring peeking from his nose.

"Are you asking because you're interested in Teague or Ondina?"

I cough, my eyes widening. "Uhm. I mean, Teague, but I'm not opposed to Ondina either."

His eyebrow shoots up in question and I notice the small slit between the hairs. *Edgy. Love it.*

"I love people. Doesn't matter what's in their pants. But I—I don't know. I'm intrigued by Teague."

"That's cool." Gabe nods a few times before speaking again. "Well, to answer your question, no. They're not together. Teague doesn't share much about his life. He's got a pretty dark past and I think he intimidates people."

Yeah, I got that. He doesn't quite look like the most approachable man. I don't know what to say in response, so I just nod and look out the window as Gabe drives.

"So, how did training go?" Gabe breaks the silence.

"Fantastic, actually. Teague taught me a flying triangle choke. I'm definitely going to need an ice bath after today though." I lift my arm above my head, feeling the soreness in my arm. My back muscles tense in response.

"He must like you."

I laugh a little louder than I planned. "Yeah right. If that is Teague liking someone, I don't want to see what it looks like when he dislikes someone."

We pull up to the apartment complex and I find myself searching for Teague's car. It's nowhere to be seen, which leaves me feeling disappointed.

I slide out of the car and stand, feeling an intense cramp run through my body. I double over from the pain, releasing a soft groan.

Gabe rushes to my side, putting a hand on my back. "Are you okay?"

I jerk a nod from where I'm hunched over. "Yeah," I breathe, waving my hand at him to shoo him away. "It'll pass in a moment." The cramping subsides, allowing me to stand back up, slowly. Glancing at Gabe, I see his face is full of worry. "I'll be fine. I swear." Gabe doesn't look convinced but nods slowly.

"Okay, well. Let me walk you up. I have to meet someone so I'm not staying but I'd feel better making sure you get back okay."

"That's fair," I agree, not having the energy to argue.

GABE LEAVES ME to settle into my apartment alone. After he leaves, the tears flow immediately. One thing I rarely share about myself is my journey with endometriosis. When I was twelve, I got my first period. It wasn't horrible, but it wasn't pleasant either. From there, it just got worse. Every doctor refused to take my pain seriously until one day I passed out from my cramping. I had been in the bathroom, puking my guts out from the intense pain. My mother's neighbor came to check on me and insisted my mother take me to the hospital.

The next month, I had my first laparoscopic surgery. They found endometriosis tissue built up all along my uterus and up to my intestines and bowels. I pull the waistband of my shorts down to run a finger over my scars.

The pain is unbearable sometimes, and others it's almost nonexistent. Now that I have my IUD, it hasn't been so bad, but occasionally, my cramping becomes so bad, I'm knocked on my ass for weeks at a time.

Pain stabs through my uterus and into my stomach. The cramps send waves of stabbing pain up my ass, causing me to fall to my knees on the floor. A wave of nausea rolls over me. Panic overtakes my body as I crawl my way to the bathroom. To suffer these flare-ups alone is terrifying to me. I've had to suffer alone for years, but now… I worry most now about the need to get up and work out tomorrow. I made a commitment, and to back out so soon…

Everyone is going to hate me. I'm going to lose everything before I even have it.

My mind attacks me, the panic causing my breathing to hitch. The cold tile of the bathroom floor feels nice against my sweaty skin. I can feel my heart pounding out of my chest as another wave of pain sends pulses through my butt again. I peel my shorts off my body, the tight waistband making me feel trapped.

I cry silently on the bathroom floor until my eyes feel puffy and my body exhausted from each wave of pain.

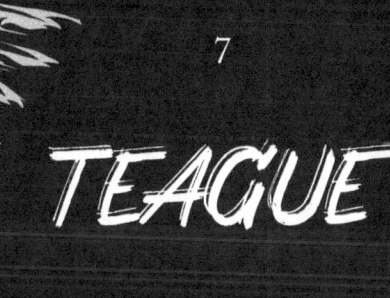

7

TEAGUE

My phone ringing in my pocket gives me the opening I need to escape this meeting with Killian. For the past hour, we've sat in this cramped office and discussed our plan, which is proving to be more arduous than expected. No one can come to an amicable conclusion, so it's a continuous roundabout of arguing and bickering. These men are all power hungry, seeking to show off their firepower and ability to get something done. It's taxing having to listen to them constantly.

I stand up from my seat across from Killian.

"I have to take this," I say as I hold the phone to my ear and step outside the office door. "Gabe." Closing the door behind me, I lean against the wall, listening.

"Something is up with Briar, and I wanted to let you know."

A thrum of concern flushes through me.

"What happened?" I try not to sound too worried.

A sigh sounds on the other end of the phone. "When we pulled up to the apartment, she doubled over like she was in pain. I think something is wrong. She refused to tell me anything. I thought maybe she'd talk to you."

I straighten. "Why would she talk to me?"

Gabe laughs quietly. "You're an idiot, you know that?" I glare at the phone as if I could send my glare to him through it. "Just go check on her. It could be nothing, but it could be serious."

I nod to myself, understanding his worry.

"Okay. I'll get out of this meeting and head over. Thanks, Gabe." I end the call and step back into the meeting. Leaning against the back door, I wait for Killian's attention to snap to me.

"I have business to attend to." Killian just waves his hand, and I turn, leaving the meeting to the power-hungry idiots.

I rush back to the apartments, my concern getting the best of me. This woman is going to be the death of me. She's going to make me soft, and I can't have that.

Taking two steps at a time, I run up the stairs to her apartment. When I reach her door, I see that it's not closed properly, which is my first sign that something is wrong. I knock lightly, hoping to get her attention.

"Briar?" I call into the apartment, but I get no response.

Making an executive decision, I pull out my gun and stalk inside, clearing it of any intruders. Once I clear the living room, I call out for her again. A small whimper comes from the bathroom.

"Briar?" There's still no response. Getting increasingly worried, I open the bathroom door and find her splayed out on the bathroom floor, her pants stripped from her body and a loose shirt covering her upper half. I drop to the ground by her side, my hands finding her body instantly. She's warm and sweaty to touch, almost as though she's sick. When I move her head, I see that she's mostly unresponsive. My heart pounds in my chest, anxiety rushing through my body. Panic.

I pull her body into my lap, trying to cradle her head in my arms. I look her over for any injuries, but when I see none, I continue to worry.

I don't know what I'm doing.

Briar moans in my arms, her eyes cracking open slightly. "It hurts," she says, weakly.

"What hurts?" I try to sound calm, but I am clearly not calm.

"Everything," she groans, pointing down to her waist. "I hurt."

"Where?" I'm trying to be respectful of her body, so I try not to look any further than I need to, my eyes darting from her eyes to her almost naked bottom half.

She huffs a small laugh. "What's the matter, Teague?" She gives me a weak smile. "Never seen a naked woman before?"

She pushes her underwear down a little, her fingers running over two small scars above her pubic bone. I watch the way her hands move across the spot, my curiosity peaking at what happened to her.

"Was this my fault?" I gaze into her eyes, searching for anger, disgust, anything. "Pushing you too hard in training?"

Her eyes squint, her gaze looking between my two eyes. "Help me up, will you? Then we can talk."

I don't help her up. I continue staring at her before I scoop her up into my arms and stand. I carry her from the bathroom to the living room, setting her down gently on the large black couch.

"What do you need?" I ask, feeling helpless and responsible. I hate feeling helpless.

"Pain meds. Strong ones. Something with acetaminophen,

pamabrom, and/or pyrilamine would be amazing though. It's one of the few combinations that will help me currently."

My understanding comes quickly. This is some sort of period thing. I may not understand, but I can try. I get up to stand from the couch, ready to walk across the room as Briar's arm brushes my leg.

"Don't leave me." Her eyes are pleading.

"I'll come right back. I promise." I place a hand on her forehead before walking out of her apartment.

A few minutes later, I come back with meds, a heating pad, crackers, and apple juice.

"Please don't ask me why I have all of this stuff. You'll hurt my brooding image," I say, trying to get a response out of her. She smiles, but it doesn't quite reach her eyes. "So, you gonna tell me what's happening now?" I sit down on the couch opposite of her, but she moves towards me to lay her head on my lap.

"I was diagnosed with endometriosis when I was fifteen…"

"What's endometriosis?" I interrupt. Her eyes widen. "What?"

"You're kind of scaring me. You're being nice to me, sweet even," she whispers.

"Would you rather me be unkind after I found you basically passed out on the bathroom floor?" I ask, drily.

"I can take care of myself."

"Right. Looks like you were doing a great job of that," I snap, immediately feeling guilty. She rolls her eyes at me, the walls building back up again slowly. Good. We're better that way.

"Endometriosis is… I like to explain it like this. You know how cancer is foreign cells that reproduce and grow in places where they shouldn't?" I nod down at her. "Well, endometriosis is a disorder where endometrial tissue grows in places outside of the uterus. So, for example, they found the tissue growing on my ovaries and up into my intestines. Basically, it causes period cramps on steroids."

Nodding, I try to absorb what she just shared with me. She reaches for the water bottle I set on the coffee table. I grab it, handing it to her along with the bottle of pills. She looks up at me for a moment, just watching me.

"In addition to endo, I was told that I have PMDD too. Which, before you ask, is premenstrual dysphoric disorder. And that causes me to have severe depression and anxiety, but it's mostly around the time when I'm on my period." Her face scrunches. "Is all this period talk grossing you out?"

Shaking my head, I put a hand on her thigh. "All good."

"Doctors say that the only way to diagnose is with surgery. I think that's bullshit because I had every external symptom outside of having the actual proof of endometriosis tissue. But then one day it got so bad that I was scheduled for surgery after a trip to the ER." She moves her head in my lap to look at me. "I've had two surgeries in total. Both not fun. But now I have an IUD and I don't have periods per se... But when I'm supposed to have a period, my body will simulate some of the symptoms without the bleeding. Not every time, but this is the worst it's been in months. And sometimes I'll just bleed randomly."

"That sounds..."

"Horrible? Disgusting? Debilitating?" she finishes for me.

"Well, yeah. You're very brave to deal with all of that."

She smiles up at me, a full bright smile. It's filled with emotions I can't quite place.

"I hope you weren't doing anything important." Her eyelashes flutter as she looks down at her hands. *I'd cross a mountain range for you.* My heart clenches. *Stop it. You can't have her.*

"I got out of a meeting with Killian." Her eyes focus on mine.

"I don't think he likes me. I've always wanted a father, but I never knew what I'd get when I found out he was a crime lord."

"I've never known Killian to be the teddy bear type, but I think he's got a soft spot for you. I don't think I would've been your watchdog if he didn't." We've never talked about that factoid. The fact that I was basically her stalker.

"I don't understand him. He acts like he doesn't know me. I'm here now and he's done nothing to try to get to know me. Not like I'm not thankful you were around, I am, but is it so wrong that I wanted it to be him?" Her voice grows sad, her cheeks reddening a bit.

"No," I say. "It's not." She rests her head on my shoulder, pulling the blanket further over her body.

"I dreamt about you." She breathes. "It was always your eyes I saw in my dreams after you held me. I didn't know you, but I stayed because you told me to." My breath catches at her words. I don't know what to say, so I just continue looking forwards, my heart beating quicker. *It's probably just the drugs talking. Right?*

Eventually, she breaks the silence. "Will you stay with me? We could watch a movie or something. I just don't enjoy being alone where I can wallow in my thoughts."

"Yeah," I say. "I'll stay with you. But no chick flicks." I tap her head, jokingly.

She gags. "Ew. Who do you think I am? I want to watch Speed. I love me some Keanu Reeves."

I throw my head back in a hearty laugh. This girl is going to be the death of me. "Speed it is."

"I wanted to know you, Teague." She lays her head down on my chest, her eyes closing. Her breathing evening out.

"I wanted to know you, too" I say, my voice barely a whisper.

Briar falls asleep, her head still in my lap. My mind wanders, curious about this woman who's seemed like someone only from my dreams. I should be working. I should be planning and keeping far away from her. But it feels nice to have this moment. I decide to let myself be selfish, just for tonight. Then tomorrow, things can go back to the way they should be. But tonight—tonight I can do this and be here with her. I can get this glimpse of what a life with her could be like.

WAKING UP, I feel the tension from the awkward position my neck was in all night. Briar is crouched in the fetal position on the other side of the couch. Looking over at her, I see her small body move with each even breath. I can only hope that staying with her helped her through the worst of it.

The feeling of my phone vibrating in my pocket sends a rush of urgency through me. I fumble, trying to grab it and get some distance between us, hoping that I don't startle her awake. Stepping into her bathroom, I answer the call and put the phone to my ear.

"Yep," I say, keeping my voice low.

"Can you come into the office now? There have been some developments with Declan that we need to discuss." Killian wastes no time trying to explain things over the phone.

I leave Briar alone, my nerves getting the best of me still. I should've told him no. When I step foot into the office, I can immediately feel that something is wrong. Killian is seated in the conference room, his hand running through his graying beard. Papers are spread around him, but he's focused on one paper. I knock against the door frame, alerting him to my presence. He doesn't even look at me when he signals me to come in.

I sit in the chair across from him. Releasing a big sigh, Killian lowers the paper, turning them and shoving them in front of me. I glance at them briefly. At first glance, it looks like chicken scratch, but the longer I look at them, I can make out the words scrawled across the paper.

Mind your own business, Killian. This is your final warning. It's not only your life at stake now. Do it for your daughter.

"They're getting worse. Cease all operations for now until I can decide how to proceed." Killian's hand returns to his beard. "There are things I can't tell you now, but her life is more valuable than my own. Take her training seriously. It's even more imperative that she knows how to protect herself."

"Understood, sir." My heart rate increases. He's being so vague. He is my *Don,* which means my loyalty lies with him.

"Do you think she's got it in her to lead?" he asks. The question throws me for a loop.

"She is someone worth undying loyalty."

His eyes soften a touch. "I wish I got a chance to know her," he sighs.

"You still can," I push. She said it last night, she wanted to know her father, crime lord, and all.

"I fear it's too late for me." With that, Killian stands, leaving me alone in the conference room.

8

Briar

It's been three weeks since that night with Teague. He stayed with me the whole night and continued to take care of me for the next few days. It's been weird between us, though. His hard outer shell began to break. For a while, he would give me glimpses of that man, but now it's like his walls are back up and completely solid. I don't know how to feel. I don't even know what I should feel. After my terrible end with River, who is still in holding I might add, I had this idea of what it could be like to love someone again. Just a taste of opening myself back up. In response to Teague's indifferent attitude toward me being back, I feel like I should snap mine back into place as well. But a part of me doesn't want that. This was progress and healing. Everything I am going to do here with the Crows, I want to feel. I want to feel something—to feel alive.

I feel most alive when I'm training, particularly since I'm improving. Living in a world where knowledge is readily accessible, I took it upon myself to teach myself anything I could get my hands on. This week, when we started training with knives, Teague was surprised to learn I already knew a decent amount about it. Daddy Dearest underestimated how much his little girl knew about him and his hobbies. Would running a gang be considered a hobby? Or maybe a career? Whatever. What matters is that I could whoop Teague's ass when it comes to knife throwing. Blindfolded.

I was hoping for some sort of satisfaction from beating Teague, but in all honesty, I just feel a little empty. The joy that I should have felt didn't come.

We've created this dangerous game between the two of us. Since he's locked his feelings up so tight, I've found other ways to entertain myself. The bets we made to motivate our training are bordering the line of feelings. It's almost like a game of truth or dare, each bet getting a little closer to the line that separates us. Maybe one day he'll break down his walls, but for now, I'm content to ride the line.

Teague's muscular arms come to my side as I aim the gun at my next target. I feel him behind me, and the thought of him towering over me from behind sends a chill through my body. Today, we're in an outdoor range. The course is set up with various moving targets that pop out at you to simulate people.

"Relax your shoulders and—" He brings one of his arms to tap my left leg. "—bring this leg back. The kickback can knock your body off balance. If you have a leg to stabilize you, you're less likely to lose your balance, or worse, fall."

My finger rests on the side of the gun, not yet on the trigger. I nod my understanding and take a breath before moving my finger to the trigger.

Bang.

My body is pushed back slightly by the force of the gun. I've shot before, but never guns as powerful as these. Releasing a frustrated sigh, I put the gun down and circle the course.

"You're a good shot, ya know? Just need some more practice. You have a good eye and good aim. It's just keeping the strength in your arms and body constant." His grip on my arm is firm. "Get into position one more time. I'll show you what I mean."

I raise my hands like I'm going to aim. His hand comes to my belly and I flinch. He lets out a dark chuckle.

"Trust me," he says into my ear. With his hand on my stomach, he talks me through the stance. "Your strength starts at your core, yeah? Keep your core tight and strong." His hands come to my shoulders. With each touch, my body heats more, but I push the feelings down, trying to hide my reactions to his touch. "Raise your shoulders to your ears. Good. Now relax." My shoulders relax. "That always helps me to figure out where I need to be. At this point, I don't even think about it anymore, but it'll become muscle memory for you eventually." Last, his hand moves to my legs, or my thighs to be exact, and it takes everything in me not to squirm at his touch. My imagination sparks with all the places his hands could be right now, and I have to bite my lip to keep from saying something I shouldn't. "Remember, spread apart, and keep your knees slightly bent."

"Spread my legs, keep them bent. Got it." I hold it a moment longer then relax. Teague quirks a brow at me. "What?" I huff.

"Nothing," he says before sauntering back toward the table where our guns rest.

That frustrates me. I hate it when he stops himself from talking. Does he not fucking trust me yet? I'm basically one of them and yet I still have to work for their trust. I mean, I guess it makes sense. I haven't even taken the oath yet, but I am not stupid enough to betray anyone even with just my verbal agreement.

"Fine. Don't talk to me then." I roll my eyes and help load the guns into their cases. I feel Teague's eyes on me like he's trying to burn a hole through my skull. I continue with what I'm doing, ignoring him. When he huffs, my eyes snap to him. I shoot him a glare, challenging. He just stares back at me like we are in some sort of competition. He throws his hands up in defeat, but then smiles mischievously.

"You don't want to know what I'm thinking," he finally says. *Oh, game on.*

"Oh, but I really do."

"I don't think you could handle this mind of mine," he taunts, tapping his index finger to his temple. His eyes darken a bit, as if some risqué thought just flew through his mind.

"What's your deal, Teague? You were so nice to me a few weeks ago and now it's like you don't know me. We've spent weeks together. It's not like you just met me. What's your deal?"

He doesn't respond.

"I asked you a question, Teague." My tone is bitter and biting. "You do know whose blood runs through my veins, right?"

"Oh, so you're throwing the blood relation card around now. Is that supposed to scare me?" He's angry now.

"No. It's supposed to get you to talk to me. One day I could be your boss."

He huffs an angry laugh. "Right. Like that will happen."

I clench my jaw in anger. "Oh, because I have a vagina, that means

I can't take over, huh? I'll fucking show you. I've been alone my whole life. At least I know that's going to continue. You can stay in your fucking bubble. It's probably safer there anyway."

His eyes squint in anger and his face twists into something I can't quite read. He growls before taking a step toward me, his hand coming to the back of my head. His hands fist my hair and my mind goes blank for a moment. I tilt my chin up to look at him. He looks pained, his eyes switching from my lips to my eyes, trying to read my expression. "

Do it," I say a little breathless. "Fucking do it." My voice is small now, but the bite is still there. He takes a breath then shakes his head. He takes a step back and turns his back to me. My eyes fill with unshed tears.

"Coward," I mutter under my breath. I stomp to the massive truck and load the few cases of guns I grabbed into the back seat then slam the door. Without looking back, I throw my helmet over my head and turn the key, my bike roaring to life. Without another thought, I drive away, leaving Teague standing there, confused and alone.

AFTER STOMPING INTO my apartment an hour ago, I stepped into the shower and let myself cry out of frustration. I don't know what I wanted Teague to do, but I wanted something. I'm not sure if I'm ready to admit to myself what I feel. What started as attraction has grown into something more. An infatuation, I guess you could call it. I don't like labels. I have never been one to try and fit myself into a box. Boxes are so confining, and I don't need that in my life.

After my shower, I went in search of the smuttiest book I could get my hands on. Something about a good sexy book calms me down and clears my head. It also takes care of some other needs too. Two birds with one stone, ya know? I really need to get laid and then maybe my body's reactions to Teague will disappear. Or maybe they won't.

I hear Teague's heavy footsteps through the hall a moment before his door opens and slams. A moment later, a knock sounds at my door and I almost jump.

"Coming," I yell out toward the door.

When I swing it open, Ondina's bright face is the first thing I see. *Not who I was expecting.*

"Hey girl!" She smiles brightly. Her hair is in a full bun at the top of her head, some natural curls left out to frame her face. "Can I come in?"

I nod, stepping out of the way, allowing her entry into my apartment. "What's up?" Closing the door behind Ondina, I walk to the kitchen and pull out two beers for us. "Do you want one?"

Smiling wide, she takes one from my hand. "Is that even a question?" She pulls out a knife from her pocket and flips the cap off before taking a long gulp. Letting out a deep sigh, she walks to the couch and plops down into the plush leather. "Teague called me."

"Oh," I grind my teeth, waiting for whatever else she has to say. "What did he say?"

"Just that you left the range pretty mad and that I should come check on you." She takes another sip of her beer then smiles. "What did he do to piss you off?" Her eyebrow arches up in question, her feet propped up on the coffee table.

I groan. "Honestly, I don't really know."

Ondina laughs, then eyes me suspiciously. I huff a laugh at the face she gives me. "Okay fine. We got into an argument, and I was thinking with my cunt, I think, instead of my brain." Ondina snorts as she coughs and chokes on her beer. I thump her back a few times before she gets a hold of herself, transitioning from strangled choking to hysterical laughter.

"Bitch. Did he deny your sexy ass? If he doesn't tap that, I will."

"I wouldn't be opposed to that." I smirk at her, then laugh when her face goes red. "Why are men such assholes?" I sigh, plopping down on the couch beside her.

"Well, men have these antennas in their penis that signal their brains any time they encounter a woman. One signal tells them to think with their dick, and the second signals to their asshole to talk through their face."

I snort, beer shooting out of my nose.

"Ondina," I shriek, laughing so hard my stomach hurts. She just shrugs in response.

"Well, what are we going to do to get back at him?" She looks at me expectantly. An idea sparks in my head, and I slowly grin as it cements itself further as a fantastic idea.

"Wait here." Running to my room, I grab my laptop and flip it open. My fingers fly across the keys, breaking myself into the Bluetooth speaker that Teague keeps in his living room. "Do you remember that speaker that Teague has in his living room?" I ask as I venture back out. Ondina nods a few times, waiting for me to explain. The last time we all had pizza, Teague opened his apartment to everyone. I took the opportunity to look around and take note of his belongings. Call it curiosity or call it insurance, either way, it has its uses. "I can hack into that and mess with him. It's really juvenile but it was the first thing that popped into my head."

She laughs loudly, then slaps a hand over her mouth. "Play some hard-core porn over the speakers or something."

I snort, tears beginning to leak from my eyes as we laugh.

"You got it, babe."

Pulling up a porn website, Ondina and I scroll through, looking for the best video to play over the speakers. Eventually, we settle on a video of a particularly dirty threesome.

"Ready?" I ask Ondina. She nods, the laugh bubbling up in her throat already. I type the command into my computer, making sure the video will connect to the speaker. I hit play and a moment later loud moans sound through the walls of Teague's apartment, the video playing at full volume. There's slamming as Teague tries to get the sound to turn off. It just keeps blaring, even as the speaker is clearly thrown across the room.

We cackle together, louder than we should be. I know our cover is blown as Teague's footsteps storm to my front door and he pounds his fists aggressively against it.

When I open the door, I plaster the sweetest smile on my face. "Yes?"

"Turn it off," he says angrily.

"No, but thank you for asking." I snort as I slam the door in his face, leaving him to the sounds of flesh slapping flesh and rehearsed moans. I press my back into the door and look at Ondina. It only takes a moment—I slide down the door, my butt hitting the floor, laughing so hard that I cry. I never realized how badly I needed a friend. Ondina came into my life at the right time, and I couldn't be more thankful.

9

Briar

The next morning, I wake up to a text from Ondina. I've got a full day of training again. This time it's split among different members of Teague's trusted circle.

Ondina texted me an address I don't recognize. I don't know much about the dynamics of Teague's team, but I'm anxious to learn more.

Pulling myself from bed, I rush to get ready, throwing my riding clothes on and my workout clothes into a backpack. Slinging it over my shoulder, I walk out the door and down the steps to my bike. Anxiety trickles through my body as I mount my bike. A trickle of pain shoots through me, my heart racing in response. It's the week before my dreaded period is due. I can't have another episode like the one before. This is my life now and I fear that my body will prevent me from standing by a team. Instead of ruminating, I brush it off, and let the fresh air clear my mind. After a ten minute ride, I pull my helmet off, shaking out my hair. The breeze tickles my face as I flick the kickstand down, and walk into the auto mechanic shop. I've never been here before and curiosity overwhelms me as I walk further inside. There's a bright red mustang parked in the garage, the sound of tools clunking from beneath it. I look at it closer and realize that it's Gabe's mustang.

"Hello?" I say into the shop, my footsteps purposefully louder. The clunking stops as I see Ondina roll out from underneath the car.

"Surprised?" she asks, pulling herself up and wiping grease off on a towel.

A startled laugh spills from me. "Actually, no. Nothing about you should surprise me anymore." Ondina grins at me, the curls piled on the top of her head spilling over a bit. "I'm a mechanic," she says. "Cars are my specialty. If you ever need a new ride, I'm your woman."

"I'll be sure to take you up on that offer," I say, a smile taking over my face.

"I brought you here today because I want you to understand what I do. I used to race illegally. I learned everything from the boys there. Now I fix cars in my free time, and dabble in racing... Or rather I like to drive really–" her eyes twinkle with excitement, "–really fast. Gimme a minute and I'll show you around." With a wink, she spins on her heels and tosses the towel over her shoulder. I watch as she tinkers with some things under the hood of the car. What felt like mere minutes later, she slams the hood shut and turns to me. "Wanna start it up?" I nod and walk to the driver's door, opening it and climbing inside. I turn the key in the ignition and the car roars to life. Ondina smiles, her eyes scrunching as her cheeks rise. "Yay! It sounds great. I don't have time to make you a car expert today, but

I do have time to show you around a bit. Come." She walks to the back of the shop and right though the back door. I follow her, trying to keep up. We exit the garage where there's a line of parked cars. The one that catches my eye immediately is a yellow Volkswagen Thing. I've always loved the look of those cars.

"I've got a collection," Ondina muses. "When we've got more time, I'll teach you all about them, but I think it's Gabe's turn to steal you away." She looks at her watch then to the side door. My brows knit together, but my question is answered as Gabe strolls through the door, dressed from head to toe in tactical wear.

"How did you know he was here?" I ask. Ondina just smirks at me, blowing a kiss over her shoulder and sauntering back inside the garage.

"It's like she's got superhuman hearing or something," he says, sidling up to me. I nod in agreement, my lips pursing.

"I'm taking you back to the gym." Gabe walks to the front of the garage. "Meet ya there."

He throws his leg over his motorcycle, revving the engine. He pulls away from the curb, leaving me standing by my bike.

This whole journey has really tested my need for control. I used to control every facet of my life and now my life is on another person's dime. Taking a deep breath, I wipe the resting bitch off my face and replace her with a smile. *More espresso, less depresso.* Think about the espresso that will be running through my veins. *Happy thoughts.*

I pull up to Teague's gym a few minutes later. Gabe is already inside, pacing around a table at the back of the room. Walking closer, I see that the table is decorated with various knives.

"Teague says you've got the fighting down, so now we're incorporating the weapons. As weapons master, I control who gets what. I hope you can hold your own." He straps a belt around his waist then stuffs various throwing knives into it.

"Can I change first?"

"No," he says. "These fights won't be happening in workout clothes, so we'll fight like this." He dips under the ropes, climbing into the ring. He turns, waiting for me to gear up. I grab a thigh holster and attach it to my jeans. *Thank God for stretchy jeans.*

After jumping into the ring, I barely have a moment to pull knives into my hands before Gabe lunges for me. I block, ducking under his arm and spinning behind him. My knife slips from my hand and I bend to catch it, taking a knee to my gut as Gabe turns to me. He lunges again and I block, using that momentum to strike at center mass.

My body stiffens as I feel Teague walk into the room. While my mind is distracted, Gabe catches me off guard and spins me, my back slamming into his chest and a blade at my neck.

He pushes me away. "One distraction will cost you."

I narrow my eyes, my jaw clenching. I release a growl, lunging for him once more. *I hate losing.* Our arms connect as I strike, and he blocks. I watch him, observing his pattern with each block. When his foot comes down to stabilize himself, I use that opportunity to strike again. I whip around, kicking him in the chest. He falters back, and I swing my leg again, knocking him to the floor and pinning him to the ground. With my knees, I knock the knives from his hands and bring my own blade to his throat.

I whip my head up to look at Teague, my ponytail flopping over my shoulder as I gaze at him with pure rage. A wicked grin spreads across my face as I look at him through my lashes. He's standing with his arms crossed, staring at us with a blank face. The corner of his mouth twitches up while the rest of his face remains stoic. Gabe groans beneath me, and I release my knee from his chest and release his neck. I stand up and offer him my hand. He takes it.

I start to yank him up as he speaks. "Not so bad, for a newbie."

I drop his hand, Gabe falling backward, right onto his ass. Teague snorts from outside the ring and my eyes find his immediately.

"Not so bad, for a ginger," I say, climbing through the ropes and out of the ring.

As I walk to the table, I wink at Teague, giving him my best pouty look. *Yeah, that's right, big guy. Try me.*

"I'm out. See y'all at home." I walk right out the door, leaving the guys staring after me. Maybe a lack of control isn't so bad after all.

10

TEAGUE

The sound of screaming wakes me from a particularly nasty nightmare. The lifeless body of my mother on top of a pile of bodies I killed was the weapon of choice for tonight. My sleep was littered with death and destruction; nothing new for me. I sit up quickly, realizing that the screaming isn't a dream. Throwing my blankets off, I throw on the first shirt I can find, pulling it over my head while reaching for a hidden Glock from my bedside table, and slowly creep toward the noise.

Panic floods through my body, my breath coming in sharp gasps as I rush to get to her—Briar. I snatch the master key from my hall table and run to Briar's door. Gabe is already awake, his sleepy form standing in his doorway.

"What's happening?" he mumbles. His concern clearly plastered on his face.

"I think she's dreaming." I fumble with the key, trying, unsuccessfully, to get the door open. *Damn it!*

"Fuck, fuck, FUCK."

Gabe stalks over to me, taking the key from my hands and glowering at me. "I know you care about her, and this is why you need to get a grip. Take a moment man. She's going to need you to be calm, not freaking out. So calm the fuck down!"

He opens the door with ease. I give him a wary smile, and step inside, shutting the door behind me. I don't think Briar would appreciate multiple men showing up next to her bed in the middle of the night.

Her screams grow louder and more intense. When I open the bedroom door, her naked body is tangled in sheets as she thrashes in her sleep.

Her naked body.

Fuck. I breathe deeply to calm my nerves as I drop to my knees beside her bed.

"Briar!" I roar. My hands pin her to the bed to keep her from thrashing, but she doesn't wake. Whatever memory she's reliving is a terrible one. Her clammy skin feels cold beneath my warm fingers.

"Briar!" I yell again. I shake her softly, hoping to snap her out of the darkness overtaking her.

The screaming stops first. Then her eyes snap open, her breathing slowing. The screams are quickly replaced by silent sobs, fat tears running down her cheeks. She blinks, the tears gleaming as she looks up to me, her voice hoarse as she says my name.

"Teague," she breathes. "We've gotta stop meeting like this." A weak smile spreads across her face.

Without warning, she sits up and wraps her arms around my neck, her face nuzzling into my neck, her hot breath short circuiting my brain. After a moment's hesitation, I wrap my arms around her waist and press her warm body to mine. Her breasts press against my chest, and it takes every ounce of self-control I have to keep my dick under control. Our breathing syncs together as we hold each other in silence.

"What happened?" she croaks, pulling away from me.

"I woke up to your screaming. I could hear it all the way from my room, and I panicked. I have a master key for all of the apartments, so I let myself in." I pull the key from my pocket.

"Thank God for that," she says sadly. She's silent for a moment. "It was River. His hand was around my throat, with my mom at his side. It's always River." She leans forward, placing her head on my chest.

"Get dressed," I say. "We're going out."

Her eyebrows draw together. "Teague. It's two in the morning. Where on Earth would we need to go at this hour?"

"Just trust me," I say. "Dress for business." Standing, I turn to wait in the next room, but a squeak from Briar stops me in my tracks.

"Don't leave me." Her voice is full of pleading and sadness. "Please," she breathes.

I turn back to face her. How could I leave her when she asks like that? "Okay. I'm here, okay? I'll stay. I'll just turn away while you get dressed. Is that okay?"

As if she's just now realizing she's naked, she clutches the sheet to her body, nodding.

"Okay." I turn to face the wall, giving her privacy. The sound of rustling sheets alerts me to her movement. Her soft footsteps pad to the closet. After a moment, she emerges dressed in black pants, a silky maroon tank top, and a leather jacket. I look to her feet and see the heeled leather boots that I bought her. She doesn't know that, though. They were just left for her with no note. Maybe she is smart enough to put the pieces together, but then again, maybe not. In the heels, she is a good three inches taller, her head coming to my shoulders now. I smile at the small woman in front of me and the power emanating from her now. So different when her mask is pulled back in place.

"Come with me to my room, then we'll head out."

Briar watches me as I dress. Her eyes roam over me, watching every move. My cock reacts under her gaze. Her eyes continue watching me, my ego fueled by her attention. I dress quickly, making a show of rolling my sleeves up my forearms. I still need to look the part even when I know that blood is going to be involved, and there will be bloodshed tonight. Anger brews within me. I let it fester, fueling the dark side of me.

A part of me fears that once I let the beast out, Briar will shrink away from me. Another part of me fears that she's more like me than she lets on—the potential for a King and Queen of the Underworld. What if she doesn't run away in fear? What if instead, she enjoys this life? I don't know what is worse, but either way, I know tonight will be a test. If she survives, I will know she is ready. The power is in her hands completely.

WE DRIVE IN silence to a warehouse outside the city limits. It's far enough away from any other buildings to be isolated from interest, making it the perfect home for people like him.

"Why did you pick this car?" Briar breaks the silence as we pull up to a shadowed gravel road leading to our destination.

"What do you mean?" I feign innocence.

"Mercedes AMG 63 Coupe. Let me guess…You have at least 630 horsepower under the hood of this beauty? This car means business… so why this car?" The car rolls to a stop, the motion-activated streetlights flickering on.

"Impressive…" I sigh before answering. "I have a reputation to uphold. I love my truck, but usually, when I am here for… other reasons, I choose this car." She nods slowly before placing a hand on the door handle.

"Wait!" I swing my door open and rush to her side. Opening the door, I nod my head to her slightly, signaling for her to step out. "Tonight, you are the queen. You deserve to be treated like one." She hesitates before slipping her hand into my outstretched one.

"Queen, huh? I don't feel like a queen."

"Oh, but you will." A wicked grin spreads across my face. Opening the trunk, I reveal several cases of weapons. "Take your pick."

Her face breaks into a wide set grin as she takes the SIG-Sauer P320 and a few throwing knives. She holsters the gun at her waist and tucks the knives into her thigh holster. I can't help but admire her as she does this. I'd like to remove every ounce of clothing on her body, leaving only the gun and knives. I imagine my fingers exploring the ample curves of her body while she wears a weapon ready to kill. I get away with staring for a moment longer before I need to armor myself with a gun.

I sling a holster over my shoulder and press the Remington 1975 into my chest.

"Ah. A classic," Briar muses as she takes in my preferred weapon. "Good choice."

She lightly punches my arm before closing the trunk of the car and slipping her arm through mine. Being this close to her does a number on my brain, on my cock. Her scent fills my nose, something like a fruity floral mixture that drives me wild.

We walk to the warehouse arm in arm. I called ahead, letting Jason know that we would be coming. The warehouse is heavily guarded and secured; from the outside, it appears abandoned, but once we make it inside, it's clearly far from abandoned. I lead Briar down a narrow corridor to a staircase that leads underground.

"What is this place?" she questions me as she inspects her surroundings.

"Our version of San Quentin."

An eerie mood replaces the excitement of a moment ago. The dimly lit hallway leads us to our destination. As we approach, I see Jason posted outside. He nods at me before stepping away from the door.

We enter as a unit. I can feel the way Briar grows at least a foot at my side. The smell is what hits me first, the nauseating stench of urine and blood. I turn off my senses, channeling the beast that lives within me.

Seated in a chair across the room is River Nolan. He's slumped over, his hands chained to the metal chair, fresh blood drying from where he's rubbed his skin raw attempting to slip the manacles off his wrists. At the sound of our footsteps, his head bobs before snapping up, his eyes having made contact with Briar. I move my hand to Briar's waist, slightly out of possession and partially out of the need to protect her. I've seen this bastard before, but this is the first time I get a good look at him. The beast roars, a grin begging to break free at the joy I feel in seeing his condition.

I lean down to bring my lips to her ear, "The power lies with you. The power to decide your future. The power to decide his fate. Whatever you decide, I support you. This is a chance for retribution or forgiveness. Or both. The choice is yours," I whisper softly, so only she can hear me.

Her green eyes shift to me, a slight gleam in her gaze as she thinks through her next move. She breathes in deeply, then nods, taking a step forward toward her nightmare.

River smiles at her from across the room. "I see you've replaced me already." He spits, his saliva landing pathetically in his lap.

"Replaced you?" she hisses. She cocks her head to the side, observing him. "There was nothing to replace. You are nothing. You became nothing to me the first time you lifted a hand to my face, not to bring comfort or love, but to wound." She stalks closer, her heels clicking lightly on the cement floor. A monster of her own claws at the surface. I see it, just there, fighting to break free. A twisted sense of arousal fills me to the brim. The mere presence of her has called to me in the past, but this power radiating from her is like no other I've experienced before. Like a lioness stalking her prey, she circles him, a finger dancing across his body as she talks. "Do you remember the first time you hit me?" River nods his head slowly, his eyes darkening like the memory pleased him. "I was too weak to leave you then." Her voice doesn't shake, doesn't betray her nerves.

Anger spurs within me. There was more to her abuse than she let on. This has been going on for years and it all came to a head with her mother getting involved. My body reacts, my muscles tightening and flexing on instinct. I remain behind her only by the small ounce of control I have left.

"Tell me, River." Briar crouches to face him, clutching his chin in her hand. "Do you think I'm weak now?"

River breathes in deeply. "You will always be that weak little girl, bleeding out on the floor because she couldn't make mommy happy. Or me." A grin spreads across his face.

Smack.

Briar shakes out her hand lightly. River spits blood and… I think that's a tooth. Briar just knocked out a tooth with the force of her smack. Well, color me impressed among other things. River lets out a maniacal laugh. He coughs a few times as more blood dribbles onto the floor. "You fucking bitch," he growls. "Your mother's pussy was so much better. Did you know I crawled into her bed at night and got off on the pain it would cause you if you knew?" He moans, his cock straining his pants. He kicks in a misguided attempt to reach Briar.

I can't help myself as I take a step forward, a growl ripping from deep in my throat. "I swear to Hades if you touch her, with your foot, your saliva, it doesn't fucking matter. I'll rip the skin from your body and feed it to you."

Briar holds a hand up to me, stopping me from approaching further. I force myself to halt. This is her fight.

"News flash, River. Your juiceless cock was never going to be enough for me. I'm *so* glad you enjoyed my mom's pussy so much." She practically hisses that last part. River growls again, writhing forward as he tries and fails to jump at her.

"We'll be done here soon, don't you worry." She pulls a knife from her thigh and spins it in her hands. *God, that's hot.*

"River, do you know what a wraith is?" He looks at her, stone faced. "I'll take that as a no. Historically, wraiths were said to be undead creatures with unfinished business in the mortal realm. You tried to kill me, River. And do you know what else?" She walks around him, his face following her every step. He shakes his head, his breathing coming out ragged. There's that hint of fear I expected from a rat like him.

"No." He's trembling now. So am I—internally—but for different reasons.

"You're my unfinished business." Her head tilts, mocking his fear. "I've thought about this moment for years. At first, I thought death would be too easy, not enough *pain*. But then I thought about it more. I'm not much of a religious person, but my father dearest prays to a God above. He believes the worst of the worst will experience eternal damnation in hell. Burning on a spit for eternity." She smiles.

Death mongering looks damn good on her.

"Do you want to know what it feels like to be burned alive, River?" River struggles in his chair, his screams filling the small space. Briar raises her leg, placing her heel directly into his chest. My eyes watch the muscles of her leg as she presses the heel in deeper until he falls backward, his back hitting the ground with a thump. Bringing her body to tower over him, she steps on his chest once more. "Answer me, River," she says with more force in her voice. Pride swells in my chest at her actions.

Fuck, I think I'm falling in love.

River squirms under her foot. "No. I don't want to know what that feels like."

She stands there a moment, contemplating, then sighs.

"Teague." She turns to look at me. "Will you help me raise him back up? I changed my mind."

In two steps I'm at her side, my skin burning to touch her. I push the feeling aside to lift the chair from the floor. Taking a step back, I look at Briar quizzically, unsure of what her next move will be.

Her hands cross in front of her chest as she moves to stand in front of the now upright River.

"You've haunted my nightmares for long enough, River. It is time for me to finish my business and say goodbye." She uncrosses her hands and presses them to the sides of River's face. My throat tightens.

"I forgive you," she says. She takes a step back and removes the gun from her waist. Raising it to his head, she pulls the trigger, a bullet flying straight between his eyes.

11

Briar

Teague won't tell me where we are going. He woke me up from a nap, decked out in a suit, and told me to get dressed. Because of the shopping trip I took earlier, I knew the perfect dress for the occasion. My floor length, green velvet dress matches Teague's tie perfectly. Was that on purpose? I can't say, but it gives me a bit of joy knowing that we look like a matching pair.

There's a thigh high slit up the right side, allowing me to show some leg. Maybe I'll be able to tempt Teague a bit with a peep of skin. At least, I hope I can.

The summer has come and gone, leaving us with a cooler night breeze. Spooky bitches like me would call this spooky season. Can't say I disagree. California lacks the presence of seasons. Instead,

California's seasons, named by me, are as follows: Holy Fuck It's Hot, We're On Fucking FIRE, It's Raining For Point Five Seconds— Freak Out and Sweater Weather. I've been a part of the Crimson Crows, unofficially, for a little over two months now. That puts us squarely in Sweater Weather territory.

After that night with River, my training picked up. Teague has apparently decided I was ready; he's started treating me more like an equal than a trainee.

That brings us to today. Exactly two months and a week since I signed my life away to the Crows. Maybe this is my first job, or Teague's way of celebrating? Whatever it may be, I'm so giddy with excitement, my leg bounces as we drive.

Teague's warm hand finds my thigh. "Relax. You'll find out soon enough."

I take a deep breath and relax my body. As quickly as I relax, the excitement comes back, sending my leg shaking again. I groan.

"I can't. I won't be able to rest until I know what you have up your sleeve. Are we going to be seeing people? Is this a party? Give me something."

"Trade secret," He replies. "Just trust me." He peels his eyes away from the road for a moment to glance at me. "You can do that right?" The corners of his mouth turn up slightly before his face turns back to the road. I roll my eyes far back enough for them to get stuck.

"Fine," I huff.

Fifteen minutes later, Teague's car careens around a corner and right into the closest parking spot. Teague nearly jumps out of the car and rushes around to the passenger side. With an easy tug, he frees me from the car and extends his arm to me. Taking it, we walk arm-in-arm to the front of a large theater building.

Gasping, I take in the beauty of the theater lobby. Blood red floors extend to the back of the room, with a large center staircase branching out in two directions. A vermillion carpet decorates the staircase; I'm walking up a red carpet. The walls are all a rustic golden color, large pillars on each side. The room is lit through a cluster of massive, stunning crystal chandeliers.

Taking the steps two at a time, we eventually round the corner into a banquet hall. Two long, family style tables are set with several dozen seats.

"This way," Teague guides me through the banquet hall to a back room. Closing the door behind him, he turns to me, a sly grin spreading across his face.

"I still don't understand what's happening." I quirk a brow at him, watching him closely for hints. He stalks toward me slowly, his eyes darkening slightly. My heart races the closer he gets to me.

"Just wanted a moment alone before you are swarmed by a gaggle of men trying to prove how big their dicks are." He closes the distance between us, leaving a small space between my face and his chest. My breathing hitches at how close he is. He rests a hand on the wall next to my head, caging me in. I step back until my feet hit the wall, my breath coming in quick bursts.

"W-What are you doing?" Drawing my bottom lip into my mouth, I turn my face up to him.

"Looking at you," he says, his eyes crawling up and down my form. My pussy throbs at the attention; fuck him for getting my hopes up. I look down, suddenly feeling embarrassed at how quickly my body is responding.

"You look so beautiful." His free hand comes to my chin, raising my face to peer up at him. "There's something I've been meaning to do." I blink in surprise as his mouth finds mine. His lips are soft, his kiss tender. He pulls away too soon, so I bring my hands to his face, pulling him back to me. My heels allow me to skip the step of raising up on my toes to meet his mouth. Warmth fills my body as our kisses become more frantic, like kissing each other is something we need as badly as the need to breathe.

I pull away, the sound of voices and footsteps outside the door yanking me out of the moment. "You toy with my heart, Teague."

"I don't mean to," he says. I want to believe him. I really do.

We don't have time to talk about it now because the voices grow louder, as though more and more people are filling the banquet hall. Teague's phone pings in his pocket and he releases a deep breath before stepping away and pulling it out.

"I'm meant to deliver the guest of honor once everyone arrives." His walls snapping back into place, the persona he has adopted so well rejoining us. I don't let it show how it hurts me to see him transform back into an emotionless machine. "They're almost ready."

"Who is the guest of honor? Is it someone I know?"

The corners of Teague's mouth turn up slowly until a full teasing grin is spread across his face.

"Oh, didn't you know? It's you." He laughs brightly, clearly enjoying my shocked face.

"M—Me? Oh fuck." I pace back and forth. "Why? Teague," I plead. "I hate being the center of attention." I'm starting to panic.

His hand comes to my shoulder. "I'll be right next to you the whole time. If you feel uncomfortable or just want to step out for a moment just… give me a signal or something."

I gape at him for a moment. "Uhm… okay. I touch my face a lot so… how about I swipe my finger across my nose or something."

"That works." His phone pings again. I groan, assuming that means it's time to deliver me.

"You ready?"

"As I'll ever be." I breathe in, taking his arm once again.

When we walk into the banquet hall, dozens of eyes turn to look at me. I only recognize a few faces in the crowd. I spot Ondina and Gabe immediately. Hal is not far away from them on the other side of the long table. My father sits at the head of the first table, two open chairs at his sides. I stand there a moment, looking like a lamb being led to slaughter. But then everyone stands in unison. A few men in the front snicker at Teague's arm in mine. Part of me wonders if this surprises them, or if they're shocked to see me.

"Gentlemen." Killian addresses the crowd. "My heir has come home to us." He pauses, allowing for gasps to sound across the room. "Tonight is her induction ceremony. Tonight is her welcome into the family. She will pledge her loyalty to the Crows and to me, her blood father." Light cheering spreads across the room. I just stand there awkwardly at first. Then a sudden sense of pride fills me. I stand a bit taller, raising my chin with pride.

"Come, daughter." Killian beckons us both to the table.

"Does every inductee get such special treatment from Teague Rossi?" I whisper to Teague as we walk.

"You're my first," he muses. "I'm usually hands-off, hiding away. But I couldn't stand to let someone else be near you twenty-four seven." He pulls out my chair, leaving me standing at the table with my thoughts. I try to keep my face neutral as I sit beside Killian.

"Briar Ruarc, as you stand before the family, you will be questioned. Your answers will determine whether or not we accept you." He speaks loudly. I can feel all eyes on me, leaving me feeling naked and defenseless before them. "Do you have your weapon of choice with you tonight?"

"I do," I respond. I remove the Heckler & Koch P30L from the holster between my legs and place it on the table. *Like I go anywhere unarmed, even in an evening gown.*

"After you leave this room today, the moment any bullet leaves this gun or anyone else's, we do not speak of what happens next. Do you agree?"

"I do." My heart races. Can I do this? Am I ready to be an heiress?

"And will you remain loyal to this family to the death?"

"I will." Will I? Are these people my family? I hardly know them.

A man appears at Killian's side, a gleaming silver platter in both hands. A needle rests on a handkerchief, a large golden bowl, and a card depicting a saint in prayer resting beside it. He places the platter in front of Killian, and I shiver as I anticipate what's coming next.

"With this needle, I will prick your trigger finger." I hesitate only a moment before I extend my right hand to him, allowing him access to my pointer finger. I feel the pain of the prick, then the roughness of the card being wiped across my bleeding finger. That was unexpected.

Killian immediately crumples the card, tossing it into the bowl before setting it on fire with matches pulled from his suit jacket.

"Should you ever betray your family, your body will burn like a saint." He turns to me, one hand extended, the other holding a golden ring. Taking his hand, I hold his gaze intently as he slips the ring onto my trigger finger. I try to keep the fear at bay. I do not fear him. I fear the future and what this means for me. *Are pit stains visible in velvet?*

He rests his other hand on top of mine, and we pause a moment. His golden eyes gleam at me. Is this pride I see staring back at me? After a moment, he raises our joined hands above his head.

"Welcome to the family, daughter." The crowd roars at his acknowledgment, loud cheers spreading across the room like wildfire. in unison. Killian's arms spread wide; "Go meet your family."

"I'M SO FULL, I might explode." I slump in my seat and rub my food baby, Ondina laughing at my side.

"Well, I have bad news, then. I'm dragging you out to celebrate—we're going clubbing." She mimes dancing in her chair, and I cackle at her absurd movements. "Besides, I want to see you grind on Teague a bit, just to appreciate the face he'll make." She winks at me conspiratorially. I snort, then my face heats, remembering our kiss earlier in the night. Ondina saw it before I could turn and hide my face. *Shit.*

"GIRL! What was that face you just made? Spill!"

"I don't know what you're talking about."

Ondina smirks. "You little liar. You'll tell me, eventually. Trust me." She pats my back, then stands. "Come on! The guys can drive together. You're coming with me, babe."

I groan. "I really need to get a car. I keep playing ring around the rosy with drivers."

"It's not such a bad thing to be driven around like a queen, Babe." Ondina winks in my direction. Walking to the parking lot, Ondina stops in front of a pearly white BMW M5. In the dark under moonlight, it's gorgeous. I can only imagine what it looks like during the day.

We both climb into her car, the engine roaring to life. This girl's got style. I take time admiring the interior of her car as we drive through the city. There's a myriad of purple and teal accents throughout her car. I run my fingers across her dashboard taking in every detail.

"Your car is beautiful," I say. "This makes me want my own car even more now. I love my bike, but I feel like I need something more substantial." My golden ring now shimmering on my finger brings a small smile to my face. Upon closer inspection, I find an R engraved into the ring along with a pair of wings. *I've finally found my wings.*

"I get that. The need for freedom."

"Where are we going anyways? People here have developed a bad habit of taking me places without telling me where we're going."

Ondina laughs. "I take it that you've been kidnapped a few times?"

"Just a few." I grimace at the memories.

She laughs again. "We're going to Elysium. A club downtown. It's Underworld themed."

"Well, that's cool. People here must really like their Greek mythology." Everything here seems to be a reference to Hades, the Underworld, or some other myth.

"You don't even know the half of it, girl."

We pull up a few minutes later to an imposing building decorated with a neon purple and blue sign. The line to get in is wrapped around the building. I groan at the thought of waiting outside in the cold.

"How the hell are we supposed to get in there?"

"Babe… You're a crow now, not to mention a Ruarc. You could just say your name and they would start falling at your feet. Wanna try?" Ondina wags her eyebrows suggestively.

I grimace. "Not really."

She shrugs in response. "No pressure, but just so you know, that name will get you far around here." Her eyebrow raises, a smirk forming on her face.

"Oh, I don't doubt that." I know the power my name holds. I don't think I'm ready for the attention or the expectation that accompanies it.

The men are already waiting for us by the time we make our way to the doors. I spot Teague immediately, his height obvious among the throng of women. As we get closer, I spy a young blond gesticulating wildly as she talks with Teague. She giggles loudly as if whatever he just said was the pinnacle of hilarity. Even from here, I can tell he is wholly uninterested. The moment he spots me, his posture changes. His body turns away from his conversation, focusing his undivided attention on me. His gaze sends electricity through my blood, a wild excitement flooding my veins.

The blond must notice the change in attention because she looks in our direction. As if she could get any more annoying, she moves her body to stand in front of Teague, demanding his focus. One more step and my body is directly behind hers. I can feel her stiffening in my presence, towering over her in my tall heels.

I lock eyes with Teague, a slight gleam in his eyes as he waits to see what I do next. He quirks an eyebrow at me, as if to say, *jealous?* In all honesty, I don't know. As much as I'd like him to, Teague doesn't belong to me. But maybe, just for tonight, I'll pretend he does.

I clear my throat loudly, close enough to breathe on the girl in front of me. She turns around slowly with a smirk on her face.

"Excuse you," She declares. *God, that's annoying.*

I cock a brow at her. The *audacity.* "You're excused."

Her brows furrow. I wave her off like a bug on my windshield, trying to make my way closer to Teague. The girl once again puts her body in my way. *I think she has a death wish.*

"What are you doing? Who even are you? Probably someone insignificant." She asks, challenging me. Gabe chuckles at Teague's side.

I smile viciously. She doesn't know who she's messing with. "Briar Ruarc. And I suggest you get out of my way."

She pales. Her thumbs twiddle nervously in front of her. "R—

Ruarc? As in Killian Ruarc?"

"The one and only," I quip.

She stands there a moment as if contemplating what to do next. Suddenly she turns on her heels, flying toward her group of friends, escaping before she can push me far enough to snap.

Ondina squeezes my arm. "Told ya." She laughs softly.

I nod in response. "I really need a drink."

The bouncer at the front door waves us right in. I've never had special treatment before. As much as I hate to admit it, I don't mind it. We make our way through the packed club to the bar. I order a rum and coke, my signature drink. My eyes glance down as the moisture from the glass slides down my arm and onto the floor.

When my eyes return to the bar, I feel his presence immediately. I turn around, practically smashing myself into Teague's chest in the process.

"Hi," I say with a small wave.

Why the fuck did you just wave?

I internally cringe when Teague laughs.

"Hi." He runs a hand through his hair. I take a sip of my drink, feeling the burn at the back of my throat. Warmth spreads through my body almost instantaneously.

Grow some balls and say something, damnit!

"Do you want to dance?" I gesture to the dance floor. *Yeah, cause that's any better.*

He raises an eyebrow at me, cocking his head as I extend my hand to him. It takes a moment, but he finally takes it.

His eyes gleam at me in the dimly lit club. The smell of alcohol is thick in the air. *Can I get drunk off smells?*

I pull on his hand until we reach the dance floor, the pulsing of music coursing through my body. My eyes flutter shut, connecting with my body, feeling the rhythm. My hips sway, moving in time with the heavy bass.

My eyes snap open when I feel Teague's hands move to my shoulders, then slide down the sides of my arms. He hooks his arms at my waist, pulling me in close to his chest. Our bodies rock together to the music. The sensual way we move makes me blush, although the alcohol surely helps. He grabs my arm and spins me around, dipping me as the music slows. The fabric of my dress is clinging to my body. We are way overdressed for this club, but as we dance, any irritation I had in the back of my head melts away.

I take a step away, but his hands reach for me, pulling me back to him. The heat of his body awakens parts of me that I didn't know I even had, that has apparently been asleep for years.

Spinning me around, he pulls my ass close to his body, grinding with the music. I feel the hardness of him against my ass and my pussy throbs in response.

I feel a sense of satisfaction knowing that my body affects him like this. The smell of him is intoxicating—sea salt and smoke. Tingles spread throughout my body as his hands roam; my waist, my thighs, my arms. My breath hitches in my throat when his hand moves to my neck, his hot breath making me ache for more than a simple touch. Teague's large hands would look so good as a necklace, snugly wrapped around my throat.

I adjust my head to give him better access. Instead of making contact with my neck, he spins me around to face him. Why does him taking control turn me on so much?

My head feels fuzzy with my arousal. To steady myself, I wrap my arms around his neck, pulling myself so close that I don't think even a molecule of air could get in. Teague's lips brush against my ear, grabbing my hands as he whispers.

"Come with me."

We barely make it down an empty hall before Teague's lips crash into mine. I respect his need for privacy, but this is still very visible. I shiver in anticipation—maybe I'm into exhibitionism after all. Cradling my head from the impact, he pushes me against the wall, deepening the kiss. A gentle stroke of his tongue short-circuits my brain. He tastes vaguely of cinnamon and alcohol. Gabe's voice pulls me from the moment. *Ugh not now.* I hear people coming closer to us. As if Teague suddenly realizes where we are and what we're doing, he pulls away from me quickly, running a hand through his hair.

His quick change in behavior confuses me. A moment ago, it didn't seem like he was trying to hide anything between us. I purse my lips. I'll be damned if I'm going to be someone's dirty little secret.

Pushing off the wall, I address Teague. "I'm going to run to the bathroom. Don't wait up." Practically running down the hall, I take the opportunity to hide away and calm myself.

When I exit the bathroom, I hear Teague talking to Gabe and Ondina. Not wanting to interrupt, I creep into the hallway.

"What's up with you and Briar, dude? She's totally into you." Gabe. That's definitely Gabe. Creeping closer, I wait for Teague's response.

"I don't date. She's just another assignment." His tone is uncaring and passive, and I feel a knot form in my throat.

Just another assignment, huh? I won't let the tears gathering in my eyes fall. Why do I feel betrayed right now? Teague is so fucking hot and cold. He can't even figure out what he wants. I just played right into his bad boy charm. I'm a *statistic.*

I rush past my *floormates*, making sure they see me and flee out the front door.

I spot the bouncer at the front door as I leave. "Do you remember the people I came with?" He nods. "Could you stall them for me?"

"Yes, Miss Ruarc."

I peel off my heels and sprint down the street to catch a cab. I refuse to leave without my dignity intact. The first cab I hail pulls over, and I quickly slip into the backseat. When I look through the back window, I see Teague running toward me in the distance.

This is not a game you want to play, Teague.

12

Briar

Killian summoned me first thing the next morning, allowing me to escape before anyone saw me.

Teague sat outside of my apartment door for a while last night, begging for me to let him in and explain, but I wasn't in the mood for a conversation. I knew he could get in–fucking master key–but he didn't push it. I'm thankful for that and thankful for the privacy to wallow alone. He was gone by the time I left, which I was also grateful for. My weak ass may have forgiven him the moment I saw him slumped by my door.

Killian is seated at a large table at the back of the hole-in-the-wall coffee shop he asked to meet at. I never pegged Killian as a coffee person. Then again, I've been wrong before–just look at Teague.

As I look at him from across the room, I have flashbacks to that first time I saw him five years ago. The time Killian keeps a secret after all these years. When he looks up from his phone, his eyes zero in on me.

"Briar." He gestures for me to sit. "I took the liberty of ordering coffee for us already. I hope you like caramel."

Smiling at him, I nod. "What is this about?"

"Right to the point." He laughs darkly. "You're acclimating well. Good for you." Was that pride?

"The first order of business is that your inheritance is now fully yours. The payment was transferred this morning."

That was not at all what I was expecting. I don't know how to react so I nod, my lips pursed into a thin line. I've never had money like this before and I don't want to get my hopes up that something *good* like this could last.

Killian continues, moving on. "I have a job for you. You're the only one I trust with this…*specific* job. I will require a team, but you will be at its center."

I purse my lips, waiting for the catch. "Okay. What do you need me to do?"

"It's a multi-purpose job. There is a neighboring gang that has gotten out of control. They've served their purpose, but they're no longer of use to me. I want them gone. The best way to achieve it is to do it from the inside out."

The barista sets our drinks down lightly in front of us and Killian quiets, waiting for her to leave. "Declan MacQuoid is the boss of the Corcoran Roosters. Simply put, they're vicious and deal in immoral trades. I would prefer to disrupt their sense of peace. Dec has something I want—valuable art pieces stolen from me."

I ponder his words. I know of these paintings. He's mentioned them before, but I didn't know the value they held.

"You're an artist, no? I want you to make forgeries and replace them. That's the first part. I also want you to get close to Declan's son, Axel." Killian brings his cup to his mouth and gulps his coffee slowly. I watch him intently—*here's the catch I was waiting for.*

"As far as I know, Axel is a piece of shit, just like his father. But if Declan dies, Axel will succeed him. I need you to be my eyes and ears, reporting back to me only." I nod at his words, agreeing. "We'll take this in stages, but my main goal is to get information. I know they're planning something, and I need to know what it is."

"Do I get to pick my team?" There's no way I'm doing this with people I can't stand. Or worse: incompetent fucks.

"Yes. However, I have a non-negotiable. Teague must be a part of your team. He is my most trusted member of the family."

I sigh, bringing my hands to my temples.

"Is there a problem with Teague?" Is that genuine concern I hear? Frowning, I take a sip of my coffee. "No. I'll make it work."

Killian looks me over for a moment. His face twists then suddenly he smiles at me. He looks at me a moment more, then laughs a hearty belly laugh.

"You look like you just saw a ghost," I say, a little concerned. He waves a hand in the air, losing the tough guy act with me.

"I did," he laughs. "I saw a glimpse of that eighteen-year-old I met five years ago." "Oh so you do remember? We're done pretending like I'm not important to you?" *Yeah, that's right. I'm still mad.*

He sighs, his hand tightening on his coffee cup. "I do. How could I forget? I know our contact has been impersonal in the past. I'd planned on keeping you away from this life."

I interrupt him, my frustration bubbling over. "So when you contacted me five years ago and sent me off to college, what was the purpose of that if you wanted to keep me away from this life? I was practically begging for you to recruit me, for you to save me from the hell I was living. I had to force my way into your life, swapping one toxic parent for another."

I begged for his attention, thinking that he was going to recruit me. My father sent me off to college in California where I met River. I remember the day that my father came to see me in college. It was the first time I saw him in person, and I was so excited. It was going to be the moment he recruited me. Instead he told me that he's sending me back home to my mother.

At first I panicked, but then I found River. It just so happened that his father was a business mogul from New York. He'd planned on taking over the family business after graduation. However, unbeknownst to me, shortly after we moved back to New York his father disowned him which is what led to the River and Iris long con.

He winces, the blow obviously hitting its mark. "I know you're angry–"

"I'm beyond angry," I counter.

"Okay beyond angry, but I did what I thought was best for you. I'd thought this life wasn't meant for you, but you've proven me wrong time and time again."

Sarcastic laughter bubbles up in my throat but I shove it down deep. "Living with my mother is the absolute worst place I could have ever been. To think I could have been spared of that life, of so many years of pain…" I rub my temples, tears threatening to spill over. "I thought that was going to be my chance for a better life. My mother was abusing me, Killian. I was at the lowest point in my life… *ever*. When you told me I was going to California I realized I finally had something to look forward to. The whole point of graduating high school early and rushing off to college was to escape and then you came in—" I point my finger at him. "—And crush every dream I had." I pause, my throat tightening as I recount this last part. "They tried to kill me," I say, my voice weak. Killian's face fills with grief. I can read the regret written across his face like a book.

"I'm sorry," he says. "I was wrong to leave you there, and to send you back."

I know that Teague's protection detail was a product of his guilt. My face softens and my heart twists. I've only ever wanted a relationship with my father. This may be the closest I ever get to that.

"Does Teague know anything about this?" I'm tired of hiding, protecting Killian's secrets.

"No. He does not." He looks down at his hands.

"Is that for a reason?" I sip my coffee again, waiting for his answer.

"No. I just wanted to protect your identity. Neveah Griffin, the identity you took on while in California, was safe and Briar Ruarc didn't exist. I wanted to keep it that way to protect you." *Protection. Doesn't he know I can protect myself? All because of him. All because I wanted his attention.*

I'm so tired of his excuses.

"I didn't need you to protect me. I needed a father, and I didn't get that. I thought that you wanted to be a part of my life. But here we are."

No wonder men like Teague can lead me on so easily. The men in my life apparently make it a point to build up my hopes, only to crush them.

"I brought you to California hoping that your mother would no longer be a problem. She didn't want children anyway. I sent you back because that proved untrue. She continued to stir up trouble when you left. Sending you back was like waving a white flag." He looks at me, his eyes full of regret and pain. I never knew the reason he sent me back like a sheep to slaughter. Killian's face focuses on me, his mouth opening like he's going to say something. Then as though he thinks the better of it, his mouth closes, the silence between us growing.

I bite my lip, nodding. I'm going to have to accept that he's just not going to be the father I've craved so desperately.

"I don't care why you sent me back anymore. I'm sure you had your reasons. I hate them, nonetheless. I'm here now, and you can't change that."

"I did want you here," he says. "After your surgery, I asked Teague to give you guidance in the direction of California, but once you got here, I panicked. Teague advocated on your behalf. That's the only reason you're here today. He saw the way you handled yourself while you stole shit from very dangerous people." He says it like he expects me to feel shame about the life I chose. As if I didn't know who I was dealing with. "I know enough about you to know that you are strong-willed and independent. Whatever happened between the two of you, just know that Teague is the reason you're here. He will be a part of the team you create, so I suggest you fix it."

My eyes narrow in anger. "*I'm* not the one who needs to do the fixing." I haven't touched my coffee this whole time. I realized that I don't have much of an appetite for anything anymore.

His stoic face tells me that this conversation is going nowhere. "I'll contact you again soon. I have a dinner set up that I would like you to attend. Consider this the beginning of this mission."

Standing, I resume the businesslike demeanor from before. I extend my hand to him, and he takes it, giving it a squeeze before releasing me. I don't return the sentiment. I'm done chasing.

"Go easy on him," he says. "I don't know what he did to deserve your wrath. Just know, I'll kill him if he hurts you." With a sad wink, he turns, leaving me standing awkwardly by the table.

Well, this is going to be a fun conversation.

13

TEAGUE

I woke up early, hoping to catch Briar before she left for the day. Now that she's officially inducted, I have no excuses to yank her out of bed for morning training.

Something about this woman is intoxicating. The pull I feel is magnetic, like she's a force all on her own. It should be a good thing, but instead it terrifies me. There are a lot of things about Briar that terrify me.

While training, I realized how quickly Briar could pick things up. Not only did that spark doubt within me, but it brought up a fear I didn't know I had. The moment she's inducted, there will be jobs and missions that don't involve me. I am well aware of her ability to take care of herself. In fact, she was alarmingly skilled. I don't doubt that she spent a lot of time teaching herself whatever she could to survive.

She had to in order to survive.

I rub my eyes, internally groaning. My tailbone rubs uncomfortably on the floor as I adjust my legs to bend in front of me. I've been sitting on this goddamned floor for hours. Leaning my head back against the wall, I close my eyes for a moment. There have been no sounds of movement within her apartment, which worries me. The only reason I haven't used my key is to respect her boundaries and privacy.

When Killian brought me on as a consultant, I struggled to feel anything. I learned to dissociate and separate myself from my job. Shutting off your feelings long-term has its consequences. When you need them again, they're buried so deep that it's nearly impossible to bring them back. I've had no need for them until now, but Briar fucking scares me. Her *mere presence* makes me feel things that I haven't felt in years.

I royally fucked up. Talking to Gabe and insinuating that she's just another assignment was a way to protect myself. I'm an ass and I did it only to protect my image, not thinking about *her* feelings. It's not the least bit true. She's not just an assignment to me. I've never viewed her in that manner. Yet, the words flew out my mouth so easily.

Footsteps draw me from my spiral of feelings. I force my eyes open, moving my head to look down the hallway.

Walking toward me, looking like a goddamn angel, is Briar. She stops at my feet, glowering down at me. I suppose I should have stood, but I was too busy drinking her in to think properly. I shrink under her gaze. How pitiful. A grown ass man twice her size shrinks under this tiny woman's gaze. I can put myself in her shoes for a moment and imagine what she's seeing. I barely put any effort into my appearance today. My usually crisp shirt is unbuttoned at the top, leaving my chest exposed. The tie I had planned on wearing today is draped around my neck and tied in a pitiful little knot. My outward appearance surely expresses what I am feeling on the inside. Maybe she'll see that and pity me. *Probably not.* I know I wouldn't.

Briar props her hand on her hip. I see the hint of her tattoo on her wrist. "Come in. We need to talk." *I wasn't expecting that.*

She takes her key from her pocket and shoves it into the keyhole. "Are Gabe and Ondina home? They'll need to be a part of this conversation, eventually." She shoves the door open, leaving it swinging for me to follow. Scrambling to my feet, I begin to speak but she slams the door closed.

"Okay. I deserved that," I mutter to myself. I knock on the door, waiting for her to let me in.

"Who's there?" There's a note of sarcasm in her voice.

"An idiot who needs to apologize?"

"Enter my cave, peasant." Pushing the door open, I find Briar sitting on the couch with her legs pulled into her chest. "Sit." She pats the seat next to her. "I texted Gabe and Ondina. They'll be here in a few minutes. Before that, you and I need to have words."

"Okay." Like a puppy with its tail between its legs, I walk over to Briar and sit across from her on the couch.

"Time's a ticking. Better talk now."

"What did you hear?" I keep my voice low and calm, even though inside I am exactly the opposite.

"All of it." She lets me sit in my discomfort for a moment, escaping to the kitchen and pulling a water bottle from the fridge.

"Well. You see..." I stop talking, unsure of how to continue. She narrows her eyes at me, impatience painted all over her face.

"Teague, cut the shit. You're a grown-ass adult. So am I. No excuses. Either talk or don't. I will not be collateral damage. You're so hot and cold and I can't keep up."

"Okay. You're right. You fucking scare me, Briar." There, I said it. "I don't feel... *things.* Then you came into my life like a hurricane and suddenly, I feel again. I don't know what I want but being near you feels like something I need." For a big bad gang member, that was pretty damn soft.

Fuck.

The knock that sounds on the door tells me my emotional moment is over.

Briar stands to answer it, pausing to face me. "Well, when you figure out what you want… You know how to find me." My heart drops a bit at her words.

You're a fucking coward.

Ondina skips into the place like a damn fairy princess. That woman is so happy all the time, and it irritates me. I don't understand how she can be so happy when we do the shit we do on a daily basis.

"Babe," she squeals. "Are you okay?" *God, how can someone be that aggressively nice all the damn time?*

She embraces Briar as they exchange secret words, the girls giggling behind their hands. Ondina releases Briar then strides to the couch and sits beside me.

When she turns to face me, she's wearing a deep scowl. Her eyes promise pain, and I know it's on Briar's behalf. Again, I'm shrinking at Ondina's side. *What is it with these women being so easily intimidating?*

She leans in close, her voice low. "You're kind of a dick, Teague. Get your shit together and stop hurting my girl. I know under all that—" She waves her hand up and down. "—Brooding facade is someone who cares. Either show it, or lose her, and maybe your dick too. Your choice." She stares at me a moment longer then rises and plops down onto the love seat across the room.

Gabe looks at me wide-eyed before taking his spot next to Ondina, his arm stretching out on the back of the loveseat.

"Does anyone want a drink? This is going to take a while." Briar stands in the kitchen, her hand on the refrigerator door. My friends chirp in response, resulting in bottles flying across the room. It's silent as Briar walks back to take a seat next to me. My stomach drops a bit, realizing that this isn't a social visit. This is serious.

Briar's mouth opens to speak, but then she stops. I notice the hesitation written all over her. The confidence I usually see is wavering.

"I–uh–I have a lot to tell all of you and I don't know where to start." She folds her hands in her lap, then decides to pull her knees into her chest wrapping herself around them. "My father and I have a rough past. When I was fifteen, I went searching for him and I found out all about the Crows and everything he had built here. He pretended like I didn't exist, so I forced him to acknowledge me. Got myself into all sorts of trouble and started picking up some rather dangerous hobbies in my free time." Her eyes lock with mine as she says, "When he finally acknowledged me, I thought that I'd finally get the chance to have a father, despite him being a crime lord, but instead he sent me off to school and then dumped me back off with my mother, who tried to kill me by the way."

Ondina gasps quietly, her eyes sad. I only know most of this because of my involvement with Killian. Killian has always known about Briar. His cool attitude and reluctance to accept her has confused me, yet a part of me understands the need to protect. Holding people at arm's length is always the safest bet for me. People get hurt when they're around me.

"I swear there's a point to telling you all of this." She laughs quietly, but the laugh doesn't quite reach her eyes. My heart clenches at her pain.

"I met with my father this morning. All of these rather unpleasant feelings were stirred up for me. So I apologize for the deviation from why you are all here today. He's requested that I put together a team." She straightens, her mask slipping back into place. I can see the anger swirling behind her eyes. "While I was in college, pretending to be a real Crow and believing my father actually wanted me, I took it upon myself to research Declan. There are some other illegal activities that are swirling around the Roosters. My father suspects that Axel has a hand in some of them."

Briar continues talking about her meeting with her father, explaining the details of her suspicion of Axel and the details surrounding the paintings that were stolen from Killian. Art is currency in this world. Some of the greatest forgeries have been created and sold by Killian who masterminds our operations. The prior leader, whom I never knew, partook in the same dealings as Declan. The word was that Killian turned the place around, cutting ties with drug suppliers and criminalizing trafficking. If a member was caught being involved, they were removed. I never cared to do more research, but I know enough to fear what Killian has planned for Declan and his men.

"So we're the team?" Gabe leans forward, his elbows resting on his knees.

"You two," she gestures between Ondina and Gabe "are my picks for this team so far." She turns her head to look at me. "The only reason you're here is because Killian requested you. That was his one condition."

Gabe scoffs, and I shoot him a look. She's still angry. Got it.

"What's the job?" For the first time today, she's smiling, but it's a wicked smile like she's about to destroy everything we hold dear. The beast within me reacts until I realize that wickedness is aimed at me.

"We're taking down the Roosters from the inside out. I've been advised to get close to Axel, but–"

"Absolutely not," I blurt. Ondina snorts, and I glare at her.

"Oh, this is gonna be good," she muses. "Gabe, do you want any popcorn?"

"And why the hell not? If I wasn't clear earlier, you're not in charge here. Funny how the power dynamics shift, huh?" Briar obviously chose violence today.

"Axel is bad news. Terrible news. Emphasis on the very." There is no way in hell I am letting her do this.

"Nothing I can't handle, Teague. Who knows? Maybe I might charm the pants *right off of him*." She raises her hand to her face, inspecting her nails then flipping it out like imagining an engagement ring.

I growl and stand abruptly. "Have fun with that. Axel will rip you to shreds. There's no way in hell that you'll tame that beast."

She scoffs, but I know better. "I'll have fun proving you wrong, Teague." I look at Gabe for help, but he throws his hands up in surrender. So much for bro code.

"You're on your own, man. She's the boss for now."

"Sit down, Teague." Staring at her in challenge, I stay standing a moment longer before practically throwing myself into my seat with a huff.

Real mature, idiot.

"Gabe, could you give me a list of names that you think could be additional members for our team? I need another hacker, some muscle, and maybe another forger, or someone with a lot of knowledge when it comes to art." Briar's taking to this leadership thing like a fish to water. "Yes, Boss. When do you need it?"

"End of the week. Killian and I meet with Declan and Axel tomorrow. Ondina, can you get me everything we have on the

Roosters, as well as Declan and his family? I don't want to go into this blind."

"What can I do?" If my hand is being forced, I might as well be useful. Briar's hand comes to her face as she thinks, her lips purse and scrunch towards her nose. She's adorable when she's concentrating. *What the fuck, Teague, get a grip.*

"Well, Teague, darling. You can sit there and look pretty, for now." The room erupts in laughter, at my expense. I roll my eyes at the condescension.

"Yes, dear."

My MIND REELS from the day I've had. Sleep isn't going to come for me easily. Not like it ever does.

If only Briar knew the way I feel about her. The way I've always watched her from afar, aching to know this woman who has always been untouchable. I'm only a handful of years older than her, but my life experience and all of the things I've done ages me. It's littered my heart and soul with filth; the kind that I would never wish to share with anyone else.

Is this aching in my body what love feels like? My hands beg to touch her, to explore every part of her. I want to know how she would react to my touch and the noises she makes as she comes.

I groan in frustration, my cock straining in my boxers. I ignore it, knowing that I deserve the frustration I feel tonight.

Bringing my hands to my face, I rub at my eyes with frustration. I'm not someone who deserves her trust or honesty. I know that it'll take much more than a meager apology to win this woman's heart.

Axel is a slimeball. She's going to be at his mercy, eventually. Nothing about this seems safe, nor smart. I've known Axel for years and nothing about him is honest or even remotely *good*. My worry is that a woman like her would be able to tame the beast within him.

Fuck.

Is that my motherfucking dick talking or is that my head? I want to trust that she can take care of herself.

I want her to tame the beast within me.

Mentally scolding myself, my arm moves to cradle my head as I stare up at the dark ceiling.

Briar came crashing into my life like a hurricane. A beautiful, dark-haired hurricane that collided with my body and soul. The day I first saw her, I couldn't get her out of my head. Those beautiful green eyes piercing. Even from afar she was the most beautiful thing I'd ever seen.

Fuck.

My eyelids feel heavy, my body overtaken by the need for sleep. My dreams tonight will be filled with memories of green eyes and the possibilities of what could be. Is there even a possibility? What would it look like if I take the leap?

14

Briar

Period cramps are of the devil. Who decided that it was a good idea to make our bodies punish us for not getting pregnant? Shouldn't my uterus be throwing a party every month instead?

I've been in bed all day until I absolutely could not be one with my bed any longer. I've got plans tonight that I cannot miss.

Period be damned. I'm going to be one hot bitch tonight.

I wasn't planning on putting much effort into my appearance tonight, but then my father called. Teague would be joining us for dinner. Something about Teague insisting there was a need for backup. As if something were going to happen in such a public place. I highly doubt they're stupid enough to pull something tonight. That sneaky fuck is trying to weasel his way into my job, and I'm not here for it.

Playing dress up is always fun, but now I get to kill two birds with one stone—make Teague jealous and woo my way into Axel's heart. That shouldn't be too hard.

Wow. So much confidence today, huh?

Mentally, I'm struggling with this whole situation. I've decided that the best way to get Axel to trust me is to skip the friend route and go straight for the romantic partner position. Except with my heart all tied up in knots over Teague, I see myself struggling to throw myself at another man.

If only Teague got his shit together and knew what he wanted.

My outfit of the day includes an extremely low-cut green blouse. When I say extremely low cut, I mean it leaves *very* little to the imagination. I paired it with some leather pants and a faux fur coat. Mafia Don's daughter vibes for sure. Rolling my eyes at myself, I slip into my heels right as I hear a knock at the door.

"I'll be right there," I call. My heels clack against the floor, announcing my approach. Swinging it open, I lose control of my jaw for a moment. Standing in front of me is a very handsome and *very* well-dressed Teague. He's in a tailored suit that hugs his body in all the right places. The sleeves are rolled up, veins in his forearm on full display. Arms are my weakness. My eyes drift upward and linger on his face, his hair, and the hint of stubble decorating his chin.

His eyes don't bother with subtlety either. Feeling vulnerable under his gaze, I shift my weight to one side, resting a hand on my hip.

"Take a picture, it'll last longer."

Teague growls as he pulls out his phone. I'm absolutely stunned as he snaps a photo. I didn't think he'd actually do it. Instinctively, I reach for his phone, trying to delete the evidence, but he clicks his tongue, holding the phone high above his head.

"You gave me permission to do that. No take-backs," he taunts. He's challenging me. Rolling my eyes, I huff a breath, pulling my arms to my chest. Apparently, that was the wrong move because now he's staring at my chest.

"Didn't your mom ever teach you it's rude to stare?" I say.

Teague chuckles. "I won't be able to keep my eyes off you all evening." He runs a hand through his hair, cursing under his breath. "It should be illegal for you to leave this apartment looking like… that." He's practically undressing me with his eyes and my pussy clenches at the thought of being naked in front of him.

"Oh-kay." I wave my hands in front of him. "I have to get going now. What was your purpose for coming here and interrupting me, other than to gawk?"

His eyes widen just as a wave of cramps rush through my body. It takes everything in me to hide the pain I feel from my face. My body aches to hunch forward, but I resist, instead holding eye contact with Teague. He looks at me curiously, almost as though he can see right through my mask.

"Why are you here, Teague?" My heel clacks on the floor as I make a show of tapping my foot impatiently.

"Are you in pain?" My cheeks redden at his question. I internally scold myself for not hiding my pain well enough. I am so used to suffering alone in silence, I don't see why that needs to change after Teague's helped me once. I can feel my face hardening, my thoughts plastering themselves on my face.

"I'm fine," I say, my hands coming to my hips.

"You don't need to hide your pain from me." Teague looks so sincere that I almost believe him.

"Like I said, I'm fine." Teague's eyebrows draw together, his head shaking slightly. For a moment, I think he's going to turn away from me and walk away, but instead he stands his ground, shaking off his disappointment or whatever that was.

"Anyway, I thought we could drive together," he says.

"And why would we do that?"

"Safety?" He takes a step toward me, forcing me further back into my apartment. He closes the door behind him, his eyes darkening.

"What are you doing?"

"Whatever I want." His voice is several octaves lower, sending goosebumps down my arms. My breath hitches as he takes a step forward.

"Teague," I'd meant that to sound brave, but it sounds more like a plea.

"Yes?" My mind reels with everything I want this man to do to me. He could bend me over this table and bury himself inside of me right now, and I would beg for more. Blinking a few times, I suck in a breath, hoping it will clear the lust-filled fog from my head.

A slow grin spreads over Teague's face, his eyes narrowing in on my chest again.

Fuck, I'm not wearing a bra.

The evidence of my arousal is on full display. My nipples are swollen peaks through the thin fabric of my shirt.

"I really hate you right now," I mutter, covering my tits with my arms.

"I think quite the opposite." He smirks.

Clearing my throat, I try to change the subject. "I'll drive myself. I don't think us arriving together will send the right message."

Teague is clearly dissatisfied with my response because his face twists into a half angry, half…frustrated expression? Whatever it is, he's not pleased. A naughty thought passes through my mind about being punished for being a brat, and suddenly I am flushed all over again.

You did this to yourself, you horn-dog. Get your shit together.

Mentally pulling up my big girl panties, I stride past Teague and open the apartment door.

"I'll see you there, Teague." I wink and wave my hand, indicating he should leave.

Oh, I fucked up.

Teague's eyes darken as he stalks towards me, capturing my mouth in a demanding kiss. His hand rakes through my hair as his other hand finds my ass, giving it a rough squeeze. My knees go weak as I whimper instinctively, then my eyes go wide as I realize what I've just done. Teague pulls away from me with a satisfied grin.

"I'll be thinking about that sound all night," he breathes against my lips. With that, he turns on his heels and leaves me alone—gaping like a fish and horny as fuck.

ONDINA TOOK MY complaints about needing a car literally because she had a brand-new GR Supra dropped off for me. I take a walk around the car, admiring my new ride. I whistle. She's quite the beauty. There's a note tucked under the windshield wiper.

Make sure you name her. She's in the color phantom for a reason. ;)
-Ondina

"Ondina, you have outdone yourself," I muse to myself. "Well, let's take you for a spin," I state as I run my hands along the hood. "I think I'll name you Callisto."

The car roars to life, immediately sending an excited thrill through my body.

Oh, I could get used to this.

I drive faster than necessary to the fancy seaside restaurant my father picked. It rests on a large dock overlooking the water. This place has a waitlist as large as my mom's audacity. I guess the name Ruarc does come with its perks.

Teague is already there when I pull up. His Mercedes-Benz is parked in a dimly lit area of the parking lot. I pull Callisto into a spot next to Teague's car.

As I step out, my phone buzzes in my back pocket. I feel the rush of blood in my cheeks as I read the message. My breath hitches as I read and reread it.

Teague: I parked in the back. What a perfect place to bend you over my car and fuck you from behind. Don't you think?

Wow. Just wow.

Is it hot in here or is it just me?

My heart rate picks up as I fan myself. *Pull yourself together, Briar.*

The moment I step inside the restaurant, I spot him. The corners of his mouth turn up slightly as I approach the table full of men. Teague doesn't alert them to my presence right away. Instead, I have to clear my throat as I come to stand behind my father.

"Ah, there she is," my father says coolly.

"Better late than never," I say. Two men I don't recognize stand to greet me.

"Hello, Briar. I am Declan MacQuoid, and this is my son Axel." He gestures to the man across from him.

Humming my response, I pause to take them in. He has to be at least six feet tall, round at the belly, and balding. Still, his face is alarmingly attractive for a man over fifty. I had expected him to be tubby and unimposing based on how my father talked about him, but that's not at all how he looks. I imagined him as one of those men who looks like he smells bad.

Axel, on the other hand, is breathtaking. His black hair is trimmed and slicked back, accentuating his pronounced jaw line. When reading his file—because who would I be without doing a little research beforehand—I learned Axel is mixed race. He is what people would call a 'Wasian.' His father is white while his mother is full Korean.

Axel moves to sit next to Teague, allowing me a seat by my father and oh-so-conveniently across from Teague. Declan sits at the head of the table, his pungent smell hitting me almost immediately.

Oh look. I was right.

As if Teague can read my thoughts, a flash of a smirk crosses his face.

The hardwood of the chair rubs uncomfortably across my back. It takes a moment of fidgeting until I feel comfortable. *Ladylike, Briar, real ladylike.*

"So, Briar. You're new to the Crows?" Axel speaks to me directly as if no one else is at the table. Smiling brightly, I nod.

"Very new." Feigning ignorance, I decide to test out Axel's ego with my next question. "Are you new as well? I've never seen you before."

A wide grin spreads across Axel's face at my question before he and Declan spit out a laugh. "Oh no, sweetheart. I've been a part of the Roosters since birth. But I'm flattered that you think I'm new."

It takes everything in me not to cringe at his use of 'sweetheart' when addressing me.

I am not your sweetheart, thank you.

I giggle sweetly, blinking a few times, trying to hold my nausea in. "Wow since birth? How cool." I place my hands on the table, cradling my head in my hands as I look across at Axel. "Have y'all ordered yet?"

Teague answers first. "We were waiting for you to arrive before we ordered."

The look that Axel gives me sends warning bells screaming through my body. He's stunning, but he's also a walking red flag. I think Axel could be a lion in sheep's clothing.

I browse the menu. I'm not picky by any means, but everything here is overpriced and complicated.

Again, as if on cue, Teague pulls out his phone and types a quick message before tucking his phone into his jacket pocket. Sneaking a peek at my phone, I see a text about getting burgers after. I almost sigh in relief. Now that my pain meds have kicked in, my appetite is back.

I feel like this is a trap. Why is he trying so hard now?

The server comes by and collects our orders. I order a salad. It felt like the safest option.

"I knew I liked you. Only good girls eat their leafy greens." Axel says from across the table. *Blech. Did he really just say that?*

When the waitress reaches Teague, he denies food, saying he ate earlier and is solely here for the company.

Lie.

I fight a smile at the gesture.

"So, Declan, I hear you are Boss of the Roosters?" I say. Declan puffs out his chest. I guess even that minor question juiced his ego. Internally rolling my eyes, I train my attention on Declan as he talks.

He tells the table, mainly my father, about his ventures as a second, eventually stepping up as Boss when his father fell ill. I like to prepare before I meet people. It's an old habit. Tonight was no exception. According to my research, Declan stepped into his new position very quickly. His father, Aaron, fell ill suddenly, almost unexpectedly. It was suspicious, but I didn't pay much attention to it until now. Declan continues speaking, his chin rising and his eyes gleaming with something like pride.

The feel of Teague's foot hitting mine under the table pulls me from my thoughts. I watch Declan closely, my eyes drifting to Teague every once in a while. His foot continues to find my leg, making me overly aware of his presence. *I won't let him distract me.* Keeping my eyes trained on Declan and Axel, my thoughts wander so much that I miss Axel's question.

"I'm sorry. Can you repeat that?"

Axel smiles, his head tilting to the side. His hand slides across the table, then stops in front of me. He taps the table a few times. "Of course, B." *Oh, so I have a nickname now?* "I asked if you enjoyed being in LA?"

"Oh, yes! I do, very much. It's different from the East Coast, but I am enjoying the weather." "I was told you went to USC for college. I'm surprised you got a degree. You don't strike me as the college type."

Oh no he did not. Was that a personal attack?

He licks his lips, his eyes lifting as though he's looking for a reaction. I won't give it to him.

"I got a Bachelors in forensics with a minor in art history. Graduated in three years."

Teague looks at me, his eyes gleaming. Axel just quirks an eyebrow at me.

"Women don't typically bode well in gangs. What makes you think you will?"

I laugh, trying to keep the sarcasm from my voice. "You should tell that to Ondina."

I don't dare entertain his question. I've got nothing to prove, especially not to him. This verbal boxing match with Axel is growing boring. I suspect he doesn't like me, for some odd reason. We've only just met.

Our conversation remains steady throughout the evening. Teague continues to play footsie with me under the table, threatening my control. From what I've gathered, Axel is a major party boy who likes to dabble in illegal things. I get the feeling that the illegal drug trade is his favorite. Declan hasn't incriminated himself–yet. My leg shakes under the table as the conversations come to a close. I've barely touched my salad and my stomach is growling uncomfortably.

"Well, it has been lovely meeting you," I say, rushing along the exit. Everyone stands, Teague taking a moment longer. My eyes narrow at him and he just shrugs. *I hate it when he does that.* "B, I'd like to take you out some time," Axel announces to everyone. "Tomorrow evening."

Oh, so not even waiting for a response.

He takes a step toward me and snatches my phone out of my hands. Teague barely restrains himself next to me. I clench my teeth and glare at him in warning. Axel types in something into his phone then a ringing sounds in his pocket.

"I'll text you the details," he says, flashing me a smile that might be incredibly handsome if I were stupid. Not leaving me any room to argue, he saunters away with his father on his tail.

I glare at my father, who has stayed silent throughout this entire exchange.

"Really?" I add a flat note of irritation in my voice. "Him?"

"Nothing you can't handle," he says. He rubs a hand through his beard and over his mouth. "Just be careful."

15

TEAGUE

Flirting with a woman has never been this fun. I told myself I was doing it just to tease her, but it turned into this dangerous game. *Why did she take the bait? Later. We'll worry about this later.*

Briar follows me as we leave the restaurant. She's cleared her throat several times, trying to act casual, but I can practically smell her arousal. Thank Hades that I've gotten really great at tucking my dick away. This taunting is going to get real dangerous real fast.

"Nice car," I say. She beams a smile that makes my heart pound.

"I named her Callisto." She looks down at her feet, fidgeting. I noticed those incredibly high heels earlier. Heels on this woman should be illegal. The way her ass moves as she walks could kill me. "Wanna go for a ride?" She winks at me mischievously.

"Hell yeah." I toss my suit jacket over my shoulder and open the passenger door, sliding inside easily. She dawdles for a moment before pulling open the driver's side door. She tosses her heels over her shoulder and into the back seat.

"I can't drive fast in heels. I want to see what this baby can do." Her nose crinkles in excitement.

Feeling like a kid in the candy store, I sit back and enjoy the ride. What a view.

Two hours later, we pull back into the restaurant parking lot. By now, everyone has gone home, leaving the parking lot devoid of cars. Besides ours, of course. Briar exits the car, coming around to my door to—honestly, I have no clue.

I watch her curiously. With each step she takes, my breath hitches. The tension in the car was high, but I don't regret teasing her like I did. Fuck, it was worth my painful hard-on to see her like that for me. Teasing her is like a love language, an addiction.

She pulls the car door open and stands in front of me. From the time it took her to get from the driver's side to the passenger's side, her eyes have gone glassy with lust.

"Get out of the car," she commands. I cock an eyebrow at her.

"I don't believe I take orders from you."

"Is that so?" What she does next surprises me. The leather of her pants quietly squeaks as she slowly lowers herself to the ground before me. "I don't appreciate being teased," she says.

She runs her palms up my thighs until her nails graze my already hardening cock. I stifle a hiss, the contact firing all sorts of feelings in my brain. I swallow thickly, my Adam's apple bobbing with the motion.

She smirks slightly, seemingly happy with my discomfort.

"What do you want?" I rasp. The lust heavy in my voice gives my need away and damn it, I don't care one bit.

She shrugs, quickly standing and turning back toward the driver's side.

Oh, hell no.

I pull myself out of the seat and catch her arm right as she rounds the back of the car. With one hand, I scoop her up and trap her body against the back of the car. I settle her head between my hands on either side of her face. Her breath brushes against my cheek as I bring my face close to hers.

"I don't appreciate being teased," I whisper against her lips, throwing her own statement back at her.

Her hands plunge into my hair a moment before my lips find hers. She draws my bottom lip into her mouth and bites; I smile into her kiss, the rough bite sending a jolt of pleasure right to my cock. She opens her legs, allowing me to step between them. Her hands crawl down my back, gripping my sides before slipping back up to tug on my hair again. As her fingers wrap and twirl through the longer stands, my lips caress her neck, causing her to gasp quietly.

Tingles of desire rush through my body and I ignite, craving the feeling of her, needing to have more of her against me. My fingers roam, snaking under her shirt and feeling the warmth of her skin under my palms. She shivers as my fingertips graze her breasts. Her legs tighten around my waist, trapping me between her heels and her core.

My lips find hers again, and our mouths battle for control, her tongue begging for entrance. I duly oblige. I caress her nipple, rolling the tight bud between my fingers. She releases the most delicious moan from her mouth, and I practically come in my pants from the sound alone.

"Do that again," I groan into her mouth.

She releases a breathy laugh before speaking. "Do what again?"

"That moan. It was the most beautiful sound I've ever heard."

"Yeah?" Briar gasps into my hair as I kiss down her neck, bending to draw her nipple into my mouth. *Fuck.* She writhes under my touch, spurring me on, begging me to continue.

We tease each other, back and forth. I feel her hand slipping to my waist, and I shiver in anticipation.

Her hand slips further…

My phone rings in my pocket, ripping the moment away from me.

"Ignore it," she says, her lips nibbling on my neck.

The phone continues to ring, and my nerves rise with each passing tone.

Shaking my head, I pull the phone from my front pocket. "I can't ignore it. If it's your father, he'll kill me." The phone screen lights up with Killian's name.

Briar scoffs as I answer the call. "Killian."

His voice fills the phone. Something about needing me to oversee some new recruits or whatever, but I'm not paying attention. Briar's body language has changed. She rigid, that stony mask slipping back into place.

"Yep," I say into the phone, my eyes locked with Briars. Killian ends the call a moment later and I lower the phone to lay it on the trunk of the car.

"What just happened?" I plant a hand on her waist.

"I get that this is both our lives, but there was a choice there and you made it."

I look at her, reading the expression in her eyes.

She sighs. "We keep playing these games, Teague." Her mouth curves down, her eyes turning glassy. "I just want to feel chosen. I'm so tired of chasing." She sounds so defeated. Her words hit me in a way I didn't expect. *I'm tired of chasing.*

I run the words through my mind several times trying to decode them. She's been chasing people her whole life both literally and figuratively. Chasing information and secrets as well as the love of her father and mother. *And now me and I've blown it. Twice now.*

I bring my hand to her face, rubbing her cheek with my thumb. Tracing my thumb across her lips, I feel her give in, the weight of her head resting into my palm.

"I know that I am not good at this. I'm still figuring this out. But I'd like to make it clear, just because I answer a call from your father, it doesn't mean I haven't chosen you." *I want you.* I bring my forehead to rest against her. "It just means I'm terrified of dying."

Briar's eyes smile, her full cheeks growing as her mouth follows. I close my eyes against her forehead, breathing deeply.

"Okay, fine," she concedes, pulling away from me. I watch as her eyes grow hungry again before she sighs. "I do need to get home. This woman needs her beauty sleep."

Without hesitation, I step out of her grasp and extend my hand to help her off the trunk.

"Well, thank you. For tonight and for coming with me on a joy ride." She smiles, rising on her toes, planting a kiss on my cheek. "You're not so bad, Teague Rossi."

BRIAR CALLED A meeting with the team today. After careful consideration, she decided on two new members. Hal and Riggs will be here any moment, and my nerves are getting the better of me. Briar has reignited a part of me that hasn't surfaced in over a decade. Feelings that I didn't know I had, creating an uncomfortable inner silence that I can never quite settle into.

Instead of our apartment building, we're convening in an old conference room I've converted into our meeting space. We need a home base, and the apartments would eventually start to feel cramped as we grew. Plus, I firmly believe in at least attempting work-life boundaries. Too bad I've never been successful on that front.

Briar saunters into the conference room looking like a snack. An absolute snack. Her curves are on full display, those dark jeans hugging her body in all the right places. If we weren't expecting other people, I would spread her out on this table and savor that delicious body of hers for hours. I don't fall to my knees often, but for her, I would kneel between her legs and worship.

"Stop looking at me like that," she snaps. She can try to hide it all she wants, but her voice is huskier than usual.

"Like what?" I'm just taunting her now, poking her to see how far I can tease her before she snaps.

"Like you want to eat me." She pulls her bottom lip into her mouth. If Gabe hadn't walked through the door at that exact moment, that would have been my undoing. My control is slipping the more time I spend with her, and I don't quite mind.

"What's happening, friends?" Gabe asks the room. After apparently taking his time reading the room, his eyes go wide before he bursts out laughing.

"What?" Briar asks, a note of defensiveness in her voice. Gabe just shrugs in response. Briar rolls her eyes and I can't help but laugh. She turns her unhappy gaze on me, her eyes full of warning. I know she hates it when people answer with a shrug. I know because I do it to her all the time.

"Where is everyone else?" Neither of us answers him. Gabe talks about something else, but I'm not paying attention. Instead, I fix my eyes on Briar. She's moved to sit at the head of the table, her legs crossed. Leading looks good on her. I've always viewed myself as a very dominant person, but the power she holds makes me want to let her use it on me.

Her eyes catch mine for a moment, and she surprises me by licking her lips before returning her gaze back to Gabe. My cock strains against the rough zipper of my jeans at just that small movement.

"We're still doing this, huh?" Gabe gestures to Briar and me and his words snap my attention back to him.

"I don't know what you mean," I say, kicking back in my chair, my tone noncommittal.

Gabe scoffs. "Why don't you two just fuck and get it over with already? If you keep eye fucking each other like that, I'm going to be sick." He crosses his arms in front of him. "I can practically taste the tension from here." He puts a finger in the air and then places it in his mouth. "Yup. That's some tasty tension."

Before I process what I'm doing, I'm up and out of my seat in an instant. My arms wrap around Gabe's neck, locking him in a headlock. He releases a less-than-manly squeal as I run my knuckles over the top of his head.

"You fucker," I grit out. I release Gabe, allowing him to push away from me. He releases a hearty laugh right as the others walk through the door.

"What did I miss?" Ondina plops into the chair next to Briar, spinning herself in the office chair.

Releasing a loud sigh, I take my seat opposite Ondina. "Nothing important." It's obvious I'm lying, but I don't care.

Briar clears her throat. "By the way, I ordered pizza for everyone. I figured we would be here a while and that having food available would be a good idea."

The last two to arrive are Hal and Riggs.

"I know we got off on the wrong foot, but I am honored to be a part of this team, Miss Ruarc," Hal says a bit timidly, his face reddening. Hal is a six foot three, three-hundred-pound monster. At six feet five, I'm not small by any means, but his stature makes him a formidable opponent. His full beard hides his facial expressions, but I know there is a small amount of fear there.

"Hal, please, it's Briar. No hard feelings." She pops him on the shoulder like an old friend and a shadow of a smile appears on his face in return. He's going to develop a soft spot for Briar. I can already tell.

Riggs, on the other hand, is a mystery. He's quiet and reserved, not much of a team player, but he's the best when it comes to tech. I have no doubt that Briar will make him into a team player. He'll have no other choice but to be. He extends his hand to Briar. He's slightly shorter than Hal, but still towers over Briar, even in her heels.

"Dominic Riggs," he says. "Tech and information." His shaggy blond hair flips into his face as he backs away.

"Thanks for being here, Riggs." Briar nods her head at him, and I smile. I briefed her beforehand on his nickname. "Alright, well. Let's get to work, shall we?" Briar's face is all business. Heads bob around the room in agreement. "I know you're all aware of the general reason for which this team is required, but I wanted to go into more specifics. However, before I get into that, I have one specific order of business I need to address." Briar stands, placing her hands flat on the table. Everyone looks at her with their undivided attention.

"Just because my father is your don does not mean you have any reason to trust me. I know that most of you don't know me, but I hope to rectify that situation soon. As your leader in this, I promise that I will not steer you wrong. I am not new to this kind of work, shocking as it may seem. I had a knack for finding trouble prior to my induction." Briar gestures to me, surprising me. "Teague will be my second in this, so if you don't trust me, at least trust him."

"You have my full support," I say, a little too eagerly.

Shit. I need to tamper that down.

It felt necessary, so I let it slip. She nods thankfully.

"Questions?" No one responds, so she moves on.

We spend the rest of the afternoon discussing plans for obtaining the paintings. Ondina and Riggs are tech wizards. Together, they'll get the layout of Declan's mansion and information on where the paintings are located. Briar believes Declan would keep it close based on what Killian said. For now, everything's based on speculation. Hal and I are serving as the muscle. I'm too recognizable to Declan and his men, so anything in-field will be up to Gabe and Hal. Not that I'm happy about that.

We have a giant folder of information, including photos of the paintings we're after.

The swap is complicated, but not impossible. Briar will forge the paintings, making them identical enough to swap without immediate notice. With planning, we should be able to get in and out of the place unseen. Emphasis on the *should*.

I know I should trust Briar, trust her intuition and her planning, but I can't help the possessive, protective beast that roars to the surface.

Briar slings her bag over her shoulder. "Well. I hate to leave so abruptly, but I have a date I need to attend." She shoots me a conspiratorial glance, then makes her way out the door. Why do I have the urge to follow her like a lost puppy?

"I have another meeting to attend." The words come out squeaky and rushed before I even think them through. I quickly excuse myself, not caring about the team's reaction.

I vaguely hear Ondina whisper to Gabe. "Do you think she really has a date?"

Gabe laughs loudly. "If she does, Teague is totally about to stalk the shit out of it."

Shit. Is that what I planned on doing?

I really hadn't thought this through.

HIDING OUT IN my apartment has proven to be the worst decision I could have made. I silently pace the room like a man deranged. I can still hear the click of her heels through the apartment next door.

Why do I feel like this?

The hum of music stops, drawing my attention back to what I'm meant to be doing. If her music stopped, that means she's wrapping up her primping and getting ready to leave.

Right on cue, the soft click of her door opening forces my feet forward. Mustering the most nonchalant face I can manage, I swing my door open.

The growl reverberating through me was totally unplanned, but I can't help it. I groan, drinking in every inch of her.

Briar makes a show of turning around to face me, a satisfied smirk toying at the corners of her mouth. She's in the smallest dress possible, quite literally. Every curve of her body is on show, making my cock twitch in my slacks.

Fuck.

"There's no way you're going out like that," I practically snarl. Her eyebrows shoot up in a wordless challenge.

"Why not? Last I checked, no one could tell me what I can and cannot wear. Particularly you." Her lips part slightly, drawing my attention to her full mouth. My mouth opens and closes several times. I look down at my crotch, scolding.

Come on, dick. You were talking so fluently a moment ago.

"That's what I thought." She saunters down the hall, leaving me astonished in her wake.

"Where are you going?" I blurt.

Big bad gang member huh?

"I'll be fine," she calls over her shoulder.

"Just in case." I make a desperate move towards her.

She stops right before reaching the stairs. "Mermaid's Cove."

And just like that, I cancel my plans for the rest of the night.

16

Briar

I knew my outfit would throw him over the edge. If he wants to taunt me with empty threats, I'll taunt him right back. Just because we had a moment on the car does not mean that I've called a cease fire. I didn't expect to be taunting myself though. The way he stares, like the stars begin and end with me, makes me break out in goosebumps. He just stands there, half desperate, half pleading as I walk away from him. The things he wants to do to me—it's written all over his face. *If only he could get his shit together and take what he wants.*

Walking into Mermaid's Cove, I didn't expect Teague to be sitting in the corner waiting for me. My heart pounds in my chest as I instead look for Axel. He stands, drawing my attention to the bar.

My racing heart doesn't slow as I feel Teague's hungry gaze on me. I can physically feel him, as if he were touching me from across the room.

Is it hot in here?

I take a few calming breaths, willing my face back to *calm* and *fake*, and make my way across the room to Axel. If I can just ignore Teague.

The bar Axel chose is pirate and underwater themed. A giant fish tank wraps around the entire building, extending up the walls and onto the ceiling. There are actresses dressed as mermaids swimming around, making stops to wave and greet guests. I smile at the redhead mermaid that spots me and gracefully waves, blowing air bubbles at me.

"Hey, B!" Axel makes a show of pulling me into his chest. I stand there awkwardly for a moment before lifting my arms and wrapping them around him. This is too familiar for someone I just met yesterday. Out of the corner of my eye, I see Teague shift uncomfortably. Mentally willing him to stay hidden, I stay wrapped in Axel's arms until he lets go, much longer than I would have liked.

I breathe in his scent—nicotine and citrus, not my favorite—committing it to memory. It may come in handy for me one day.

"Can I buy you a drink?" His voice is higher pitched than Teague's. It's not unpleasant. But it isn't Teague's. Not the husky, sex-filled voice that caresses my ears and makes me clench my thighs together whenever I hear it.

Remember the mission, Briar.

"Rum and coke please." Taking a seat, I drop my purse to the floor and move it between my feet. Axel grins, clearly pleased with my drink choice.

"My kind of girl," he says. His arm has snaked its way across the back of my seat It takes way too much self-control to let him stay there. Axel signals to the bartender. "Can we get menus?" A moment later, two menus appear in front of us.

The first thing my eyes see is fries. Any form of fried potato calls to my soul at all times. I will never turn down a fried potato.

I decide to order chicken tenders and fries while Axel decides on a bacon burger. He teases me about my childish order, but I wave it off like it's no big deal. "Comfort food, Axel."

He hums his agreement, taking a gulp of his beer. *He's being surprisingly pleasant.*

"So why the Crows?"

I cock an eyebrow at him, confused. *Excuse me? What kind of question is that?*

"Because of my dad?" I blink at him a few times, realizing that answer wasn't enough for him. I sigh. I'm not getting out of this one easily. "It felt like a simple decision for me. I have familial ties and honestly, I didn't know the Roosters existed until my father told me."

Lie. I totally knew. Research is one of my specialties.

"Ouch. I wonder what could have been. We're lacking some tits in the Roosters. It's full of cock." He grins at me, as if his chauvinistic comments shouldn't nauseate me. I err on the side of caution and choose to laugh to stroke his massive ego. The delivery wasn't the best, but he clearly believes it.

"Oh. What could have been, huh?" I purr. "What could have been, Axel?"

The feel of his breath on my face heats my cheeks as he moves his face close to mine. Axel's lips find mine in an unpleasant, aggressive kiss. It's not the gentle yet urgent kisses that Teague supplies. As Axel's lips explore mine, the only person on my mind is Teague. I gasp a little as he bites my lip lightly.

He pulls away a moment later, his eyes meeting mine. "If you were a Rooster, I would be more inclined to make you mine."

He looks over my shoulder and I can't stop the feeling of being watched. A chill rapidly spreads through my body, and not the good kind.

Danger.

Pulling away from him, the hard metal of the barstool rubs on my back uncomfortably. "I need to go to the ladies' room," I say without giving him a moment to protest.

Weaving my way through the tables, I find the narrow hallway leading to the restrooms. The hairs on the back of my neck stand, warning me of danger nearby. I feel like I'm being followed the further I go into the bar, but when I look behind me, there's no one. My breathing picks up and I slip inside the small restroom.

Shit, I left my purse.

With my hands on either side of the bathroom sink, I look at my reflection in the round mirror above me.

"Okay," I breathe. "You have sixty seconds to get your shit together and figure out what's going on here." I let my mask drop for a moment, the scared little girl shining through.

My hair is in loose waves down my shoulders, and my dress leaves me feeling vulnerable. I'm an idiot for leaving my weapon in my car.

Think. Think. Think.

The sound of the door opening draws my attention away from the mirror. A man slips into the small bathroom, closing and locking the door behind him. The hairs on the back of my neck stand straight up again.

This is bad.

A cold sweat drips down my spine, fear seeping to the surface. Throwing the mask back in place, I lock eyes with him through the mirror.

I trained for this.

Gray eyes, brown hair, tattoos. He's in blue jeans, work boots, and a white tee. There's an identifying scar across his right eyebrow.

He smirks at me, a flash of gold teeth twinkling at me. I turn slowly, not taking my eyes off him.

At least he's recognizable.

"I think you're in the wrong bathroom," I spit.

If only he'd speak, I could remember his voice.

He grunts. Okay, so maybe he isn't an idiot. He widens his stance, readying himself to attack. *Alright then. Not how I saw tonight going.*

"I can't help you if you attack me. What do you want?" I put on my bravest, most forceful voice.

Mama's not here to play.

He growls again, taking a step forward. Reaching into his pocket, he flips out a knife and lunges towards me.

Fucker fights dirty.

I let him just close enough before I slip out of his way, moving behind him. He doesn't expect that, and I use his hesitation to my advantage. My hand comes down on his head, smashing his face into the bathroom sink. His hand comes up to push me away, but I've got the advantage now. I smash his hand against the wall. The knife clatters to the floor.

With both hands occupied, I've left myself vulnerable, something I don't realize until it's too late. He sends his elbow into my side, causing me to fall back into the wall. Using it as an anchor, I send a well-aimed kick straight into his stomach.

"You bitch!" He growls at me.

There's the voice. He's got an accent. Even better. *Gotcha.*

He grabs my foot and whips me to the ground. I gasp, feeling the air leave my lungs. My stomach clenches as I try to suck in a sharp breath.

Where the fuck is Teague?

His foot comes to my ribs, crushing me beneath him. I shriek as pain blooms in my side.

It hurts to breathe. I panic, looking around for anything I could possibly use to take him down. On my right, I spy the knife is close enough for me to grab.

Wrapping my fist around the cool metal, I slam the blade into the side of his thigh, forcing him to release me as he cries out in pain. Bringing my legs up, I wrap them around his waist, forcing his back to the ground as I unsheathe the knife from its wound.

Ignoring the pain in my side, I rush to my knees, using them to pin his arms to his sides, the knife in my hand coming to his throat.

"What do you want from me?" I yell at him. He spits in my face. *Wrong move dude.* His defiance only makes me angrier. I drive the knife harder into his throat, a bead of blood trickling down the blade from the pressure.

"Why are you here?" I yell, louder this time. He laughs darkly. "I'll give you one last chance." I move the knife, slicing a cut into his arm. "What do you want?"

He's silent for a moment, his eyes darting between me and the door. "You." he spits out. "They want you."

"Who wants me? Why?"

Before he can answer, someone knocks on the door.

"Hello, are you okay in there?" They knock again. I groan in frustration.

How fucking convenient.

My eyes dart to the door again. I realize my mistake immediately as my head kisses the floor, and the world fades to black.

A CRASHING NOISE pulls me from the darkness. Axel busts through the door, a man I don't recognize at his side.

Axel looks at me with… concern? He blinks looking around the small bathroom, his fists clenched at his sides. I try to move, but he drops to my side.

"Don't move. You hit your head." His voice isn't kind. I can't tell if that anger is directed towards me or the situation. The nameless man walks back down the hall, returning a moment later with the bartender.

"What happened?" The bartender questions from the door, obviously too uncomfortable to enter a woman's bathroom. *Asshole.*

"Someone attacked me," I grit out, my voice rough from the pain spreading through my body.

"I called 911," he replies. "They should be here any minute."

"I'm fine," I say, my face still pressed to the cool bathroom floor. I realize then how disgusting a bathroom floor is. I try to sit up, but immediately regret it when my vision fizzles on the edges and my head swims.

"Stay down," Axel commands. Loud sirens wail outside the building, the rush of footsteps lulling me back into unconsciousness, but not before I hear Axel speak.

"I'll take care of this," he says.

What does that even mean?

THE FIRST THING I hear when I wake again is the steady beeping of a machine.

My eyes flutter open, blinking a few times to take in my surroundings. A woman walks into the room right as I realize where I am. She smiles at me sweetly.

"Hi, hon. How are you feeling?"

"My head hurts," I croak.

She nods a few times. "That's to be expected. You hit your head pretty hard. Do you know where you are?"

"A hospital?" I take a wild, albeit obvious, guess.

"St Adam's hospital, to be specific. Do you know what year it is?"

Clearing my throat, I mutter, "2021. October. I don't know what day it is or how long I was out. But the day this happened was the sixth." She smiles at me.

"Good. I'm going to check your vitals now. Is that okay?" She hovers over me waiting for my response. If she had reached for me, I don't know how I would have reacted. I nod my response, which was the wrong choice. My head pounds almost immediately.

The nurse runs through the motions of checking my blood pressure, temperature and monitoring me for signs of a concussion. The doctor questions me about my attack and asks me if I have anyone at home available to monitor me there. When my face scrunches in question, he clarifies that I would be more comfortable healing at home. I assure him I can find someone to stay with me, and he seems pleased enough with my answer to stop questioning me.

An hour later, Dr. Harrow sends me home with a healthy number of painkillers, symptoms to look for, and instructions to care for my bruised ribs and hands. Before the nurse leaves me to change, she hands me my phone and purse, telling me to call my family to let them know. I thank her as she rushes from the room, closing the door behind her.

My phone feels heavy in my hand. As my fingers type in my passcode, a sick feeling in my stomach overtakes me. I have zero missed calls. Something feels very wrong. I can't shake the feeling that something horrible happened while I was incapacitated. Almost as though the universe is listening, my phone rings, an unknown number flashing on the screen. It's a video call. My gut tells me not to answer it, but I do anyway.

Heavy breathing comes through on the other end of the call before a masked face pops across the screen. He wriggles the phone in his hands before flipping the camera to show my father.

My heart stops.

The pit in my stomach grows, leaving a sickening roil in its place.

Killian is slumped in a chair, blood dripping from his face. His eyes peel open when the man pushes a gun into his temple. "You've got thirty seconds," the masked figure says. "I love you," he gasps, a tear running down his face. "Do good and live." The camera shakes, Killian's eyes closing. "I love…"

BANG.

My brain goes blank as Killian's body slumps, blood spraying the phone and the floor. The man doesn't care to flip the phone back to him.

"This is the last warning, Briar Ruarc. Stay out of our business." The call ends abruptly, leaving me alone with my panicked thoughts. I'm panicking. Breaths are coming shorter and closer together, my vision blurring.

The fear from earlier creeps in and instead of pushing it down, I let it consume me. The tears fall freely and with full force, my body shaking with silent sobs. Somehow pushing myself to dress, I rush through the hospital at almost a run, finding my car parked in the guest parking lot.

Did someone drive my car here?

I rummage through my purse, finding my keys to let myself in. The sobs coming more urgently, louder and harsher now that I'm out of anyone's earshot. I gasp, trying to catch my breath.

I wasn't ready for this.

A frustrated scream tears from my lips as my panic and fear overtake me.

17

Briar

When I compose myself enough to see clearly, I throw my car into reverse and peel out of the hospital parking lot. My heart is broken, ripped from my chest, and utterly destroyed. I've felt grief before, but never like this. The only living parent I've ever remotely cared about is dead, ripped away from me in some fucking grab for power.

I drive faster than I should, but the creeping feeling of dread won't let up. I don't know how to deal with this—how to feel about anything.

Dozens of rapid-fire questions plague my head, my thoughts cloudy with emotion. It feels like a geyser ready to burst at any moment. I shove it down again, not ready to process it. I need to be alone, to hide and bathe myself in darkness. My natural tendency is to want to disappear, wrapping these feelings up and throwing them away, but a part of me knows that's not possible. So instead, I drive to the one place that I can call my own, a safety net that will protect me from others, *for now*.

Thank fuck for the continual green lights, allowing me to pull into the apartment complex parking lot in under ten minutes.

The chill spreading through my body has me pulling my gun from my glove compartment and securing it to my side. The apartment complex is silent. I know there are people that live on the first floor, but today it seems like it's completely empty.

I take my heels off and hold them at my side as I run up the stairs, taking them two at a time. When I get to my apartment, the door is cracked slightly. *Well, that's not a good sign.* Upon further inspection, I see shards of the door frame dusting the floor. My breaths come in quick gasps as I take a step to the right and knock on Teague's door.

I knock again, but there's no answer. Moving across the hall, I try both Ondina's and Gabe's doors, realizing that none of them are home.

Fuck.

I yell into my apartment, alerting the intruder to my presence. When no one answers, I kick the door open, holding my gun out in front of me. The gun shakes in my hands, but I do my best to steady myself as I cross the threshold. Looking to the left, I clear the kitchen and then the living room. Someone trashed my apartment, leaving things overturned and broken all everywhere. Making my way into the bathroom, I shove the shower curtain aside and check behind the door.

Clear.

Walking through my bedroom is the hardest part. The intruder took a knife to my bed, slashing through the mattress and all of my decor. This place was finally feeling more like home, and now they had to go and ruin it. My body heats with anger and fear. *Now that's an emotion I can work with.*

I pull out my phone and flip through my contacts until I find Teague.

It rings twice before he answers.

"Briar!" His voice is full of relief and urgency. Teague has become my beacon in the darkness. Everything about him calls to me in a way that I've never felt before. I have never believed in fate, but today, maybe I do.

Before I can stop them, the tears fall, not so silently. "Teague," My voice breaks.

His voice grows dark. "What happened? You know what, never mind. Where are you? I'll be right there."

"Apartments," I choke out through my tears. The sound of a car roaring to life in the background calms me.

He's on his way.

"Stay on the phone with me, gorgeous. I'll be right there."

TEAGUE

PANIC, DREAD, FEAR—feelings flood my system. I was already in a mood when I saw her kiss Axel, but that shifted into anger when I got the call from Killian.

"They bombed the office building."

I play Killian's words in my head over and over again.

Two people dead, and our headquarters, with all of its art,

destroyed.

Fucking Declan.

I suspect this was a hit meant to cripple us. Thankfully, we have backups, but Killian is pissed.

I hated leaving her with him, but Killian needed me.

Now I'm paying the price. Her voice was broken. Something happened—something bad.

I find her on the floor outside of her apartment in the fetal position. She's sobbing silently with her phone laid in front of her. My body goes stiff, my mind wandering with all the things that fucker could have done to her to leave her like this, so fragile and not *Briar*.

I drop to my knees beside her and pull her into my arms. She adjusts herself, nuzzling her head into my chest. Her body shakes with her silent sobs, leaving moisture on my shirt. Somehow, I coax her into letting me take her downstairs to my car. Settling into my truck, I make sure she's buckled and safe before shoving the keys into the ignition.

"Where are we going?"

"Somewhere safe."

We drive in companionable silence for the relatively short drive to my home. I bought it as backup for emergencies and it's mainly storage, but it'll do for now. I turn down the gravel road to the private entrance of my home.

"You're not going to kill me, right?" She attempts to tease, but there is still that note of sadness in her soft voice.

"No. I promise." I place a hand on her thigh, giving it a comforting squeeze. Well, at least I hope it translates as comforting. Headlights illuminate the large, imposing gate that signals the start of my property. I click the button on my rearview mirror, swinging the gate open to let us through. The crunch of gravel beneath the truck's tires sounds familiar and comfortable.

Pushing open my door, I drop from my truck, flick the lock over the gate, and flip open the control panel. Disabling the remote control and tapping on the security system, I feel more comfortable knowing that no one can get into our safe haven tonight.

As the truck rolls down the driveway, the lights flicker on, illuminating the outside of the house. It's not huge by any means, but it's not small either. If I was being honest with myself, I would admit that I bought this house in hopes of one day having a family to fill the halls. It felt like a stupid wish until Briar came into my life like a hurricane. Briar could be family enough tonight.

"Where are we?" I help Briar out of the truck, while she takes in the house. Something about seeing her in front of my home makes me feel... excited? She looks like she fits in perfectly with my space, like it was meant for her. She shivers, wrapping her arms around herself.

"Are you cold?" She nods at me as I strip my suit jacket from my body and I toss it around her shoulders, rubbing her arms to warm her. "Let's go inside."

I jerk my head toward the front door. Small footsteps resonate beside me as she follows up the small path. A wince escapes her mouth and I realize she's barefoot. Without a second thought, I scoop her into my arms and over the threshold. Kicking the door closed behind me, I flick the lights on before setting her down to look around.

"I would like a tour... maybe tomorrow, but right now I just really want to sit down." She sounds weak, and the thought makes me wince. Her eyes squint closed as I carry her into the living room.

"Of course. Is the couch okay for now? I need to empty rooms for us." She hums a yes. Even that hum has me weak in the knees. She's a masterpiece. My saving grace and my kryptonite rolled into one, deadly package.

Finding solace on the roomy leather couch, I set us both down into its warm embrace. She reaches for my hand, interlacing our fingers. A spark runs up my fingertips when she touches me. She's rested in my lap and I want nothing more than to remain like this with her forever.

I gently remove her from my lap, and she protests, but I silence her with a look. She frowns but settles back into the couch. Moving to the fireplace, I pull some wood from the pile at the side, arranging them carefully. With the starter paper and a lighter, I ignite it, poking at the wood until I can feel the warmth filling the room. When I return to Briar's side, she remains attached to me, letting me go only for the necessities; it's like the contact of our bodies brings her comfort.

"Do you want to tell me what happened?" I feel her head shake into my chest. Her whole body is curled up into mine.

"Tomorrow," she murmurs.

Her breathing slows into a steady rhythm, and I can't help but watch the way her chest moves as she breathes. Every once in a while, she whimpers, breaking my heart in the process. *What happened to her?* I move her head to my lap, finding a pillow for her head and throwing a blanket over her back. I could watch her sleep for a lifetime.

I rest my head on the back of the couch, letting my eyes close. Her body against mine reminds me that all is well…for now.

18

Briar

Stirring from sleep, the first thing I feel is the incredible weight of Teague's arms wrapped around me. By now, the fire has gone out, but the warmth from his body keeps the shivers from the chilly morning at bay.

With Teague asleep, I take the time to study my surroundings. I didn't ask him any questions, but I find curiosity getting the best of me now. I try not to stir too much as I move my head for a better vantage point.

We're in his living room, I realize. Teague's home is beautiful, a kind of cozy industrial. A steel gray brick wall where the fireplace rests accentuates the white of the living room, creating an open, airy feel. I don't know if Teague has an interior decorator, but if he does, triple her pay. The gray leather couch we lay on is not only stunning but extremely comfortable. My body sinks into it, enveloping me like I imagine a cloud would. The TV rests in a nook with expensive-looking speakers at the sides. I imagine watching action movies would be an experience with the surround sound in this room.

Teague's chest rises with a deep breath a moment before one of his eyes peeks open at me.

"Hey," he rasps out. *Wow, even his morning voice is sexy as hell.*

"Hey." His hand finds my cheek, rubbing his thumb lightly over the curves of my face. My eyes flutter shut at his touch, and I lean my head instinctively into his comforting hand.

I don't know when it happened, but my heart began falling—falling for someone I may never have. *Aw shit.*

Shifting my head on his chest, I open my eyes, trying to convey my feelings without having to say anything, without having to be vulnerable, willing all of my emotions forward as I gaze at him. His eyes flit between my eyes, his eyebrows growing closer together as he studies me.

A silent tear escapes, the wetness sliding down my cheek. *Damnit emotions, not what I had in mind.*

"Do you want to talk about it?" Silence encompasses us for a long time. It could be seconds or minutes, but Teague stays patient, an emotional rock at my side. His hand finds mine, his thumb roaming gentle circles over my palm.

Pulling the blankets off my body, I sit up fully, allowing myself to look at Teague. My ribs ache, with movement and I wince. Teague notices and immediately shifts allowing me to find a comfortable position once more.

I finally speak, the words coming to me now. "Killian is dead." Teague's face goes pale white, his breathing becoming erratic. His face shifts, and I can tell there's something more he's not saying. My throat tightens with unshed tears.

"What happened, Teague?" I wrap my feelings into a little box and shove them away. I'm not ready to confront the full weight of my grief yet. I'll pay for it later. I know that. But I can't do it now.

"An act of war. The thing we've been waiting for." I can practically feel the color drain from my face. "They bombed the office building and everyone in it. Thankfully, someone warned Killian. We were able to get most people out." Teague closes his eyes, breathing in deeply. "How do you know he's dead?"

"I saw it happen." I almost choke on the words. *I watched it happen. I saw him die.* "Those bastards face-timed me, letting me watch them shoot Killian in the face." My fists clench in anger before I release them, trying to calm myself. *Not doing a great job at it, gotta say.*

I hate feelings. I tilt my head up at Teague, reading everything I need to in his face. His sadness, guilt, and panic. "I don't know much about who Killian was to you… I haven't even thought about what is going to happen next. I'm not ready to, yet. But when I'm ready… When we're ready. We can do it together." It isn't much, but it's the best I can do for now. He nods, his face still a vortex of emotion. "That's where you went last night? I couldn't feel you watching me anymore." My voice comes out as a whisper. The admission of his presence creating an impact on me feels freeing and terrifying at the same time. I fear his rejection, and his repulsion, but it never comes.

His expression softens, a look of understanding crossing his face. "I found you outside of your apartment last night. Why?" His thumb continues to rub soothing circles on my palm as his other hand rests on my leg, now entangled with his.

"Someone broke in and wrecked everything. It was a warning to stop digging into the Roosters. Their plan to break me, I'm sure."

"And where was Axel?"

I cringe at his question, my face twisting with the frustration I feel. "Gone. I don't know. He disappeared after the bathroom incident."

His eyes go wide as his hands dart forward to rest on my shoulders. "Did he hurt you?" He speaks with urgency, laced with venom.

The tears fall freely from my eyes now. "I don't know." Teague's features twist with confusion. "It was someone else who physically hurt me, but when Axel found me… he looked so angry." I still don't know why he looked so angry.

"I'll kill him," he roars. His breathing deepens, his body shaking in anger.

I can feel myself starting to retreat back into my shell. This is too much, Teague, the Roosters, my father, all of it. Teague's strong, tattooed arms pull me forward until I'm wrapped in his embrace and fully seated in his lap. He's so careful and gentle. He doesn't know the full scope of my injuries yet, but I suspect he'd be gentle without that knowledge.

"I'm sorry," he whispers. "Axel will pay for this. I *will* kill him." Teague's fingers comb through my hair as he continues speaking. "I apologize for not thinking about how my reaction may affect you, though."

"We need to tell everyone else if word hasn't gotten out already." My control threatens to snap, the tears begging to fall, my heart wanting to break wide open. But I'm a Ruarc. Does this mean that I'm the boss now? If so, I can't have emotions.

"What will happen with the Crows?"

Teague grimaces. "It will go up for a vote. By name, you should take over, but because I am his second, I could also step in. The people will decide."

I nod, the admission sending something like relief through me. Maybe I won't be responsible for the fate of the Crows after all.

"Let me take care of it all. I'll do anything you need," he says. I nod weakly, unsure if I can handle speaking. He holds me, allowing the silence to pass on. It's a comfortable silence, like we know everything will be okay as long as we stay inside our little bubble. "Hal is medically trained. Do you want him to come look at your injuries?" Teague rests his hand on my thigh, his thumb stroking circles. A shiver shoots up my spine as I shake my head.

"I'll be fine. I don't think I can stomach human contact right now," I say.

"Are you hungry? I don't have much food here, but I can run to the store to—"

"Don't leave me… Please." I gasp into his chest and grasp tightly onto his shirt. *I can't do this alone.*

"Okay, okay." His palm rests on my head. "I won't leave you. I can call someone to pick up groceries, or we can go together later. What do you think?"

"Let's see what you have and then we can go together? I just need some time…" The thought of entering the real world again makes my whole body shake with panic. He nods his understanding, and I relax a bit. Who knew I'd be finding comfort in a mafia man?

"Okay," is all he says, and it speaks all the words he doesn't need to say. It's every bit of understanding and comfort I need.

Teague and I find fixings for pasta stashed away in the cupboards. It's not an ideal breakfast, but we both need to eat *something*. I can feel the ache in my body spreading the longer I neglect the medication in my bag.

Doing something so mundane feels oddly normal. Being in the kitchen together, working as a team; just feels like something I could get used to. I try to do more, but Teague insists on caring for me. I suspect that I am allowed to do the bare minimum only to protect both our sanities. The small tasks he does allow me to do keep me busy enough, so I won't complain.

THE DAYS PASS quickly, spending time with Teague. He's given me time to process what happened without pushing me to share, and in return, I allowed myself to be vulnerable.

After day four of being holed up in the house, I ache in more ways than one. We've made a habit of falling asleep together on the couch every night. *Maybe he fears what would happen if we made it into a bed.* With his hands running through my hair, I ache for the moment he stops being so gentle. I want more than the light touches I've been given so far. Even with my body still healing, I want to feel him between my legs, to have him claim me for himself.

Teague set me up in the master bedroom, saying it would be more comfortable for me there than the couch, and yet I still choose to fall asleep in his arms downstairs. *Take a hint.*

The thick tension between us has created this innate need for him. His scent covers everything, throwing me into a constant state of arousal. I was hoping he would make a move, but maybe it's time to take matters into my own hands, literally. I know he's trying to be sensitive and understanding, but a girl's got needs, okay?

Grabbing my phone from the bedside table, I connect my phone to the wireless speaker in the bathroom. Scrolling through my music,

I settle on my sexy time playlist, starting with "Ride" by SOMO. I smirk as I undress, letting myself into the bathroom, padding across the cool tile to the shower.

This master bathroom was designed to fit Teague and his needs. Teague is a big man, so everything is taller, wider, and more suited to a giant than a woman my size. Because of that, the tub is big enough for at least three of me. My mind wanders to the dirty things that could be done in that tub. On my second night here, I indulged in a heavenly bubble bath, jets and all.

The shower is like a room of its own. Gray tile flooring accents the raw stone wall at the back of the shower, like a spa or a natural spring. It's incredible. *And incredibly well suited to my plans.* I turn the water on to heat up, steam starting to billow out of the open shower door.

Standing there naked as the day I was born, my thoughts follow along with the song lyrics still blasting from the stereo. My first thought is to be self-conscious. Don't get me wrong, I love my body, but there are days that I look in the mirror and see my endo belly full of bloat and I feel incredibly unwelcome in my own skin. The scars that pepper my body make me unique, and I've learned to love each one. *I am beautiful just the way I am.* It's not easy to love myself, but I learn this love as time goes on. I can smell Teague's scent on everything, which does nothing to tamper my arousal. My body feels like it's on fire, the need for physical touch becoming overwhelming. I cross my legs, pressing my thighs together, feeling my wetness already pooling. Just thinking about him is foreplay enough, but he doesn't need to know that.

I can't help myself, my fingers glide through the slickness, sliding up to my already sensitive clit. Rubbing in little circles, I drop my head back, releasing a small moan at the feeling. I squeeze my eyes shut, imagining Teague's hands on my body, exploring every inch. My breathing increases and the small circles grow more urgent, my weight shifting between my legs as I touch myself.

I feel his presence behind me before I hear his footsteps approaching. My face heats, not only with desire but with embarrassment. I'm afraid to turn and look at him for fear of rejection.

The air grows thick, making the enormous bathroom feel small. I hear his footsteps as he pads closer to me. I breathe deeply, anticipating his next moves.

His mouth comes to my neck, the feel of it raising goosebumps down my spine. My knees almost buckle from that touch alone. He sighs into my neck as his hands rest on my shoulders. Teague's hands run down my sides until his fingers interlock with mine. He guides me in a turn to face him. I keep my eyes closed, not quite ready to see the look on his face.

Finally finding my courage, I open my eyes meeting Teague's dark gaze. He's shirtless, his tattooed body visible in all its glory. His gray joggers hang low on his waist, accentuating the deep vee leading exactly where I want my hands to be. I see a hint of black ink peeking from his waistband that I've never noticed before. My eyes lock there for a moment, admiring his sculpted body and the swirls of ink covering it. When I find his face again, his pupils are so dilated that his eyes look black. He drinks me in like fine wine, making me shudder in response. Each second I stand there exposed to him, I think about the move he'll make.

Will he touch me? Will he indulge in me, or will he reject me? I don't know if I could handle the devastation of his rejection right now. The feral look on his face sends a wave of desire coursing through me. He clears his throat, Adam's apple bobbing with his swallow.

"You have a tattoo." His voice drips with desire and lust. I nod. It's a flower decorating my spine. I was told that spine tattoos symbolize strength; I am beautiful yet strong. *I could use some of that strength right now.*

"What do you want, Teague?" I breathe slowly, waiting for his answer.

"You," he rasps. There's no question there. His answer is full of confidence and determination.

"Then take me."

Not missing a beat, he drags my bare body to him, our hot skin making contact, setting sparks off throughout my body, sparks flying where we touch. His hands roam over me, starting at my shoulders and working their way down. He stops at the large bruises on my ribs, his fingers exploring and testing, his lips turning down with a frown.

"Did he do this to you?" His hand moves up my back and down my spine, tracing the curves of my tattoo. I gasp at his touch, clearly so deprived of loving touches that my brain is on overload.

"No. Someone else." I'd love to find out, but now's not the time. I gasp again as his hand moves lower, finding my back dimples and grazing my ass. I wiggle, urging him to move lower. He chuckles.

"I plan on taking my time with you, Briar." His lips find my neck again, the act so sweet and intimate, in complete contrast with what I know his words imply.

"What do you want?" I ask again.

"To worship."

In one swift movement, he throws me over his shoulder. His hand comes down on my ass, a welcome sting sending a shiver down my spine. I'm practically dripping, my desire for him so strong I can feel it drenching his shoulder.

Teague walks into the shower, the hot water grazing my skin as he walks through the spray. He sets me down on a wooden bench against the shower wall. I'm seated with my back against the cool stone wall.

"Spread your legs." I oblige him, baring myself completely to him. My eyes go wide as he kneels before me, keeping his gaze locked with mine the whole time.

His arms twist under my legs, his fingers interlocking at my back. Dragging my body toward him, his face moves to my core. With the first swipe of his tongue, I know I'm a goner. My orgasm is already so close, purely from anticipation. The feel of his tongue pushing inside me sends a shiver through my body. With each flick of his tongue, my orgasm builds, making my body tense, my moans bouncing loudly off the shower walls. Teague's hand comes to my sensitive clit, tracing circles while his tongue moves, in and out, in and out. My legs wrap around Teague's neck and he moves his right hand to my mouth, urging my lips open to take his fingers into my mouth. I suck them willingly, swirling my tongue over the tips. He groans into my core.

"You taste like fucking heaven," he moans. He pulls his hand from my mouth and moves a finger to my throbbing cunt. I moan in pleasure as he pushes his fingers in just the right way.

"I'm so close," I gasp out. My hands are in his hair, tugging and pulling as he grunts his approval. With one last flick of his fingers on my clit, I come undone, my orgasm shaking my body so violently that I must have briefly blacked out. My pussy pulses around his fingers, Teague not letting up his brutal pace while I ride out my ecstasy. My body goes limp as he withdraws his fingers and stands, a wide smile on his face.

I scramble to compose myself, reaching for him. He steps towards me, allowing me to yank down his soaked joggers. I'm so eager to have him naked that I don't even care that he's laughing at me, the sound like magic to my ears.

He reaches to remove his boxers, but I whimper in protest. There's no need for me to question how he's feeling. The evidence is highlighted quite clearly by the *large* tent in his boxers.

"Let me." Hooking my hands in the waistband of his pants, I push down, freeing his cock from the fabric barrier.

Taking a step back, I admire him for a moment. His thighs are covered in ink, the tattoos traveling down his legs and wrapping up his waist. When my eyes trail down, my eyes catch on the ink decorating his cock. *I'll examine that further later.*

I lick my lips, taking in the size of him.

"I want *that* in my mouth," I say, wrapping my hands around his cock. I stroke the thick length of him as he pulses beneath my fingers, a bead of pre-cum forming over his tip. He's larger than any man I've had before. *I'm not one to back down from a challenge.* I hesitate only a moment before looking up at him.

"My turn," I say practically drooling.

His breathing hitches as I take him into my mouth.

"Fuck," he hisses, bringing his hands to my now-wet hair. He fists my hair, his grip encouraging me to take him deeper. Unable to deny him anything at this point, I relax my throat, sinking down further, my eyes watering as he hits the back of my throat. My hand comes to his balls, the other working his shaft. His knees bend slightly as I work him with my mouth.

"Baby," he grits out between breaths. "As much as I love this, I really want to bury myself six feet deep in your pussy right now." I stroke him again, a moan escaping his lips again. "Babe, I mean it. I won't last long like this."

I chuckle around his cock, his hands twisting further into my hair.

Letting him go with a pop, I peer up at him, desire clouding my vision.

"I have an IUD… but if you give me any diseases, I'll cut your dick off." He chokes out a laugh.

"Deal." As if it's no effort at all, he lifts me off the floor and slams my back against the wall. Shoving my leg over his shoulder, he fists his cock, lining himself up with my opening.

With the first thrust, my vision illuminates with sparks, like fireworks going off in my brain.

"Fuck, you feel so good," he grits out, withdrawing himself and thrusting back in with the same force. I moan with the impact, his cock filling me up completely. His mouth finds mine, our tongues battling for dominance. I nip at his lower lip, wanting, *needing* to mark him as mine.

He pumps in and out of me as I'm pinned against the wall, his hand gripping my ass with each one.

"Teague," I breathe. God, I sound wanton; he's ruining me. His mouth comes to my neck, his tongue licking the drops of water from my body. My breath hitches; my mind goes blank, almost like he's short circuiting my brain with each lick.

"Yes, baby?"

"Harder," I moan. "Fuck me like you mean it." It's a command, not a request.

"Yes, ma'am." His pace increases, his cock pounding into me with such force I'm sure I'll have bruises tomorrow. My body shakes with each thrust, and I know I'm close.

"I'm going to come," I warn, my body warming with my building orgasm.

"You don't know how long I've waited for this," he says, his thrusts becoming more erratic as I near my release. "Touch yourself, baby."

I don't question it. Bringing my hand to my clit, the other to my breast, I play with myself. In a matter of seconds, I come undone. My body clenches around Teague's cock, milking him as he finds his own release seconds later.

Our bodies are still linked when his breathing slows against my chest. "Fuck, I think I'm in love," he moans, his voice husky. I laugh it off, a piece of me thinking he doesn't mean it seriously.

"Come, let's actually shower," I say, encouraging the use of the shower for its true purposes. *What fun is that anyway?*

Pulling himself from inside me, he sets me down on shaky legs. I relax under the stream of water, letting the warmth wash over me. Teague follows me, taking the opportunity to run his hands over my body as he helps me wash.

I stare at the wall, my fears starting to manifest, taking me away from the moment. Teague knows me well enough at this point to know the small changes in my demeanor. His arm comes to rest on my shoulder.

"What are you thinking about?"

"I'm scared of getting hurt again." I want to lock my heart in a box and leave it there.

"What can I do?" I didn't expect that. He doesn't try to encourage me, nor does he jump to his defense. Instead, he's asking me what he can do—I could cry.

"Words are just empty promises without actions," I mutter plainly.

"Actions speak louder than words," he agrees. "Nothing I can say will ease your mind, but I will try my hardest to make you feel loved, safe, and worthy of all you deserve." He brings his mouth to my ear. "Maybe it's early for love, but my heart is yours."

My heart jumps to my throat at his declaration. We've been riding this line for months, my heart waiting to fall, but never quite tipping over the edge. This could be the moment I finally walk the ledge and jump.

19

TEAGUE

This will *never* get old. Briar's naked body is wrapped in my arms, and it's pure bliss. Is this what home feels like? This feels so natural, like a married couple waking up in *their* bed. I don't want to worry about what-ifs or the next steps. She's all that matters right now. My feelings for her grow and deepen the more time I spend with her. She has utterly destroyed the man I thought I was.

She lays by my side, a book in her hands as she reads that smutty romance she pulled off my bookshelf. My hands skim across her skin, wanting to be in contact at all times. She is an addiction that feeds my soul instead of destroying it.

Briar sighs loudly the moment I pull my hand away from her hair. I am constantly touching her. I want to commit this moment to memory. I chuckle at her frustration, bringing my hand back to her head.

g out of

food, and you can't wear my t-shirts forever."

"Just one more day," she groans. Her gaze flits from the book to my face. "And is that a challenge? I will wear whatever I want, *Sir.*"

"I don't mean that I want you to stop wearing my shirts, because you look sexy as fuck walking around in my clothes. But I truly think you will want your own clothes, eventually."

"Nah," she says, her eyebrows wiggling in challenge.

"Wanna bet?" I wink at her. She sets her book down, moving to climb on top of me. She brings her face close to mine, our noses touching. My face twitches as I fight a smile.

"You're on. Hit me with your worst." She kisses me quickly, then leaps out of bed. I'm on her in an instant.

"Oh, no you don't." I catch her, wrapping her up in my arms, making her squeal happily.

"What're you gonna do about it, huh?" She wiggles in my arms. As if she's moving in slow motion, Briar opens her mouth wide and chomps down on my arm. I feel her tongue wiggling on my skin while her teeth bite harder.

"Ouch!" She keeps biting down, eventually moving to suck on my arm. When she finally releases me, a string of drool follows her mouth as she wipes her face with her hand. She giggles, looking pleased with herself. Staring at the bite, I see the purple bruise formed from her sharp sucking.

"Mine," she growls, playfully.

"Who are you and what have you done with Briar?" Her face falls, her body no longer fighting against mine. "Hey. Hey. What's wrong?"

"This is me," she whispers. "The real me—the playful me. I don't let her out often…" Her head falls to her chest, her eyes dropping to the floor. My chest constricts at the thought of her feeling so ashamed. I gently tip her face to look at me.

"You never need to hide around me. If you can accept the devil inside me, then I can accept the goofball, murderess, heiress, bookworm inside of you. I will accept every one of your personalities without question." Briar crashes her face into my chest.

"Where did you come from?" The fabric of my shirt muffles her voice as she speaks into my chest. "I don't deserve you." I drop to my knees, purposefully making myself smaller than her. My heart hurts realizing that she truly believes that. I don't deserve *her*, not the other way around.

"You deserve the world, Briar. If I could give you more than that, I would. Don't discount yourself. You've done nothing to warrant a less deserving life." My hands hold hers to my chest, keeping our physical contact. She nods weakly. Eventually, she'll understand her value and her worth, but for now, I can accept her understanding.

"Come on. I have to make you regret wearing my clothing." I wink at her, bringing myself to my feet.

BRIAR WALKED INTO the guest room bathroom like she was told. She's clarified that she doesn't mind wearing my clothing. As much as I love that, a part of me worries she's afraid to go back to her apartment. I would stay here off the grid with her, forever, but there's work to be done.

Grabbing my choice of shirt for her, I knock lightly on the door, alerting her to my presence. Briar opens the door, sticking out her hand to retrieve the shirt.

"Give me ten minutes," she shouts from the other side of the door. I know the minute she sees the shirt because she yells a myriad of curse words at me. "I HATE YOU," she yells, laughing. I chuckle to myself, waiting for the big reveal.

I walk down the stairs and right into the kitchen. As I'm grabbing mugs for coffee, my cell phone rings in my pocket. My spine straightens when I see the name on the screen.

"Gabe," I say, the phone pressed to my cheek.

"They counted the final vote this morning." I put the mugs down, on the counter, waiting for him to continue. "They voted in favor of blood. Briar is the new Don."

Gabe's words register slowly. I'm not disappointed. At one point in my life I would have said that I wanted this more than anything. Now, though, the tightening in my throat is not a result of the loss, but because I know that this bliss we've been living in is over. Briar is being thrust into this position with little to no warning.

"Thank you for letting me know," I say, my voice tight. He ends the call, and I slip the phone into my pocket.

Ten minutes later, the guest room door opens, revealing the full splendor of the shirt I chose. Her hair is up in a messy bun, a touch of makeup on her face. She swears by carrying backup makeup in her purse, and it clearly cheers her up. I'll never understand makeup. She's beautiful, with or without it. I try my hardest to smile, but I know she'll see right through me.

I twirl my hand at her, waiting for her to give me a spin. She does, giving me a double middle finger as she spins.

"Really? A spring break shirt?" She's obviously not impressed. I throw my head back in a laugh. The shirt reads, 'I came to get my balls wet,' with a big red solo cup and a ping pong ball. She smiles brightly, finally laughing with me.

"You want to take me shopping like this? Or are we going to my place first?" She props a hand on her hip, eyeing me. It's then I know she spots it.

"What's wrong?" I run my hand through the stubble at my chin.

"You're the new Don."

Her eyes widen. "Are you upset?"

"No," I say, taking a step toward her and resting my arms on her shoulders. "No, not at all. I just hoped there was a way to ease you into this. It won't be easy."

"You'll be with me the whole time," she says confidently. "Will you be my second?"

"I'd be honored," I say, placing a kiss on her forehead.

"Okay good, because I have no clue what I'm doing."

I shake my head at her, a grin overtaking my face.

"Where are we going?" I say, my eyes roaming across her body.

"My place please," she bounces on her toes in anxiety. "I miss thongs."

I laugh. "Your place it is then."

BRIAR WALKS OUT the front door of my house barefoot and sporting my spring break shirt like it was made for her.

"I'm seriously so turned on right now," I groan. She gives me a half-assed glare before walking to the truck door.

As we load into the truck, she turns to look at me. "I'm not ready to go back to the real world." "We can continue staying here, you know. The office is destroyed. This can be our home base from now on."

Her eyes brighten at my words. Taking that as a yes, I pull the car out, unlocking and locking the gate behind me.

"So… are you gonna tell me about the house? And why you were living in an apartment instead?" Her voice is teasing, but I can hear the question behind the humor.

"I bought it…" I stumble over my words for a moment, unsure of what to say. "I've always wanted to settle down. The apartment was both to be close to you and to force me into feeling like home wasn't a place I deserved." The look she sends me is full of sadness.

"I'm happy you wanted to be close to me, but everyone deserves a home." Her palm comes to rest on my thigh as she continues. "Can I be honest?"

"Of course."

"For the first time in my whole life, I feel like I've found a place that could be home. These past few days with you have been like nothing I've ever experienced before. I've felt… safe." My heart thrums in my chest at her confession. Why haven't I locked this woman down already?

You fucking idiot.

"I guess that's kinda weird considering it's not my home." She's receding, and I see it happening slowly, almost in real-time.

"Do you want it to be?" Her eyes snap to me. They're filled with something that looks a lot like hope. The car rolls to a stop, the red light giving me an opportunity to concentrate on her fully instead of driving. The silence is deafening as I wait for her response.

"K—Killian… I hadn't even thought about it. I—I know he had a home and I've momentarily considered moving there…"

"Stay with me. At the house." My heart panics with urgency. Removing my hand from the wheel, I move my hand to her leg, my foot on the gas, rolling the car forward again. "Otherwise, I'm going to move in with you. You can't escape me," I tease.

Not joking.

"Do you mean that?" She looks at me almost incredulously, like

I'm going to take it back at any moment.

"Which part?" Pulling the truck into the apartment parking lot, I can feel her waiting for the truck to stop before she answers me.

"All of it." She stills as we hit the cement parking block.

"Yes. I mean every word. You can have your own room for your own space, but I mean it."

"Okay." She swings her door open and runs to my side of the car, bouncing on her toes. Before I can step out of the car, she flings her arms around my waist.

"I've never had a home before," she says into my chest. "I never got to be a kid either. Thank you for allowing me to have the chance for both." "

You're making me soft, Briar." I chuckle. "Let's go. You're making my dick hard and we still need to go shopping." She reaches for my hand, linking our fingers.

"Then let's hurry so we can go *home.*" She giggles at the word.

We walk, hand in hand, up the stairs and through the apartment hallway. When we make it to her door, the sound of opening locks draws my attention. Part of me thinks to drop Briar's hand, but she holds firm.

Ondina steps out into the hallway, her eyes dropping to our hands immediately.

"What the fuck happened, Briar?" Her voice is serious, but I don't miss the wink she sends her. Briar's face drops significantly before she snaps her protection back in place.

"He pulled his head out of his ass, that's what." Briar gestures to me then looks back at Ondina. "Is that what you were asking? There's a lot that's happened."

Ondina cackles loudly. "For now," she says. "Now if only mine would do that," she huffs.

"Hey, speaking of." Briar's face falls again. "Teague and I won't be staying here anymore. Teague offered his house as the new home base. I want everyone to come tomorrow. We have some… developments we need to talk about."

Ondina nods knowingly. She pulls Briar into an easy hug; they stand there for a moment, Briar visibly relaxing into Ondina's arms.

I enter the apartment first, stiffening slightly when I take it all in. The place is trashed. Drawers are thrown all over the place with their contents spilled on the floor. The dachshund lamp she picked out was shattered on the floor.

I could tell that Briar was scared to see this place, and now I understand a little better. I suspect it has something to do with past trauma, or maybe this is simply a hard process for her. Whatever it may be, I will be her rock through it all.

As soon as Briar steps foot into the living room, her legs immediately give out. I move so swiftly I surprise even myself, catching her before her knees hit the ground.

"Hey, hey. It's okay. Look at me." Her hands hide her face. Seconds, maybe minutes later, she looks up at me, her face full of fear.

"I'm sorry." She pants, her eyes going glassy with tears. "I need a minute."

I nod my head and lower myself to the floor next to her. She breathes deeply a few times, then wraps her hands around her legs.

"My mom hit me," she says. I still, my body tensing. I *knew* that. "She chose these deadbeat men who liked to prove their masculinity through violence." Silent tears stream down her face. Her voice shakes, her face twisting in anger. "One day in high school, I came home to a heated fight between my mom and her newest man. They trashed the apartment as if they had been throwing things at each other, or she was hiding from him. Whatever it was, it was violent and nasty." She shakes, the tears falling more freely now. "Wrong place, wrong time, I guess. He turned on me, deciding I'd be a good substitute to take his anger out on."

Where the fuck was I for this? My body heats with rage.

You couldn't protect her from this. You've failed her twice now.

It takes everything in me to remain seated. My fists ache to punch something. I see red as she continues talking, but I focus on the sound of her voice to ground me.

"She allowed it to happen. I *know* she knew. She had to. It wasn't enough that she hit me. Now the men in her life could too." Her hand gestures to the room. "Being here, seeing my place like that... It brought back memories of that girl. She died that night. A week after, Killian reached out to me, and I was on the first plane out of NYC."

Killian didn't post me as her silent security detail until after she moved back to New York. There's so much I missed, so much trauma that she is living with. How could I ever think that she wouldn't understand mine?

"Can I hold you?" I ask.

She nods. "You don't have to ask. In case you haven't noticed, I feel safe with you." Her admission calms my beating heart.

"I understand that, but I never want you to feel pressured, or forced in any way. Promise me you'll speak up if you're uncomfortable."

"I promise, but please don't stop touching me just because I've shared this with you. I'm not fragile, and I want you to."

"I can agree with that. Let me help you, let me share your burden. We'll get through this together."

Briar packs up two suitcases of things that were salvageable. I know with her inheritance money she could afford to rebuy everything, but I think the sentiment behind everything is what's most important to her. I laugh, realizing that she's most concerned about her books. A heavily tabbed one was the first she wrapped in her arms after seeing it survived.

Dork.

"My laptop's gone," her voice calls out from the bedroom, panic notching her tone up an octave. "All of my files on Axel and Declan were on there. They're going to have everything, Teague." Anxiety is written all over her face. "I just got here and I'm already going to fail Killian. I couldn't protect him, Teague. I couldn't help him when he needed me the most."

"Briar, listen to me. Whoever is responsible for this will pay one way or another. We just need to think out of the box for now."

"One thing I know *for sure* is that the Roosters were responsible for the thrashing of my apartment. I don't know why they'd need to murder Killian, but I've got no reason to believe they didn't do it either. I want Declan gone. I don't want to take over the Crows with this mess. If the Roosters can't agree to peace, I'll take more drastic measures. The fact that I even want to offer peace surprises me." "

Thinking like a Don already." I wink at her. "I'll take care of it. We'll fix this. Send your text out now to the team. We'll have an emergency meeting tonight."

WE SET THE meeting for 8 tonight. I tasked Gabe with bringing supplies, including a new computer for Briar. My little hacker needs her legs in order to run.

The trip to the grocery store was quite the scene. Briar, still wearing my shirt with the addition of her own ripped jeans, wandered off in search of snacks. She returned shortly with arms full of chips, candy, and juice. Dumping them all into the cart, she looks at me through her lashes. I give her an incredulous look after noticing all the sugar and carbs.

"What? I'm paying and I want fried potatoes with flavor sprinkled all over them." She sticks her tongue out at me and I roll my eyes at her.

"Your money, your body."

"Are you judging me, Teague?"

"Absolutely."

"I'm judging you too." She holds the bag of brussels sprouts in front of me. "What the fuck is this? Gross." Her nose crinkles in disgust.

"*That gross stuff* is healthy. Trust me, if you don't like it, you can spit it onto my plate and I'll eat it."

Her nose crinkles in disgust. "That's nasty, but you're on."

It was how her eyes lit up over the mention of enchiladas that made me put the extra effort into tonight's dinner. I'm cooking for more people than normal, and enchiladas were the first thing that came to mind outside of pizza. Plus, Briar needs to eat some home-cooked meals.

Five hundred dollars later, we have enough groceries for a month. Thank goodness because after the looks Briar was giving me, she'll be lucky if I let her leave my bed again.

The drive *home* is full of light touches, heated looks, and loud singing. *Perfection.*

I pull up to the gate, letting myself out to unchain the lock. When I climb back into the car, I'm met with bare legs, her hand extended to me with her panties hooked around her finger. I growl, my cock growing hard in my jeans.

Fuck it.

20

Briar

Teague guns it, lurching the car forward, leaving the gate completely open. Everyone will be here soon, so it's not a big deal anyway.

Practically throwing himself out of the car and yanking me from my seat, he tosses me over his shoulder, cave-dweller style.

We plow through the front door, Teague kicking it closed behind him, then barreling up the stairs and into the master bedroom. My shrieks and giggles resound through the hallway the whole way there.

When we reach the bedroom, his hand comes immediately to my core, one of his thick fingers slipping into my pussy. I gasp, feeling excited by his touch, and by the sudden intrusion.

"I want your cock. I need it. Right now." I'm so wet, ready to take him just from the drive home. We couldn't wait to even unpack–everything is still in the car waiting to be unloaded, melted ice cream be damned.

"You sure?" He sets me down on the bed, pulling my hips until I'm resting barely on the edge. His hands push my shirt up, revealing my breasts to him. His mouth comes down on me, his tongue swirling around my hardened nipple.

"Yes," I beg breathlessly. He trails his mouth up to my neck, tracing kisses up to my mouth. His hands fumble with his pants, eventually freeing himself from the denim prison. Lining himself up, his pushes in slowly until he's fully seated within me, swallowing my moan with his mouth.

"Fuck. Why did we wait so long to do this?" He groans as he drops his head into the crook of my neck.

"Your fault," I gasp as he thrusts into me. His mouth finds my neck, sucking lightly on the sensitive skin. "You wanted to play hard to get, tough guy. I would've jumped your bones earlier," I tease.

"Oh, you would have?" His fingers come to my clit, rubbing small circles as he thrusts. My orgasm builds, my body tensing with the pressure. I hum a yes, unable to form words. Sweat glistens on Teague's forehead from the exertion. His hands grip my hips, tugging and gripping hard enough to leave bruises. I moan, the pain increasing my pleasure.

"I want to talk about that tattoo later," I say right before Teague's phone rings in his pants and I hear honking outside the house.

"You've got thirty seconds," I hiss. He smirks at me, his thumb flying over my clit, pushing me over the edge. I pulse around him as he groans his own release.

The doorbell rings right as Teague pulls his cock from my pussy. I sit up, reaching my hands to grab him. Pulling him toward me, I pull him into my mouth, a hiss passing Teague's lips.

"Christ, Briar. They're here."

The doorbell rings again and I regretfully pull my mouth from his cock with a pop.

"Coming," I yell. "Go take care of that, while I take care of this," I gesture to my now dripping cunt.

"Again, I think I'm in love," he says, pulling up his pants and waltzing out of the bedroom door.

The sound of voices floats up through the house. I can hear Ondina clear as day, talking about how Teague has hidden this side of himself from everyone and she's jealous I got to see it first. Their laughter brings me so much joy.

I run the shower, getting a moment to myself before business commences.

My trauma is something I've held on to for so long. It will take time, but Teague has opened me up to the idea of fully healing, what fixing my fractured soul could do.

I wash myself, then realize I have no clothes to change into. I have two options: walk out in Teague's clothes or yell down for my suitcase.

Not ready to expose myself as a full softy, I opt to yell down to Teague. A moment later, he opens the bedroom door, two suitcases in tow.

"Thanks," I say, planting a kiss firmly on his lips. Sadness flicks behind his eyes a moment before he blinks, and then it's gone.

"You okay?" He nods.

"Fine, love. Just don't want to share you," he says. I smile shyly.

"One day."

"I WANT TO host a fight," I announce to the room. "If we can get all the important players into one room, we could have the upper hand. If we host a fight at your gym," I gesture to Teague. "We need to make it a high-profile fight, attract the attention of both good and bad people." Teague's hand slides under the table to rest on my leg and my brain short circuits for a moment. "Declan and Axel are messy. I've been doing more research, despite their warning, and I've found small trails of their transactions." My eyes lock with Teague's when I drop the next truth bomb. "I think my mom helped them with their trafficking business. I found evidence linking her to Declan. It's not solid proof, but it's something." I pause, thinking about what to say next. Looking at Teague again, I search for some sort of approval or comfort or something. *A leader is nothing without her second.* I don't want to elaborate fully, unsure if I can open that can of worms yet. "Any questions so far?"

"Yeah, uh, I have a question," Hal says. "What's going on there?" He gestures between Teague and me. My face goes red, unsure of what to say. We haven't really talked about it yet.

"She's my girlfriend," Teague says without hesitation. My eyes snap in shock from Hal's to Teague's. Ondina snickers across the table.

"I—I'm his girlfriend," I say, my cheeks flaming.

"Well, about damn time," Gabe hollers. "Y'all fuck yet?"

"That's the question of the century, huh?" I manage to say it without choking on my own tongue.

"So that's a yes," Gabe announces, and I roll my eyes.

I observe the heated glance that Ondina shoots toward Riggs. Riggs' only response is an indifferent glance back. My stomach drops for her. That earlier comment suddenly makes sense.

"Okay, seriously. What are your thoughts? Could this work?"

Hal speaks up first. "I used to fight. I was pretty good once. People will recognize my name if you headline with me and Teague."

Teague nods his agreement. "It would be a decent fight. I don't think Declan could turn it down. It's good for his business."

"Okay, so we headline with a big fight between you two? Or open it up for other competitors to challenge?"

"Either or, maybe both," Teague says.

"I think we could open it up for amateurs to fight but headline you two as the big event. If we invite Declan and Axel under peaceful pretenses, they may accept solely to see you two tear each other apart," I declare. My confidence only wavers slightly.

"We need an ironclad plan. There needs to be security at all entrances, strict monitoring of attendees full of trusted individuals and everyone will need their roles down pat," Riggs chimes in. This is the first time Riggs has spoken all night. I take a bite of my enchilada, not able to wait any longer. My earlier orgasm has stolen all of my energy.

"What would you do, Riggs?" I throw out between bites.

"The Roosters conduct most of their business on the dark web. If we could set it up like a business exchange was going down, something that competes with Declan's business, we could draw everyone out at once. Take out Declan, his suppliers, and supporters." He taps his fingers on the table, thinking. "We would need to prepare for major casualties. This won't be easy to keep out of the spotlight. Law enforcement will swarm the moment they get word of a major event."

"Good. That's what we want. Riggs, I need you to erase the existence of the Crows. Anything that could be linked to us needs to disappear. Ondina, make yourself available to Riggs, whatever he needs is your only job." Riggs starts to speak, but I hold my hand up to stop him. "I know you prefer to work alone, this is a team, Riggs. We need to work together if we want this to go smoothly." I say. He jerks a nod as Teague gives my leg a squeeze. I've not once forgotten his presence there; it feels as though I'm siphoning courage from him.

My phone pings in my pocket, drawing my attention away from our conversation. I silence the room with a hand up.

Axel's name flashes across my screen. I only hesitate a moment before answering it, placing it on speakerphone in the middle of the table. I hold my finger to my mouth, signaling everyone to remain quiet.

"Axel," I say coolly.

"Briar, Briar, Briar," he taunts. "I knew you were stupid, but I didn't think you were this stupid."

"I'm not sure I know what you mean." Teague's posture turns protective like he's ready to launch himself at the phone.

"You should've stayed away from all of this. Your father thought he was the boss. He thought he could just snap his fingers and his problems would go away." He tsks, the sound of a car door slamming in the background. I try to hide the pain on my face as a knot grows in my throat.

Push. It. Down.

"Did you know your mommy was going to kill you after she took all of your money? Get rich, eliminate the competition... two birds with one stone, right?" His voice sounds bitter and disgusted. Out of all the people in my life, Axel is the hardest to read. I can't yet tell if he is a villain or a hero in this story. Everything about him seems so calculated and I haven't figured out why. Maybe he doesn't like me, but a part of me believes there's something more here. I stay silent, listening as heavy footsteps sound around Axel, the movements sending waves of unease through me. As if Teague can sense the shift, he silently instructs Riggs, pulling out the laptop and shoving it toward him.

"But mommy had traces of her heart still intact." I mouth for Teague to record this. My gut is telling me Axel is going to dig his own grave. "Big surprise that the adults in our lives are incompetent. You still listening, Briar?"

What is that supposed to mean?

"Yep," I say, bored, my emotions firmly tucked into place... for now. "I don't know if you heard, but she did try to kill me. Old news, Axel."

"Do you want to know why mommy dearest was so willing to throw you to the wolves? She was so driven by money that she would do anything to make a buck. Convincing her to dump her daughter for money was easier than I thought. She doesn't have a single maternal bone in her body." He laughs, the sound cold and bitter.

Why is he telling me all of this?

"You don't say," I respond, my voice cold.

"You should've stayed away, Briar, but now that you're here, I'm willing to help you. I've got something you need."

"What's that?" I ask.

"Information. I know something you don't."

"You've shared quite a bit already." My body shakes as I speak.

"Either you come to me or I'll force you here. Your choice."

"Is that a threat, Axel?"

"Was your dead father not enough to stir you into action?" *Was it him?*

The zip ties on my control snap. My breath comes in sharp gasps as the room closes in on me. I've always been my own protector. Now in this circumstance, I can feel myself crumbling, my need for control and the desire to protect kicking in. What does he have planned?

Feelings make you weak, vulnerable. The only person left I care about is Teague and I can't lose him. What if he threatens my team next? My body shakes uncontrollably as my mind loses its grip. Teague rips the phone from the table and puts it to his ear. I panic, not ready for Axel to know he exists, that I care about him. A small shriek spills from my mouth and Teague shoots me a confused look.

What do I do? What do I do?

Teague's voice comes out as a growl, dripping with venom. "War is coming—a war you just started. Enjoy seeing your entire world painted red. Red is a rather unpleasant color, Axel." He ends the call, nearly smashing the phone on the table.

I don't wait for the others to speak. Running out the front door, I feel the gravel beneath my feet before I feel the pain. I keep running, embracing the pain, allowing myself to feel something other than emotions. Before I reach the gate, the sound of someone gaining on me brings me to halt. I gasp, trying to catch my breath, clutching at my sides. My vision is blurry, blinded by the pain-filled tears.

"Briar!" Teague calls out to me. Bracing myself with my hands on my knees, I suck in gulps of cool air. I wave a hand at him, encouraging him to speak while I attempt to ground myself.

"I can't," I gasp. "I can't fucking do this. Axel wins. He kills Killian, he wants to threaten me and the Crows, he can have it all. I'm not ready for this. He wasn't supposed to fucking *die*." I'm screaming now, my fists clenched at my side. I feel the need to punch something to let out this pent-up anger. Teague just watches me as I internally combust, his closeness calming me enough to avoid a complete meltdown. I see Teague's decision before he's made it.

"Axel's right, you know. You're stupid. If you let something like this stop you, something as minor as a half-ass provocation from that asshole, you're not the woman I thought you were."

He's provoking me and I'm overly aware of it.

"You don't mean that," I say, letting my anger surface.

"I do. You just said it. You're not ready. Guess that means we'll have to fight so I can take your place. It was always supposed to be me until you showed up."

I charge forward, giving in to the anger and hurt that his words bring me. "Well it's *me*. You want to fight? Let's fight. Say what you're really thinking, Teague. Are you mad that spoiled little Briar was just handed this position instead of you?" My fist connects with his chest harder than I anticipated. I wince in pain, forgetting how solid his muscles are. "I've never cared for anyone truly until you," I poke at his chest. "Then my father. I believed he was a different person behind the mask, but I never got to see it and Axel took that away from me. I have *nothing*. I have nothing left," I sob. Teague pulls me into his chest, my face resting against the smooth material of his shirt. "I have nothing." My knees threaten to buckle beneath me right as Teague's arms wrap around me. "He's gone." My voice chokes over another sob. I suck in a sharp breath, breathing in Teague's smokey scent.

"I know," Teague soothes, rubbing calming circles along my back. "But you're wrong. You do have something. You have a team of people who care for you, whether you believe it or not. And you have a…" Teague clears his throat. "A boyfriend… if you'll still have me."

A throaty sort of cry-laugh escapes my mouth into his chest. My face is streaming with tears, a small pool of drool gathering where my face is pressed into his shirt. It's probably a horrendous sight to behold. With the back of my hand, I wipe away my tears and the drool, most definitely taking my mascara with it.

"At first, I wanted to ask you if you were okay, but then I realized it was a stupid question." His voice quiets as he speaks. His presence brings a wave of calm over my body like a drug taking effect. I stand straighter, moving my hands to wrap around his neck.

"Yeah, that is a stupid question." My thoughts wander as my emotional pain resurfaces. My father wasn't everything, but he was the only family I've ever really had, grandma notwithstanding. *My mother doesn't count. I'm not claiming her.* But Teague is right. This team that we've created. I care for them. They've only been in my life for a short time, but I need to stop pushing others away and create a family for myself. Teague interrupts my thoughts with his next statement.

"I want to take you somewhere," Teague says, grabbing my hand. "The team is coming too. It may seem unconventional, and not the right way to handle this situation, but I promise it has a purpose." He gives my hand a firm squeeze, his touch grounding me. I nod, not sure what to say. "There's no right way to heal from this. I can see you want to push me away Briar. Please." His voice breaks. "Let me help you. Let me be there for you." Fresh tears fall from my eyes at his declaration.

"I can't hide from you," I cry out. "Loss is something I have no experience with. It feels weird grieving a man I barely knew." There is anguish laced in my voice. "I can't lose you too. Whatever's happening between us, I can't risk it. If he knows you matter to me, he can take you away from me too." I shake my head, trying to find a coherent thought.

"Briar. I can handle myself. Don't do that. Don't push to protect. I'm not letting you get away with that." Teague's voice is devolving into begging.

I don't know what else to say to him, so I settle for a simple *okay*. It's all I can promise for now.

"If okay is all you can manage, I'll take it." He brings his lips to my forehead, placing a tender kiss between my brows. "Let's get the team. I have something I want to show you.

21

TEAGUE

riar and I ride in silence, the team following behind in their own cars. Being strong is something I consider extremely important. I sometimes forget that feelings and anything remotely human is not a weakness. For the first time in years, I feel things again like fear, envy, jealousy, anxiety, and sadness. The lockbox of emotions has opened because of her. This life is difficult, full of trauma and death. Briar's been thrown into a life that I would never wish on anyone. Axel truly deserves the worst outcome possible. If I could deliver that myself, I would.

Briar's hand finds my thigh. "I love that you're angry for me, I really do, but I can literally feel the waves of anger coming off of you. If I weren't incredibly turned on right now, I would have half a thought to be terrified by that rage."

"Axel is a piece of shit. I've known it for a long time, but I never thought he was capable of something like this." My fingers are white where I'm gripping the steering wheel.

"Power makes people do crazy things. My mom, Axel, they're only two examples. There will be more." Briar plays with a rip in her jeans as she speaks. "I lock my emotions up so tight, trying to be strong, but I don't think I can be strong for much longer."

We pull into a gravel parking lot, the lights from the car the only thing illuminating the open space. Shifting into park, I turn to look at her, her features barely visible in the darkness.

"The team doesn't need you to be strong for them. They need a leader. You don't need to be perfect or put on this front." My hand finds her leg, giving it a firm squeeze. "I used to drive up here with my friends when I was in high school. We would mainly fuck around, but this has become something of a safe space," I say.

Lights illuminate the truck as two cars pull up on either side of us. I make a show of climbing out of the truck before walking around to let Briar out. I can feel her eyes on me as I walk to her side, a sly grin spreading across my face as she stares. Yanking the door open, I extend my hand to her, waiting for her to accept. "Come, I'll show you." She hesitates only for a moment before her small hand grasps mine. "This way," I call out, the other members of our team following close behind.

Leading the group to a dimly lit path, I stop before we reach the stairs. On my right is a switch that Killian and I installed. Flipping it, I watch as the lights flicker on, brightening the stairs and the large lookout at the top. We climb up a series of steps to reach the overlook, taking it slow. Briar tenses the higher we walk. She grips my hand tightly, and I do my best to steady her, letting her know that I'm with her every step of the way. The more time I spend with Briar, the more in tune with her emotions I become, the more all of those little gestures and ticks make sense.

Footsteps sound all around me as the group walks closer to the overlook. Ondina rushes to Briar's side, her hand grasping her free hand in her own.

Her voice is quiet as she speaks to Briar. I decide to walk ahead of them, giving them some privacy. Unable to keep my ears from prying, I listen to their hushed words.

"Briar, you don't have to go through this alone. I lost both of my parents when I was young. Killian saved me from a really disgusting situation. You may not realize this, but your dad brought in a lot of young people who had nothing left. Everyone here has lost someone. It's not called a family for nothing. We suffer these things together, love." Ondina releases an exasperated sigh, I'm assuming at whatever face Briar just made.

"I don't know how to let people in," she admits.

"There's no better time than the present to learn," Ondina says. She's right. There is no better time than now to learn. Just like Briar, I've been alone my whole life. This is something that the team will tackle together.

As I reach the top of the steps, I take in the familiar view of the lookout. It's a fairly large building abandoned years ago. After they rebuilt the main road, this lookout fell out of use, since it branches off a less frequently used side road. The white structure has four large pillars, and the two walls not overlooking the edge of the cliff are covered in graffiti and art. What Briar doesn't know is that I've spent years painting the walls with pictures, each one filled with the shame and desire for what could have been.

"Thank God," Ondina groans, walking up the last step. "Steps are my worst enemy." She laughs.

"Not mine. I didn't get this ass by walking on flat ground," Briar teases. I've seen that ass and I can agree that it's a *spectacular* one.

"Oh, is that your secret?" Gabe yells from behind us.

"Yep," she calls out to him. "Stairs and good genes."

With the last step, Briar takes in her surroundings, no doubt noticing the special pieces of art along the walls. Walking closer, her eyes catch on a cluster of Celtic Runes. There are three: courage, strength, and protection.

"My dad had that tattooed on his body," she murmurs.

"Your dad found me here after a bad day." I walk close to the wall, running my hands over the runes. "You haven't learned this part of me yet, but I like to think I'm an artist. I used to come here and paint." Pointing to different areas on the wall, I continue, "those Celtic symbols are things I needed at that point in my life. The swallow over there symbolizes loyalty. Not everything has a meaning, but I came to paint and draw to create the things I needed in my life through art." Briar nods her head in understanding, taking a step closer to me and linking her arm through mine.

"I've never related to anything more. Creating things brings me peace and comfort." She looks up at me with doe eyes that make my heart beat faster.

"I'm quite the artist myself," Hal chimes in.

Great, thanks for ruining the moment, asshole.

Flinging an arm over Briar's shoulder, he looks at us sideways. "Remember when I almost kicked you out of the office? I'm sorry about that by the way." He looks at her with hesitation, sending a shivering laugh through my body.

"Hal! Are you being nice to me because I'm technically your boss now? Like big boss?" I see Briar raise a teasing eyebrow at him.

"Don't be a kiss ass," I say, punching his arm lightly. Hal laughs, taking a step back to join the rest of the team.

"We need to talk." Briar pulls away from me, taking a step to the side where she can see all of them at once.

My team.

Our team.

A team that needs her to be there for them, just as much as she needs them to be there for her.

"I'm sorry for storming out on all of you earlier. I know Teague made you aware of what happened to Killian. But I'd like you to hear it from me as well." Taking a deep breath, Briar recounts her encounter with Axel, then the unnamed call resulting in Killian's death. She explains her suspicions, and how dramatically Axel changed.

"This is war. I don't know what Axel gets out of this. Power maybe? What puzzles me most is that he isn't even the one in charge, so I must assume that Declan's running the show," she says.

I recount something Axel said earlier. He talked about adults being incompetent. The context was alluding to Briar's mom but everything Axel says has meaning. I don't think Declan is smart enough to facilitate something like this on his own, if at all. If not that, some of his hatred for his father is seeping through the cracks.

Briar purses her lips, moving them to the side in thought. She does that when she gets emotional. It's one of the many things I've learned about her. "I will need time to grieve. He was my dad." Her voice breaks over the last word. "He was my Don. And despite our difficult past, a part of me loved him. But don't walk on eggshells around me and don't keep me out of things. I know you all are hurting, too. Let's all hurt and move on together."

Ondina smiles sadly, wiping a tear from her face. "We could have a private celebration of life for him," she suggests. My head bobs in agreement.

"Let's do it now. I say we all go around and say one thing we appreciated or remember about Killian and then we scream away our frustrations off the cliff." My eyebrows lift in suggestion, looking at the team for a reaction. Briar smiles at me, her gaze full of gratitude.

Hal speaks up first, walking to the edge of the lookout. "Killian is the first person I met while in California. I used to sell street art to make money and one day he stopped at my spot. He looked down at me and said, 'Get off your ass and come with me.' I never looked back."

Briar releases a loud cackle, the rest of us following.

"He would say something like that," she says, crying through her laughter. Ondina crouches low to the ground, laughing. I can't help but laugh too, seeing all of them in tears over Hal's statement. Hal raises a hand pointing to his chest.

"He asked me what I wanted to do with my life. I was practically a kid then," he says. "I'd never had anyone ask me that. So I told him the truth, that I'd always wanted to be a doctor." His eyes smile as he recounts the memory. "He didn't laugh or tell me it wasn't possible. He just said simply, 'Then do it, kid,' and walked away." Killian was a fixer, that's for sure.

"I tried hacking into his system once," Riggs says casually.

"Tried?" Briar teases. "I successfully did that. How did you get caught?"

"I was a dick and left a signature after hacking in. Your father wasn't stupid with technology." Riggs rolls his eyes. Releasing a chuckle, I look at Briar. She's enjoying this. I'm glad that she's allowed this moment to live vicariously through her team.

Gabe walks to the edge of the lookout. "My favorite memory with Killian is when he put me on a job to recruit this 'lil lady over here." He places a hand on Ondina's shoulder.

"Oh buddy 'ol pal. Thanks for being my knight in shining armor," she teases. Hal looks between the two of them, Ondina looking at Riggs and Gabe staring at Ondina.

Briar looks at me sideways, giving me a smirk. Standing on her toes, she whispers in my ear.

"I think Ondina is in love with Riggs. And maybe Gabe is in love with Ondina?" I snort at her statement.

"We'll talk about this later," I say, nipping at her ear. Her eyes close at the affection. Her warm breath is shallow along my neck as she slowly lowers back down. Clearing her throat, she looks at me, waiting.

"Killian let me steal a pet lizard," Ondina chirps while bouncing on her toes. I seriously don't understand how this woman is *so* happy all the time. Riggs laughs beside her. Briar elbows me, mumbling something about being cupid. Riggs laughs again, speaking up.

"Was that when we found out about Declan's drug supplier? We created this petty mission to inconvenience them. Took out the supplier—"

"—And stole his pet lizard," Ondina finishes. "Yeah, that was it." She smiles widely at Riggs. Riggs returns the smile before looking down at the ground. The sound of crickets increases as the night goes on. Looking out, we can see the entire city. The stars are a million times brighter out here, where the light pollution of a big city can't reach.

I'm not sure what part of myself I want to share. I haven't told Briar the gory details of my past and of my parents' passing. There will be a day when I'll share that, but for now, it'll be my burden to bear.

"I fought illegally. Got myself into some real trouble. When Killian found me, I was on the fast track to death." I feel Briar tense beside me, her eyes growing sad as her attention focuses. "I've got plenty of demons to battle. After some particularly hard days, I came up here to scream some fucks at the world and throw some paint around. It was healthier than murdering someone," I say, half-joking, half-serious. "Killian found me one night and we let off some steam together, screaming off this cliff."

"Screaming off the cliff?" Briar asks me curiously.

Without warning, I turn to face out toward the city. A grin spreads across my face before I yell a string of profanities off the side of the cliff. Everyone looks at me stunned before Briar balls up her hands into fists and bends forward, belting out a scream.

"AHHHHHHHHHHHHHH!" she yells, and the others follow. Our collective screams fill the night air. Something about screaming for no particular reason is extremely liberating. Briar takes my hand in hers, letting out one last scream. We stand there a moment, the silence turning into a calming presence. I don't know how long we stand there in silence, but after a while, Briar speaks.

"A hui hou…Aloha au iā 'oe. Until we meet again. I love you." Tears shimmer on her cheeks as she speaks. "I'm not ready to let go. I want to go home," she cries, her voice breaking. My heart breaks for her. I know then that the breakdown is coming, and I will do everything in my power to be there for her.

BRIAR WALKS UP the path to *our* home on autopilot. I can see it in the way her body is taking over as she processes her emotions. A last goodbye is something that I don't believe anyone was ready for tonight.

Killian tended to take in some misfits. This gang isn't normal. Killian was great at putting up a front for all of this, but in reality, it was like his life's mission to bring others in for an opportunity of a better life. His intentions were pure, but not always executed in the best way. It surprised no one to find out that he had done the same with Briar. The moment he would have found out about her dreadful mother, he would have created a plan to leap into action. I admire that.

A small huff of frustration leaves Briar's mouth, pulling me back to her quickly deteriorating control. The tears filling her eyes are more visible now, sending a pang of dread through my body. I take the keys from her shaking hands. Her ragged breaths grow louder the longer we're standing outside the door.

Pushing it open, I stand behind Briar, allowing her entrance first. The door shuts closed behind us with a quiet creak, and I sense what is about to happen a moment before it does. Shooting my hands out, I pull Briar into my chest before she can fall. Her body goes limp, sobs pouring out of her. She buries her face into my chest, her body shaking with her silent sobs.

"He's gone. He's gone," she repeats through sobs. This is grief, unlike anything I've witnessed before. My own grief is something I've not processed. The tightening of my throat becomes more noticeable as her sobs become more violent.

"He's gone," she repeats until it's no more than a whisper. The burning in my chest increases, her feeling of brokenness that I know so well breaking my heart. I knew this was coming. Her grief was just waiting to be released. The only thing I can do now is support her through it.

Gently pulling her into my arms, I carry her up the stairs and into the bedroom. I slide us both down onto the bed, Briar curling herself into a ball, her head finding my legs to keep some contact between us.

I've seen loss and death around me continuously; I've even caused untold amounts of it. This is so different, this feeling of not having the closure to heal and move on. Amid all of this, she hasn't had an opportunity to heal, grow and cope with this loss and the loss of her freedom. Instead, she's been thrown to the wolves and given a whole gang to mother. I have never once thought about the possibility that she wasn't ready, or that she didn't want any of it. This was an escape for her and may have been the only escape she'd ever had. Did she really want to do this, or did she feel like she had to?

My mind takes me to the depths of my darkest thoughts. The weight of what I've to do and see on the daily grips at the edges of my mind.

The shaking sobs of Briar draw me back. I need to be here for her—present for her pain and her grief. I promised. Tugging her close to me, her quiet sobs slow and her breathing evens out. Her previously shaking hands come to rest against my chest as if she's stabilizing herself.

"I'm sorry," she rasps, her hand grasping at the material of my shirt.

"No apologies, Briar. None. You are allowed to feel and I will be here with you through it all." Briar eyes soften, her lashes fluttering as she tries to blink away tears. I want to share myself with her, to open up this door of vulnerability.

"Have I told you that I lost my parents when I was young?" My hands brush through Briar's hair. Her long hair sways as she shakes her head. "My father was the worst of the worst. He hid his drug use for a long time, but after a while, it was impossible. There were days that I'd come home from grade school and find used needles on the coffee table because he passed out before I walked home." My hand grazes the stubble on my chin, as I think through my words. "He became abusive and my mother was always very timid when it came to his vices."

I clench my teeth, remembering the way he'd grow increasingly impatient, his temper growing more erratic. Briar's chest rises and falls, her arms fidgeting lightly. When our eyes connect, her eyes are full of sadness, but she moves her hand to my bicep, giving me a reassuring squeeze.

I take a deep breath before continuing. "I guess he was borrowing money to buy his drugs. The people he owed were dangerous and threatened my family to scare him into paying off his debt, but little did they know it would have the opposite effect. My father's a runner."

My body tenses as I recount the last of this story. Briar must notice because her thumb begins rubbing small circles on my arm, her touch calming me. "I went to school the morning of the incident. He'd been acting strange, pacing the living room and mumbling, but at barely thirteen I thought nothing of it. When I walked home from school, my house was quieter than normal which was the first indicator that something was wrong. Then my father walks out, a gun in the hand hanging at his side. One second I'm dropping my backpack, the next he's aiming the gun at my mother. He'd rather die than deal with his problems, so after taking care of my mother, he turned the gun on himself, leaving me alone and with his mound of debt."

Briar gasps, her hand stilling on my arm. "Teague, that's terrible. You were so young."

"I was. There's more to the story though. The men my father pissed off came for me. At that point, I'd become a really angry kid. I fought at school, got into a lot of trouble. I used it to my advantage and started fighting for money. I was able to pay back every penny my father owed. Then I started saving and eventually bought the gym, among other things."

We sit in silence for a moment, Briar absorbing the story of me.

"Thank you for sharing this with me." She reaches up and kisses my cheek, the moment tender and loving. The motion twists in my heart.

Love.

Is that what this is? Love?

I've never known love like this before, only lust. It wouldn't be such a bad thing to be in love with a woman like her. Like Briar Ruarc.

22

Briar

M y mind is clouded with doubt and insecurity, grief and emotions leaving me feeling heavy and weak. I wasn't ready for this. The more I think about it, the less confident I feel as the leader of a team. Anxiety claws at the corners of my mind, flooding me with all the 'what ifs' of the situation. This fight will either be the end of the Crows, or the beginning of my reign as queen of the criminals.

Queen of the criminals? That's stupid.

I groan internally at my own stupid commentary. What the fuck am I supposed to do now? There is no time to not be ready for this. There's no time to be a normal human being.

Killian's words breeze through my memory.

The only way out is through a body bag.

Did he mean that? Was that the only way for me to have a drop of normalcy? Shaking my head, I sit up in bed, finding myself alone. I hadn't noticed that Teague's body wasn't next to mine. I pull the warm blankets over my body as I turn to the clock on the nightstand. Eleven thirty AM. I slept almost into the afternoon. I toss my head into the pillow and groan. It's time to join the world again.

Walking to the bathroom, I flip on the shower and undress, taking a moment to look at my reflection in the mirror. This girl is someone I don't recognize. I wanted so badly to be someone worthy of a life like this, but my fears have started to creep in, making me believe that I'm just not ready. It's too soon.

I sigh, stepping into the warm stream of water, letting it wash away the tears and emotion from the night before. The warm water is welcome, soothing the tension in my body.

Stepping out of the shower, I find Teague on the bed, dressed in jeans and a gray t-shirt. He looks at me expectantly, but instead of going to him, I walk to the dresser, dropping my towel as I rummage through to find my clothes. The only sign of his movement is the small creak of the bed as he stands to his feet. His hands slide up my sides as I pull out a lacy thong and matching bra. I don't need to look cute, but it doesn't hurt to feel cute under my clothes. The feel of Teague's lips on my neck sends a chill down my spine. I can't help but sigh in relief.

"What's going on in that beautiful head of yours?" Teague runs his hands up and down my arms as I rest my weight back into his chest.

"I'm confused," I admit. "I don't know what I'm doing. And the more I think about it, the less ready I feel."

"No one is forcing you to be ready, Briar," he says into my neck. "Least of all me. That pressure is coming only from you." His words hit me like a freight train.

That pressure is coming from me.

What about all the people counting on me? My team, the entire gang, who I haven't even spoken to yet. They all are counting on me... right? Teague spins me to face him, and I suddenly feel extremely exposed under his gaze. He doesn't look me up and down though; instead, his eyes are trained on my face, reading the thoughts I'm letting through. His eyes move back and forth between mine, his face softening as he realizes what he's seeing.

"If you're not ready, that's okay. We'll figure something out. We'll get through this *together*."

He constantly reminds me of the togetherness of it all. For the first time in my entire life, I realize that I'm not alone.

Like a weight being fully lifted off my chest, I breathe fully for the first time in days. Sucking in a breath, I feel that reassurance soothing my building anxiety. Emotions lump in my throat and I swallow around it.

"I don't deserve you." I press myself into his chest again, my bare breasts squished against him.

"You deserve me and a million times more." He says it with such conviction that I almost believe it.

Almost.

"What are we doing today? I haven't even begun to think about it."

"Well..." Teague's hands slide up and down my body, hesitating slightly. "Gabe gave me a box to look through. Since the office building was destroyed, he grabbed some of Killian's things from his home office. If you're ready, I'd like to look through it for evidence against Axel and Declan."

I nod absentmindedly. "Okay. Let's do it."

An hour later, I find myself sprawled out on the floor amid piles of paper and photos. Teague and I have been rummaging through the various paperwork looking for *anything* we can use. The longer we sort through things, the less it all makes sense. The anatomy of the Crows and how they functioned never quite made sense to me. I saw no 'missions,' and even more suspicious is that I never knew how my father got his art, which was the foundation of the Crows. Looking over to Teague, I feel the confusion on my face before he registers it.

"What?" He sits up from lying on his back, and I watch the way the muscles in his arms flex with his weight. *Focus, Briar.*

"None of this makes sense. I knew the Crows existed, but it's like once my dad took over…" I shake my head, trying to find the words. "Look here."

I shuffle through some papers until I find the one I'm looking for. "My father took over the Crows almost twenty-four years ago. That means he would have met my mom while he was Don. The story was that she got pregnant and then he left shortly after to take over the Crows, but if they met while he was already with the Crows…" I pause, thinking. "It just doesn't add up." I scan the paper again, pointing to the bottom of the page.

"I'd heard that when Killian took over, the Crows were nearly bankrupt, their dealings going south with the wrong people. But as soon as he took over, the financial records were wiped clean. I remember digging a while ago and seeing one large deposit from some encrypted name and contact. It was like it was a plant? Or— Or something. None of this makes any sense. He was set from the get-go like he had someone backing him." Teague's eyes watch me as I rummage again. "And look at this. He wasn't even really keeping records. Everything was around Declan, not the Crows. A paper trail of meeting minutes with some contact that is always listed as R and nothing else. This R would correspond with him, and they would speak in some sort of code."

"What are you thinking?" Teague rubs his temples.

"Let me ask you this: did you ever really do anything outside of monitor Axel and Declan and, of course, be my watchdog?"

He thinks a moment before speaking, his lips pursing together. "Killian really was hands-off. I ran the gym and attended meetings, kept up on Declan, and spent *years* watching you."

"What is so important about Declan that basically everything stopped to focus on Rooster activity?" I pull out my phone, dialing Riggs as Teague speaks.

"That's the question, isn't it?"

Placing the phone on the floor in front of us, it rings twice before his voice sounds through the speakers.

"Yes, Boss?"

"Did you find anything when you were trying to wipe our slate clean?"

I can hear Riggs typing, his fingers flying across the keys. "Actually, yes." My heart pounds as I wait for his next words. "I suspect that someone else besides your father was pulling the strings. I tried a complete wipe, but the amount of security on this stuff is beyond what it should have been."

Teague speaks up, "Riggs, can you find the address for Killian's private homes? The level of privacy he had surrounding his residences makes me suspicious enough to want to look into them." I look at Teague gratefully. I never thought about searching Killian's home.

"I'll text you over the addresses now. He's got an unregistered property in Palmdale. I'd start there if I were you. The others check out," Riggs says.

"Can we go to my dad's home office? There must be more there we can look through. This is just a small part of the puzzle." Pulling my legs into my chest, I eye Teague curiously. He nods, standing and grabbing his keys off the coffee table. Extending a hand to me, he helps me to my feet. I put the phone to my ear.

"Let me know if you find anything else, Riggs. It's imperative we figure out what's happening here. If this fight is going to work, I need to know everything." Riggs agrees, the call ending a moment later. Teague looks at me, a seed of doubt on his face.

"If we keep digging into this, I'm afraid I'll learn that my whole life has been a lie," he admits. "I never once thought to question him." We walk out the front door, straight to the truck. I climb in with ease, loving how powerful I feel in Teague's massive vehicle.

"It's just a little sketchy. I don't want you to think everything has been a lie, but I also think we need to learn why Declan is the primary target. He is either extremely dangerous or he pissed off some powerful people off."

"Or both," Teague adds, the truck roaring to life.

We pull up to my dad's home an hour and a half later. Los Angeles traffic is the absolute worst. Seeing that I relied on public transportation in New York, it's weird being driven around here in LA. Not to mention driving such a short distance, it takes an hour to get from point A to point B, which could only be ten miles away.

When Teague walks around to open my door, something I don't think I'll ever get used to soon, I climb out and stand in the driveway. I can feel the knot forming in my throat as we walk together up the decorated pathway.

"Gabe came by early and changed the lock to keypad access." He punches in the passcode. With a small beep and the sound of the lock moving, Teague pushes the door in. I take my first step over the threshold and realize immediately that I am not ready. I'm not ready to take in his environment and I'm not ready to learn the truth of his activities. This man I knew for a few years of my life had become one of the most important. And now that he's gone… I don't know how to feel. My breathing catches in my throat as I walk further inside.

I swallow past the lump in my throat, the rising anxiety making me feel shaky and uneasy.

"Let's grab what we came for and get out." I can hear the desperation in my voice as I speak to Teague's back. He turns to look at me, nothing but understanding on his face.

"Agreed."

We explore the place a bit, learning the layout of the home. Down the long hallway to the right is an office, one I expect is his personal home office. When we enter, the background looks slightly familiar, but there is something *off*. Something just feels wrong. I open the drawers of his desk and rummage through the paperwork shoved inside. At the very back of the bottom drawer, I find two folders, both labeled with simple letters. Deciding to take them with me, I hand them to Teague to put into the box we brought. Before I close the drawer, I pull the files for every member of my team, determined to find something. I look around his desk and spy a ripped piece of paper with my name on it. On the note is my father's messy script. I feel Teague move behind me, allowing him to read over my shoulder.

Briar,

What are men to rocks and mountains?

-Dad

"What does that mean?" His hand rests on my shoulder, his touch soothing my raging heart.

I shake my head, unsure. Suddenly, an idea comes to my head.

I spin to my right, scanning the large built-in bookshelf. I walk in front of it and spot *Pride and Prejudice* immediately, grabbing it from the shelf. As soon as I do, the lights in the room go out, a loud mechanical whirring sounding from the walls and the floor.

Click.

The sound of movement causes me to flinch before the lights flicker on and I find Teague has moved to shield me from the motion.

We stay there a moment, waiting, watching for something to happen.

"Nothing's happening," I whisper to Teague. As if on cue, the mechanical whirring begins again, a panel in the wall moving to reveal a door within the bookcase. In the center of the door is a circular panel lit up with green lasers, scanning the room. After a few moments, a voice sounds throughout the room, making me jump.

"Identified… Briar Ruarc and Teague Rossi." It goes quiet for a moment before speaking again. "Cleared for entry, please move away from the door." In unison, Teague and I step backward.

Click.

The door rubs along the floor as it slides open, revealing a small staircase leading down towards a basement of sorts. I feel Teague's eyes on me, and I turn to look at him. Silently agreeing, we decide to walk through the door, Teague leading the way. Ducking into the small space, I watch his large frame crouch to fit. His footsteps echo on the concrete steps, comforting me as memories of old Barbie movies flood my mind. I remember the sounds of a princess walking down an enormous staircase, her heels clicking along each step. Reaching the last one, Teague turns back to me, eyes wide. He signals over his shoulder for me to continue after him.

The room is enormous. It probably spans the entire house, which is wild considering I would have never guessed Killian even had a secret space under the home. I tuck my hands into my pockets, suddenly feeling extremely uncomfortable. A large screen drops from the ceiling, a control panel or desk of sorts rising from the floor, causing me to jump back in surprise. The screen clicks to life, my father's face filling the screen.

"Briar, if you are seeing this, it means that something has gone very wrong, and I am dead. I am not who you believe me to be. There is a lot to this story, but the most important thing I should tell you is that the Crimson Crows do not exist."

Confusion washes over me the moment the words leave his mouth. What does he mean the Crows don't exist?

"I was born into a poor family in Hawaii. My mother was Irish, and my father was Hawaiian, which you know. What you don't know is that both my parents died when I was very young. After that, I went to a home where Niamh's mother found me." He turns, looking to the right, another person joining him on the screen. "This is the Dullahan assistant director Niamh Connors. We can't tell you everything now, but I want you to see Niamh's face as a friendly one. Please know that you can trust her."

My eyebrows scrunch in confusion. I don't understand why he is telling me this. "The Dullahan's are a group of mercenaries. We have ties in every country all over the world. We are neither hero nor villain, but simply exist. Our job is to maintain the balance in the world, keeping the good and bad in check. By now, I'm sure you are wondering what's going on. All I'll say is that we created the Crows as a way to maintain equilibrium." His hands move as if showing a balance between them. Teague's hand comes to rest on my shoulder as I take in all of this new information.

"For decades, Declan has been damaging the balance of the Pacific Northwest. Dec is ruthless. We learned years ago that he is the brains behind the operations of the Roosters, but things took a turn for worse when his father passed. Declan was left, unchecked in charge, to do whatever he pleased." Teague shifts by my side, his eyes narrowed as he watched. Something about the way he reacted makes me curious. I mentally make a note to question him later.

Images begin to flash across the screen, various photos of crime scenes and evidence, women, gagged, bound, and bloody, all shoved into shipping containers and cement rooms, spread out on the floor. Women dressed in beautiful dresses and standing in rings like a trophy or a prize to be bought shuffle across the screen. I feel sick to my stomach. The last set of photos shows multiple women in rooms, all pregnant and drugged. One girl, in particular, stands out to me, a beautiful young girl with glorious brown curls holding on to a woman who appears to be extremely high. The photos continue, showing the woman not moving, the girl sobbing at her side, trying to wake her. My heart breaks, tears spilling from my eyes.

"Ondina," I cry out, my eyes shooting to Teague. His fist clenches at his sides, wetness forming in his eyes as well. I suspect he knew some of Ondina's past, but never the full scope.

"Declan has been breeding women for slaughter, sale, and essentially anything these monsters desire. Kidnapping women, bringing in men to impregnate them, selling the children. This is his business. These women give birth over and over again until he finds no use for them anymore. At that point, they're either killed or sold to someone who wants them. Ondina is a product of this process. Her mother was stolen away at a young age and gave birth to Ondina at fourteen. I was able to rescue those in her camp, but her mother was too far gone for us to save." My father's voice goes on, but my eyes close, listening and fighting back the sickness threatening to spill from my stomach. I open them again, a knot forming in my throat at the sadness I feel.

"I feel sick," I say to Teague. His comforting hand finds my back and rubs soothing circles.

"When I left you, I hated myself, but it was the only way to protect you, both from the Dullahan and from Declan. You never existed, and I needed it to stay that way. After Teague reported on River attacking on your mother's behalf, I reluctantly brought you in. I couldn't leave you in that situation." Killian's face returns to the screen, the pictures gone.

"I took over the Crows myself in an attempt to get closer to Declan and his family, but if we are here now, something has gone wrong." He sighs, the woman at his side looking sympathetic. "I never wanted to pass this on to you, and I hope Teague is here with you, listening to this as well." He looks at my side briefly, almost as if he could see us both in this moment. A wide smile crosses his face. "I hope, Briar, that Teague has finally won your heart." Raising an eyebrow, I look at Teague with a suspicious smirk. His face reddens a bit.

"You're the only two that I can trust. Please don't think ill of me. When this message ends, all the evidence I have collected will be transferred to you, Briar. Dullahan is involved now, and they will help you, only if you ask. You're under their protection now. Save those girls, Briar. Stop this before he can destroy countless more lives." His eyes bore holes into my soul.

"I love you, Briar. I loved you the moment I saw you as a baby. I'm sorry I couldn't be the father you wanted or one that you could be proud of. You have a heart of gold. Use it to your advantage, but don't let others dim that light of yours." He pauses. His voice is quiet when he speaks again.

"One last thing: the Dullahan is larger than both of us. Niamh's mother was the founder of our organization. Although they are not blood, this is your family. You are the legacy of the Dullahan if you choose to accept your position. They could use a leader like you." He says it with a bite of bitterness. I suspect there's something he couldn't say which sends a chill of fear down my back. Niamh's face twitches beside him. *Something's wrong.*

He lingers for a moment longer before reaching toward the screen, his face disappearing a second later. My breathing increases as I process what I've just learned. Just as I start to turn away, my father's voice rings through the speakers again.

With a whir, the screen disappears, a series of digital files appearing on the touch screen desk.

"Hello, Briar," the automated voice says again. "I have been programmed to assist you with all of your needs. Your father named me Shay. If you need anything, you can simply say my name."

"What do we do now?" I stare at the files on the screen, unsure of my next move. This is all too much. My father had been a part of a mercenary group this whole time. Everything about the Crows was a lie.

"He said the Dullahan will help us if we ask." Teague's hand comes to my back again as we look down at the files. "How is this not enough to take him down already? Do they not have anything linking him to all of this?"

"That is an excellent question. There must be a gray area." I speak to the computer now. "Shay, will you please send over this information to Dominic Riggs?"

"The information is sent," Shay responds.

"I want to know how the Dullahan operate. This is all so much at once. Why can't they touch Declan?" My mind races with possibilities.

"Declan is hands off with his businesses," Teague says. "It looks like Killian worked with the Dullahan to remove Declan many times. However, Declan has countless ties and trusted allies who are willing to die in his place." He looks at me, his eyes hesitant. "I don't think Declan is the mastermind behind this. It makes sense considering Declan's age, but all I've done is watch and observe. This isn't like his usual patterns. It would make sense for someone else to be feeding him information or for him to have an inside source."

"What about Axel? What does he get out of all of this?" I ponder this for a moment. This is too much. What the fuck is happening?

"Shay. Do we have locations of these houses Declan runs? If he's hands off, who's overseeing them?"

"I'll pull the files for that information now."

"What are you thinking?" Teague maintains contact with my body, as though he can't bear to let me go. My heart aches a bit at the thought.

"Everyone has favorites. Maybe if Declan believes we're going to hit multiple places at once, he'll show us the place that is most important to him. Eventually, we can hit him where it hurts. Someone clearly wanted me dead. Let's remind them that I'm alive and well." A wicked smile crawls over my face.

Let's play.

23

TEAGUE

The scowl on my face grows the longer I sit on the bed. Briar is hidden in the bathroom, not allowing me in.

"What's the purpose of this again?" Groaning, I lay back on the bed, waiting for her to make her grand entrance.

"It's your birthday and I refuse to ignore it," she says from the bathroom. I was told to slick my hair back and wear a black pinstripe suit and tie.

"I'd much rather celebrate with you as dessert into the wee hours of the morning." At the thought of splaying Briar out on a table and feasting on her, my cock twitches in my pants. I can hear her breathing hitch in the bathroom, giving me a small prick of satisfaction. She clears her throat before stepping out into full view.

I groan as I take in every inch of her. She's wearing a tight black dress that accentuates every curve of her body, her full hips on display. The slit rides up her thigh giving me a delicious view of her leg. The rest of the fabric flows down to the floor like a waterfall. Although the dress is long sleeved, the deep vee of the front plunges to expose her breasts. My gaze grows feral, eyelids getting heavy the longer I stare at her. Briar shifts, taking a step toward me. My cock swells against my pants, causing an almost painful tightness.

"Fuck," I breathe. "You look absolutely sinful. That dress should be illegal." She grins, her bright red lips drawing my attention. Oh, how I would love those lips on every inch of my body. I bring a hand to my face, gripping my chin and mouth allowing me to breathe deeply for a second. My face, usually dusted with stubble, is shaved per her request.

I watch her like my life depends on it. Briar inhales deeply, her strappy heels hanging in one hand. I spread my legs wider, allowing her to step right into me. She brings a hand to my throat, before hovering her lips above mine.

"You can have me for dessert later." Her voice comes out as a husky whisper. "Right now…" I see the slow rise and fall of her chest. "Right now, I need you to help me into my shoes." She places a gentle peck on my lips before raising her shoes to my face. Taking them from her, I guide her leg up to rest on my thigh. I place a kiss on her leg before guiding her foot into the heel and adjusting the buckle to fit her ankle. She watches me the whole time, her gaze like a heat lamp on my body.

"You're lucky I'm not going against my better judgment and stripping you naked right now," I say as I fasten the buckle on her other heel.

"Later. I promise." She brushes her hands down her sides, smoothing the dress. "Right now, we have a birthday party to attend."

Kneeling to the ground, she grabs two black storage tubes. "Can you grab the masks off the dresser, please?" She points with her free hand. I nod before taking two wide strides to the dresser.

Two intricately woven metal masks rest on the dresser. The larger of the two is an intricate linking of lace-like swirls depicting a large skull. The smaller one is a half mask that covers the eyes and swirls up into a feather accent at the top. A teardrop jewel sits where the nose would be. Briar has definitely outdone herself with these outfits.

"We'll put the masks on before we walk in, but for now, we have to go or we'll be late." Briar saunters out of the room, leaving me staring after her as her ass sways, the black dress making it impossible to keep my dick under control. I sigh again, thinking of the least sexy things I can muster up as I walk down the stairs. I find Briar seated on the living room couch with her laptop open.

"One minute. There's something I need to take care of first." Her fingers fly across the keys at lightning speed. A moment later, she pulls a piece from a small case and lightly places it in her ear.

"Riggs." She nods a few times before speaking again. "Security is down. We've got maybe 5 minutes before they notice their camera feeds are on a loop. Can you take it from here?" I watch her while she listens for a response. "Great. Don't be late. We have a party to attend." She listens again then laughs. "Sounds good. Be safe please." She pulls the piece from her ear and places it back in the case. "Let's go."

BRIAR EXPLAINS ON the drive that the party is being hosted in a castle along the coast. I don't know how she was able to pull that one off, but in less than a week, she was able to throw this party together in time for a Halloween birthday celebration, even if the party is a front for tonight's real purpose. While everyone gets wasted and happy, our message to Axel and Declan will arrive, assuming all goes as planned.

We pull into the parking circle, a valet member meeting us up front.

"Miss Ruarc." The young man nods to her, then to me.

"Keep close by. We don't plan on staying long." Briar winks at me, the corner of her mouth curving up as she takes my hand in hers.

"Yes, ma'am." He slides into the car and pulls away.

Fastening our masks to our faces, we walk hand-in-hand toward the entrance of the castle.

As we approach, the large accents of red tapestry become more prominent. The castle is unexpectedly homey for such a large space. Lit fireplaces warm the space as we enter. Making our way into the ballroom, I see a few familiar faces gathering in small groups around cocktail tables. The room goes silent a moment before I realize they're staring—at me and Briar. Our linked hands show us as a united front, a force to be reckoned with.

"This is the first time we've been out in public like this," I say. Briar shifts at my side, her body language unreadable.

"Are you okay with it?" she asks. I don't hesitate when I answer.

"Absolutely. Let the whole world know. You are *mine*." Her cheeks flush a bit at the heat in my voice. Giving her hand a squeeze, I pull her farther into the room.

Immediately, Briar tugs on my arm, leading me toward a couple standing at the side of the ballroom. She addresses the woman with a bright smile on her face.

"June! It's so nice to see you." June turns with a wide grin on her face. The man standing beside her towers over her by several feet. We lock eyes and I nod.

"Briar! Nice to see you, darling. You've met my husband, Randall, right?" June gestures to the man beside her.

Briar nods, shaking his outstretched hand. "Nice to see you again, sir. Thank you for allowing us to use your beautiful home."

"Oh that's all her. She's the boss." I smile knowingly as Randall places a kiss across June's forehead. *Smart man.*

"That I am," June agrees with a laugh. "This must be the birthday boy."

I extend my hand, but June pulls me into an unexpected hug. I stiffen, not used to unexpected touches from strangers, but I force myself to relax.

"You're basically family now, Teague. Get used to it," Randall says, slapping a hand across my back in a hard pat. I purse my lips and force a nod. "Well. Happy birthday. I hope y'all enjoy the party." We exchange quick goodbyes before wandering further into the ballroom.

"This is an awfully dull party," someone calls from behind us. We turn in unison to see Axel entering the ballroom, completely out of costume.

"Axel," Briar muses, her voice sickly with fake sweetness. "Glad to see you made it."

"I do have to admit I was *very* surprised to get the invitation. Can't pass up the opportunity for a party." Axel's smile is vicious, almost evil, igniting my body with fury.

Briar's fingers brush my hand, her touch reminding me why we're here. It takes everything in me to match the smile that Briar has plastered on her face. My fist aches to connect with Axel's face, causing as much damage as possible, inflicting as much pain on him as he did Briar. Anger pulses through me as I force the smile to remain unwavering.

"Happy birthday, bro." He smacks his hand on my shoulder, a friendly gesture that only rouses my anger more.

I'm not your bro.

"Thanks," I grit out between my teeth. As if on cue, Declan arrives, the room going quiet as he approaches. I feel Briar tense before nodding to someone across the room.

"You'll have to excuse me, gentleman. Hostess duty calls." She smiles at me before walking to the stage. Standing upon the stage, her whole countenance is exquisite. I have no doubt in my mind that Briar could command a room and be a leader worthy of worship. I eye the microphone passed to her before her voice echoes through the ballroom.

"Welcome everyone," she says. Her voice is like honey, thick and cloying. "Thank you for being here on Halloween. I am sure many of you had other things you could be doing, but instead, you are here, to celebrate the birthday of our very own Teague Rossi." Her hand extends out toward me, heads turning in my direction. Or at least that's what I assume the reaction is. I'm not looking at the crowd, my eyes trained only on her. "Without further ado, let's kick it off with some dancing!"

The live music begins on cue; a medium paced song, enough for couples to move toward the center of the room, dancing together.

Meeting Briar at the base of the stage, I offer my hand to her. "May I have this dance, milady?"

The answering grin spreading across her face makes me want to scoop her into my arms and walk right out the front door. We walk together to the dance floor as the next song begins. The heat of everyone's stares lands on my back, but I ignore it, my attention fully on Briar. Her eyes never leave mine, her mask drawing out the gold at the center of her eyes.

We move as one, Briar letting me lead her the whole way. I don't have much experience with ballroom dancing, but I know enough to keep attention locked on us. With each dip, turn and spin, Briar captures the eyes of everyone.

Classical music whispers in our ears, setting the rhythm for our movements. Each step is methodical, choreographed yet graceful. We move as a team, Briar's feet keeping time with mine. The room spins around us, shimmering lights becoming beams. The sound of the violin reverberates through the room, sending a pulse of excitement through me.

"You look magnificent. Have I told you that yet?" I dip her, not missing the way her cheeks redden. Her back arches, head falling back to accentuate the line of her neck.

"You have. But I'll hear it again," she says. Her eyes smile as the song ends. I raise her back to me, our mouths so close I can feel her breath. Our lips meet a moment later. It's a gentle kiss, not the desperate kind. She tastes like sugar, and I devour her like an addict.

On cue, our team walks in, Ondina nodding in our direction as she walks to a back table. We break apart, looking slightly disheveled. I spot Axel and Declan staring, obviously disgusted. *Good.*

"If only they knew why they're here," I say into her ear, indicating for her to look. She laughs naturally, her head falling back, my eyes snapping to the exposed flesh of her neck.

I groan, the need to drag her from this place and into my bed intensifying with each passing second.

Winking at me, Briar leads us toward where Axel and Declan stand. "Declan. How nice to see you." She extends a hand and he hesitantly takes it.

"Sure," he quips.

"Well, enjoy the party. Birthday boy and I have business to attend to. Stay as long as you desire."

Riggs and Hal join us in our walk to the back office. Stepping foot inside, Hal pulls the door shut behind us.

"How'd it go?" I ask.

"The switch went great; everything went according to plan. Your forgeries were amazing, by the way. It'll take him years to notice the real paintings are gone," Ondina says, the corners of her mouth tilting in glee.

"Where are the real ones?" Briar's hand grazes the desk in an attempt to hide her excitement.

"At your fathers. Shay brought out frames for them and they're safely hidden," Hal replies, a wide grin on his face.

"Shay is so cool," Riggs chimes in. "I would love to spend more time with that tech. Killian was holding out on us." He's practically drooling as he talks. *Nerd.*

"He really was," Hal says.

Gabe's face falls beside him. "Don't take it personally. No one knew. Not even Briar," he says. Briar nods, her lips settling into a tight line. I can see the emotion churning behind her eyes before Ondina wraps an arm around her.

"It's okay, girl. They'll get what's coming to them." She squeezes her tightly, then steps away, pulling a container out of the mini fridge. "We brought cake."

"Happy Birthday, man." Hal claps me on the back, jerking forward with the force of it.

"Thanks, Hal" I laugh, steadying myself.

"Come on! Cut the cake," Ondina sing-songs. "My mouth is watering just looking at it."

"Who said you get cake? It's not your birthday." Gabe pulls out plates, clearly planning on claiming a piece of cake for himself.

Scowling at him, Ondina bumps him with her hip, knocking him off balance. "Oops."

Briar snorts, grabbing a plate and handing it to me. "Here. It's time for the real celebration. This may have been a petty personal mission, but I need to thank all of you for making it happen." She makes eye contact with the room. "Those paintings were important to Killian, so getting them back was the least I could do." I can see the words she doesn't say written on her face. She's worried about failure, this being the one thing she could do successfully.

Hal takes a piece of cake.

"It was a no brainer."

"Well from here on out, the real shit begins." Briar cracks her knuckles before taking a bite of cake.

24

Briar

O ne of my favorite feelings in the world is warm sand between my toes. California's general lack of weather makes for a warm and sunny climate most of the year. I can't say that I mind it, particularly when my weenie ass was frozen from October until April in New York. The four seasons don't exist in California. California is predictable. Although it could be chilly, chances are that it won't be cold enough to prevent most activities from happening.

Today, fortunately, is a perfect November day. A week after Teague's birthday, our plan is in motion. It's a day that I've been dreading from the moment I recognized it as a necessary step.

In my father's culture, black isn't the color that is worn to funerals. Instead, everyone dresses in bright colors or traditional Hawaiian attire. Today, I chose to wear my blue and white floral muumuu. Blue was Killian's favorite color. Under my muumuu, I'm wearing my bathing suit because of our plans to go out into the water during the ceremony. While braiding my hair into an intricate updo, a knock on the bathroom door draws my attention.

"You look beautiful," Ondina says from the doorway.

"Thank you. So do you." She's in a pink and white muumuu matching the one I'm wearing. She grins at me, twirling softly.

"Teague sent me. It's time to go." I nod, readying myself to leave.

"I just have one final touch." Grabbing a mermaid tail pendant from the dresser, I drape the cool necklace around my neck, Ondina rushing to help fasten it.

"Perfect!" She admires the necklace before turning to walk out of the room. "Gabe offered to drive me. I think he's trying to kiss ass or something."

I snort at her off-handed comment. "Kiss ass why?"

"He pissed me off yesterday. I really don't want to talk about it. But I think he's trying to make up for it."

I raise an eyebrow at her as we walk down the stairs. "Well, let him. They have to learn somehow." I nudge her with my elbow.

She rolls her eyes, shaking her head. "Yeah. He'll learn, alright."

"Ladies, less talking, more walking. We're going to be late." My eyes go wide at the sight of Gabe. "What?" He says, blinking. *Less talking, more walking my ass, Gabe.*

I just shake my head in response, walking into Teague's open arms.

"Can I drive?" My voice is muffled by his chest, but I know he can hear me by the deep laughter I feel.

"Yes, you can drive," he says, his voice the calm beacon I love so much. *Love?* Pulling away, I smile wide.

"Great, let's go."

I PULL INTO the parking lot with such speed that the car almost bounces off the parking block. I truly don't mind going fast, and I am quite the speeder, but I think I may have overdone it a bit.

"Speed racer today, huh?" Teague releases his death grip on the door handle and sits back into the passenger seat for a moment. He looks at me, his face full of emotion.

"What's wrong?"

"I'm… I don't. know. Worried? About today." I maintain his gaze while I speak.

"Why?"

"I want you to have this day. But I can't convince myself that something isn't going to happen."

"It might. It might not. But either way, we have a plan and we're going to stick with it. The guys have security handled and I doubt Declan would be stupid enough to make a move so publicly. Making a move today would paint a target on his back, which I doubt he wants."

"You're right, but I still worry. I want to protect you and I feel like I can't."

"I'm a big girl. I'll be okay. I respect that you want to protect me, but I promise you, I can take care of myself." I give his hand a reassuring tap, unsure if it is the right thing to do or not.

"Why are you so calm about this?" Teague's tone is teasing but I can hear the slightly panicked undertone. I shrug in response. "Well do you have your gun?"

I tap my leg. "Strapped to my thigh."

That seems to calm him a bit. People pass us in Hawaiian shirts and colorful clothing. "People are showing up. It's time to face the crowd."

I leave my shoes in the car because who wears shoes to the beach? Only psychopaths. The warm sand welcomes me immediately. I felt at home the moment I stepped foot onto the beach, Hawaiian music filling my ears.

In my many stalking adventures, I learned of Killian's love of Hawaiian music. I wish that in our short time together, I could have been able to learn directly from him which artists were the best. My personal favorite from his collection is Keali'i Reichel. Since living with Teague, my dreams have been full of possibilities and things that could be. One of the many dreams was of Teague, holding a baby girl on his arm and dancing without a single care in the world. Tears well in my eyes, my heart clenching at the thought.

"Teague, have you ever thought about… being normal? Like getting married, having children, any of those things?"

"All the time. I think about what my future could look like without the Crows. Why?" He looks at me expectantly. I purse my lips, thinking of the right words to say.

"I was just thinking about having children one day. Would that even be a possibility for me?"

"Do you want it to be a possibility?" Teague's fingers thread through mine.

"I think so. I haven't really thought about it."

"We can talk about it more later if you want. That seems like a conversation *normal* couples have, right?" He brings my hand to his lips, placing a gentle kiss on my fingers. I scrunch my nose at his comment about normal couples. *We're anything but normal.*

"I guess so," I say.

One of my favorite Hawaiian songs, *Ipo Lei Momi,* plays over the speakers. The closer we get, the louder it is. Music is something that I've always been passionate about; music allows me to feel alive. In this moment, I feel alive listening to this song with the sand in my toes, pure *joy.*

Teague reserved a private beach for Killian's celebration of life. Without the worry of random people, I feel more relaxed than I have in the past week. As we reach the tent, I see tables set up full of food, photos that serve as memories of Killian. Although this is part of the plan, I want it to appear real and genuine. Every photo I chose shows my father's loving *mundane* life.

A member of the band greets us, going over the set for the day. After asking for a specific song for the water portion of the ceremony, Teague and I find our seats, waiting for guests to arrive. Looking down at my watch, I notice it's five to noon. Everyone should be arriving in the next few minutes which gives me just a moment to breathe and take everything in. The next few minutes pass in a blur before I'm brought back to Earth by Teague's sultry voice.

"Go take your place behind the podium, love. I'll be right here." He gives my hand a reassuring squeeze before releasing me.

The music slows as I step to the podium. Looking out at the small group of faces, I recognize some fellow Crows, as well as people in the Roosters, come to pay their respects. Who I didn't expect to see is Axel in the back row, his face indifferent. Nausea rolls through me at the sight of him.

Teague must see the way my face falls because he glances over his shoulder at Axel. His anger is evident when he turns back to me. With fire in his eyes, he nods.

I close my eyes before speaking. "Thank you all for being here today to celebrate the life of my father Killian Ruarc."

THE MOST BEAUTIFUL thing about watching hula is the way the body moves in a fluid and controlled way. As *E Ō Mai* plays, a young woman dances hula as a parting gift for my father. I know that at this moment, he would be looking down and smiling. Hula is such an emotional, expressive form of dance. Every emotion, every feeling, and every word is spoken through the way the body moves. I'm captivated by her movements, tears coming to my eyes as I watch. Teague's hand on my leg reminds me of the now as well as the comfort I have found in him and in my friendships.

Applause sounds around me as the dancer finishes, bringing a smile to my face. My body warms in joy for this moment and the people here. These last moments will be beyond difficult, but I am ready to let go and be at peace.

I force myself to a stand and walk back to the podium. I smile brightly at my friends and family.

"Thank you so much. I know he would've loved that so very much." My voice breaks a little. "To end the ceremony, I will be going out onto the water for the last goodbyes. I have requested that this portion be private for me and mine. However, everyone is more than welcome to stay and observe from the beach. Thank you all again for coming. There is food at the tables for everyone. Go eat and enjoy the rest of the celebration!" I nod at Teague and Ondina before moving from the podium.

"Briar. That was lovely." A woman's voice greets me as I step away from the podium.

"Niamh, thank you for coming," I say as she pulls me into her arms as though we've known each other for years. I keep my guard up, unsure if I can truly trust her yet.

"Thank you for extending an invitation. I wouldn't have missed it for the world." She clasps my hand in hers. "Do you have a moment to talk?" Her voice is hushed and urgent.

Teague comes to my side immediately, placing a hand on my arm. "I'll be right there. Can you grab the board with the guys?" Teague nods, placing a kiss on my head.

"What's wrong?" I ask Niamh. Now I'm getting worried.

"I worry that your father's cover was compromised before he passed. I've never seen anything like it. Our systems are impenetrable, and someone must have gotten in."

Or someone spilled the beans like a traitor.

"After a period of inactivity, Declan is making moves again. Girls are being loaded as we speak to be moved into one of their homes. We haven't confirmed the location, but we know it's happening."

I want to play my cards right. At this moment, I trust no one but my team.

"What do you need me to do?" I say, our voices hushed as we walk away from the crowd.

"In our messages, you mentioned a fight. I need you to go through with it. We need their eyes on something else outside of the raids we want to execute."

"I'll make it happen." My jaw feels sore, immediately making me aware of the fact that I had been grinding my teeth and clenching my jaw. I release my jaw, hoping to reduce the tension in my face.

"How are you doing with all of this?" Niamh's face softens to an almost motherly gaze. Something about her doesn't seem right... Or is that the paranoia talking?

"I'm okay. I've had some time to think about it. But it's still so weird and… unexpected." That's the truth.

She smiles softly. "I can understand that. He didn't want to lie to you. I hope you know that."

"I do," I say. *Do I?* I twist the ring on my finger to release some of my pent-up energy. "Can I ask you something?"

"Anything."

"Does Ondina know? Where she came from? About all of you?" Niamh's eyes flick toward the water where the rest of my team sit.

"No. Killian oversaw the rescue, keeping everything anonymous. She was very young. Young enough where those memories get muddled if replaced." *Replaced?*

"By the time she was old enough to be recruited, Killian had already taken over the Crows. Teague was doing his rehab thing with the gym, so it worked."

Pursing my lips, I nod a few times. Thinking over my next words, I decide to play it safe.

"Axel or Declan wants me dead for some reason," I blurt. I don't know why I said that out loud to her. *That wasn't safe, you idiot.*

"You're a threat to him. I can't really tell you why, because I don't know what goes on in that sick mind of his, but you're new. One thing I know for sure is that they really hate change." She points to Teague and the others. "You've changed them. They're different. That alone is enough of a threat. People are drawn to you, and I don't doubt that you will be an amazing leader one day."

A creeping feeling of sadness invades my head. I don't know what's going to happen next. I don't know what the future holds, which is what scares me most. This whole life I've built… I've planned every moment I could control. There is no control in this. Teague catches my eye, a slow smile spreading across his face.

"Go. Be with your family. I'll be in touch." Niamh taps me on the back lightly before walking in the opposite direction. Taking a deep breath, I pad through the sand to the water. Teague takes my hand in his, his touch promising questions later.

We paddle out onto the water together. I thank God for the beautiful day paired with the sun blazing high in the sky. The heat licks at my skin, evening out the chill from the water.

We float in a circle on the water, the waves moving us lightly as we bob up and down with the flow. I lock eyes with everyone in the circle in turn.

"Typically, at this point, we would scatter Killian's ashes. However, Axel has chosen to deprive us of that kindness. I will have to settle for the reading of a poem and then tossing our leis. If anyone has anything to add, please feel free to do so after the reading."

"This is a poem I wrote. It is inspired by another poem called *Aloha Oe* by Don Blanding."

I read the words out loud, emotion filling my throat as I speak.

Aloha Oe.

Aloha is more than just a simple hello or casual good-bye

It is a happy greeting or a see you later

It conveys the words we all wish we could say, but cannot bring ourselves to

In a simple Aloha, a lifetime full of emotion is held

It is found and seen in every hug and kiss and in every flower gifted

In both sadness and in joy, we express

Aloha to those we love

Aloha means "I love you." So I say "Aloha Oe."

I breathe in the ocean breeze and enjoy the comfort, the sounds of the waves crashing provides. Sea salt fills my nose, a calming invasion to my raging heart. My chilled hands brush my neck as I wrap my fingers around the delicate petals of my lei. Gently removing it from around my neck, I rest it on the board between my legs as I wait for the others to do the same. As each of our leis are removed, we toss them into the water, watching them float with the bounding waters. The ocean continues to foam and welter around us, each minute passing within the company of my found family.

Riggs breaks the silence with the rumble of his stomach. "I hate to ruin the moment, but I think my stomach is eating me alive." We all laugh in unison; the first real belly laugh I have had in a while. Teague looks at me with awe in his eyes. His jade eyes match the ocean; I could stare into them for days.

Honestly, who am I kidding. I could lose myself in the essence of Teague happily forever.

"Let's go back," I say as I drop Teague's hand. Leaning forward, I rest my chest on the board and bring my legs back behind me to paddle back to shore where reality will inevitably set in. This is the final goodbye—the beginning of the end.

25

Briar

An unsettled feeling rests low in my belly. For the first time in a long time, the future is uncertain. I don't know what fate has in store for me. Will I live or will I die? This feels like a war that I will pay for with my life. If that's the case, I willingly give it. I've always been the one for self-sacrifice. In the past, I never had anything worth fighting for… until now.

Fight night is tomorrow, the raid that will determine which future will occur. Will it poke the bear and stir up a bigger war, or will it end the problem at hand and set this bird free?

A warm body wraps around mine, the weight of Teague's arm casually draped around me making me feel small. With his other arm, Teague draws my body to him, my back resting within the warmth of his chest. His breathing slows again for a moment before I wiggle against his crotch, earning a small groan in my ear. His usual scent of earthy smoke and ocean-kissed skin fills my nose. I'll have to ask him one day how the smell of him encapsulates my love for the ocean. Everything about him calls to me, like he was made just for me.

"You're gonna pay for that." The heat in his voice sends a thrill of anticipation up my spine.

Drawing my lip into my mouth, I fight a smile as I twist my upper body to look at him.

"Good morning to you too, handsome." Arching a brow at him in challenge, I wiggle again, feeling his arousal pressing against my ass.

His eyes never leave mine as he flips me, his body now resting above mine. Before I have the chance to say anything, he disappears under the covers, his hands yanking at my thin sleep shorts. I shriek as he rips them away, tossing them across the room.

"I warned you," he growls from under the blankets. He pops back into view, his gaze full of heat. "I want you to stay very still. Don't you dare make any noise."

"Or what?" I challenge. *I'm a brat, I know.*

His gaze darkens again before he takes a finger and drags it through the slickness at my core. A small whimper escapes my lips at the touch. Drawing the finger into his mouth, his eyes lock with mine. My heart stops, every fiber of my being screaming to be touched.

"I'm not sure you want to find out." Not daring to argue any further, I nod my head, encouraging him to continue.

Teague tosses the blankets off the bed, leaving no shield for me to hide under. I want to be in this moment with him forever. My heart aches for the possibility of a normal life with Teague, a forever with this man. My mind roams over the dreams I've longed for—the small wedding ceremony in the woods, a home to call our own, the pitter patter of little feet in the mornings, and the simplicity of normal. Is it so much to ask for simple? Emotion clutches at my throat, the sting of unshed tears gathering behind my eyes.

Teague's body tenses as he senses the shift in my mood. Immediately, I feel his large hands on my face, his warm skin on mine. "Tell me what's wrong?"

"I can't do this. I can't be the person everyone wants me to be. I—I want to live." My breath comes out in a gasp.

I want to live.

"Darling, no one wants you to be anything other than yourself."

"I can't be a leader. I just want to be me. I just... I just want to live for the first time in my life without the weight of everyone's expectations. I don't even know what Niamh expects of me after this point. Do we keep up this ruse of the Crows? I can't run a fake gang..." A wave of relief crashes over me.

Let go.

Teague stares at me, allowing me to let it out, so I continue. "I want *you.* I want a future. I want to be free." Teague's eyes dance over mine, his expression plain. My heart sinks a bit until he speaks.

"The one thing I can promise at this very moment is that you have me." His hands move to hold mine. He seems to think over his next words carefully before speaking again. "Why do you feel like you can't do this?" His question hits me like a ton of bricks. Am I doing this out of fear? Why do I feel this way? Do I really believe that I'm not capable of doing this?

"I feel too broken, damaged, and scarred to be a leader worth following. I can hardly lead myself; how can I lead others?" Teague moves to kneel between my legs, allowing me to take him in. The way his thighs bulge from the position and his body, chiseled through hard work, looming over mine. His tanned skin gleams under the morning light, giving me a better look at the marks and scars littering his skin. Although ink decorates his body, these marks are still visible.

"We all have scars, Briar. Scars tell the stories of survival and strength." I prop myself up on my arms to look at him. His hand brushes a strand of hair away from my face. "You are not damaged goods. You are capable of anything you set your heart out to do, including leading a gang. Whether you believe it or not, people listen to you. Your presence commands a room. You are made for this." His voice is more urgent now. "Don't let the opinions of others snuff out that light of yours."

I think on his words for a moment. The girl I was before went through a lot to get where she is now. Those moments won't define me any longer, but they can become my scars—my stories of strength and survival. I am determined to live, to live fully. Fear will not hold me back any longer.

I breathe in this new sense of confidence. "Thank you," I say to Teague, a small smile taking over my face. "Healing is a journey. I won't always believe I'm not damaged goods, but at least for now, I can fight for the future."

"I'll never forget to remind you." He leans in, kissing my forehead. "With my words." A kiss on my cheek. "With my actions." His lips brush against my neck. "With subtle looks and touches." I shiver at the contact. "Do you feel better?" His gaze darkens again as my breath slows.

I nod, unable to form words.

"Good because I'd very much like to bury myself between your legs and enjoy the sweet moans from your lips while I do it." A giggle bursts from my lips and I immediately cover my mouth. My eyes go wide as a grin spreads across Teague's face.

"Maybe pull my hair a bit," I say as his gaze darkens in challenge.

"So bossy," he says as his lips move across me, my body igniting with desire for *him*. I've never known feelings like this. Is this love? My whole being is on fire for him, every thought and feeling peppered with Teague.

His mouth makes contact with my clit causing me to writhe under his touch. Almost immediately I remember his request to stay still and relax. My eyes lock with Teague's, his gaze promising retribution. With another flick of his tongue, his hand comes to my center, teasing the area I need him most. A small whimper escapes me, the need for him growing. He quirks an eyebrow at me, his green eyes full of warning. I grin sweetly and he nips at my inner thigh, eliciting a yelp. I mime zipping my lips and lower myself to the bed, tossing my head back on the pillow.

I'm rewarded immediately by his fingers and tongue. His thick fingers fill me in a way that makes me ache for the full stretch of his cock. As he moves his fingers in just the right way, his tongue continues to flick and swirl around my clit.

I grab the pillow beside me and shove it over my face, stifling the moans I so badly wish I could release. My body tenses around his fingers as I ride them, my release sneaking up on me quickly. One last swirl of his tongue and I'm a goner.

"Let me see you," he says. I pull the pillow away, as the orgasm rips through me.

Teague's hands grip my hips, restricting my movements as waves of pleasure roll through me. I'm unable to remain quiet any longer, his tongue lapping at the evidence of my pleasure. I lay there, panting, until I see Teague draw each of his fingers into his mouth slowly, tasting me.

"Gimme," I say, my voice a bit wicked as I crawl across the bed to him. He rises to his knees giving me better access.

Hooking my hands under the waistband of his pants, I pull them down in one swoop. His cock springs free, slapping against his waist. The sight of it sends an intense shiver through my body. His gaze is feral now, but gentle; there's something soft and calculating about it. Breathing in, I gain a new understanding of this thing between us.

I capture his mouth with my lips. Unsaid words pass between us with each kiss. Love is a scary thing. Is that what I'm feeling each time my chest pounds and I feel an overwhelming draw to him?

I hear the breath leave him as I reach behind me, gripping his cock within my hand again. Stroking slowly, I tease him just he teased me. With each stroke, his eyes never leave mine. This is a challenge and an invitation to take control.

"I'm going to ride you now."

His laugh quickly turns to a groan as I impale myself on his cock. My hands find purchase on his chiseled stomach. Using his body for stability, my hips circle and lift, the feeling of him inside me bringing a rising sense of pleasure. I moan as I move, ever so slowly.

Unable to control himself any longer, Teague's hands find my hips, gripping me while he flips us, pinning me on my back once more. Before I can complain, he draws my nipple into his mouth as he thrust into me—hard. I moan, tossing my head back, enjoying the way our bodies move together. The only sound is the moans exchanged between us and the sounds of our bodies meeting with each thrust.

Teague's free hand moves to my clit, his thumb circling the sensitive bud. "Come for me," he breaths in my ear, his mouth nipping at the flesh of my neck.

With one last thrust, I tumble over the edge, my release coming in shuddering waves. Teague follows me immediately, his body tensing. Before collapsing beside me, he flips a few locks of dark hair from his face. Sweat glistens on his body. Resting my head on my hand, I admire Teague in all his glory.

"I'm sorry," I blurt. "I feel like today has been a whirlwind of emotions and mess."

"Never apologize to me for your feelings. I want you to be able to have these moments with me. I want to know what goes on in that head of yours." He kisses me on the forehead before disappearing to the bathroom. I watch and admire that ass of his as he walks. With a squeak, the shower starts, steam immediately flooding into the room. When Teague returns, his gaze is full of promise and love. Rising to my feet, I step into the bathroom, and right into the arms of comfort and safety.

26

Briar

Teague's swift breaths fill the room as he lands punch after punch on the dummy. We've been here for hours so that he can train. We should have trained more over the course of the last few days, but our circumstances have prohibited it. Worry fills my chest as I think about the possibility of Teague getting hurt. I've never seen Hal fight but judging solely off his size and build, he's definitely a worthy opponent.

Teague's got a few inches on Hal, but what Hal lacks in height, he makes up for in pure muscle. If I didn't know he was truly a teddy bear under all of that armor, I would be intimidated by the guy.

Sweat glistens over Teague's chiseled body. I thank God he chose to toss his shirt during training. With each punch he throws, his muscles flex in all the right ways. My vagina tingles from the sexiness of it all. I imagine the moment he walks near me with that sweaty body, I'll be like a bitch in heat.

Wiping the drool from my face, I turn my attention back to the mural I was drawing with chalk markers. With the fight mere hours away, I wanted to make it appear that we were putting real effort in.

The gym is now fully decorated and presentable for the public. Although it isn't the biggest space, we anticipate a great turnout. Just as anticipated, Declan couldn't turn down the opportunity to enter one of his fighters.

A sense of pride sweeps through me at the mere fact that Teague is one of the headliners. Glancing over my shoulder, I see him still pounding away at the dummy and I smile. His headphones thankfully keep him locked in the zone of whatever headspace he needs to be in for training. Footsteps draw my eyes to the front door, and I notice Ondina walk in with Riggs following close behind.

"Hiya," she exclaims. "We're here to help with whatever you need." Riggs stands at her side awkwardly and grumbles until I see Ondina nudge him with her elbow.

"Yeah. Whatever you need, boss." I laugh at the two of them and pull Ondina into my arms.

"Thanks. I appreciate it," I say into her shoulder. She just squeezes me harder. Addressing Riggs, I gesture towards the outside of the ring.

"Can you set up the sound system and make sure the DJ table works?" He escapes to the ring immediately, leaving Ondina and me standing by the front window. "Care to help me with the mural?"

"Girl, of course."

For the next hour, we giggle and shit talk while painting the windows. It's the most normal relationship I've ever had with another female. I could get used to this. By the end of the hour, we've created a mural of a face, half Teague and half Hal, with lettering across the top spelling out 'Fight Night'. The earlier unease begins to creep in again.

"Is he coming tonight?" Pursing my lips, I nod.

"Accepted the invite yesterday. And Declan entered his man into the schedule so I can guarantee they'll both be here."

"That's what we want, right?"

"Yeah. I mean we do, but it doesn't help my unease."

Ondina wipes her brush on a paper towel at her side. "What can I do?"

"I just really want tonight to be over so that we can move on." Tensions are high. I felt it from the moment I woke up this morning. Looking down at my watch, it's a few minutes to two in the afternoon. I nod my head towards the back office, and we make our way into the small room away from the boys. The door clicks closed behind us, giving us some privacy.

"Niamh is supposed to call me in a few minutes, and I would like you to listen in. If, God forbid, anything happens to me tonight, I need you to know what to do." She looks at me stunned, then furiously nods her head, the emotion hiding in her eyes. Taking a seat next to me, I flip my laptop open and navigate to the zoom call.

Minutes or maybe seconds later, Niamh's face pops into view. Her background is new—a cramped office or working space. People move behind her as though they're in a small space. My guess is a van of sorts.

"Briar." Niamh's hand adjusts the camera, moving it down more to allow her face to fully fit the frame.

"Niamh. I wasn't aware that the assistant director was so involved in these things."

She smiles, but there's a note of bitterness there. "They don't. Not until me. You don't know the shit I've been through to get here."

"I can imagine."

"Anyways. I wanted to update you on our progress. The shipment is due to arrive tonight. We have teams ready to intercept the trucks before the raid to avoid putting any lives at risk. We don't know the state these women will be in." She looks over her shoulder as someone leans in and speaks into her heart. She nods, mouthing something back to the man. Looking back at the screen she continues. "Ondina. Do you have any tips for making these women feel comfortable?" That last bit felt forced. Her face is now impassive. I can't shake the feeling that something isn't right with Niamh.

Ondina's eyes shoot to me before speaking. "Only women. Don't let any men be a part of the team. Female doctors, female staff, the works. Fresh clothes, food, comfort." Niamh nods a few times, her face still disinterested.

"If you think of anything else, please let me know." She hands off a list to someone on her right then turns back to the screen.

"Do you need us to do anything specific? I have eyes on Declan and Axel, but outside of that, is there anything I can do?" I can feel myself growing antsier as time passes. Restlessness sets in, the need to move and do *something* overwhelming me.

"Just stay safe. I want to send a plane for the two of you once the operation is successful. I would like for you both to be involved in the recovery process. These women will need strong leaders to look up to. I believe Teague's gym will become a place of solace for them as well." Ondina looks at me thoughtfully. The warmth in my chest grows. The feeling of having a purpose outside of this gang alleviates some of the restlessness I feel. Our eyes lock again and Ondina nods beside me in agreement.

"Absolutely. Tell us when and we'll be there."

"Great. Stay safe, ladies. And please, don't forget to actually enjoy the event. A good fight is good for the soul." She winks before the screen goes black.

A knock at the office door startles me out of my head.

"Come in," I say a little too loud. Gabe's lithe body slides through a small crack in the door, shutting it behind him like he's sneaking around.

"Boss." I raise my eyes from the blank screen to observe him. "Yes?"

"We've got loads of fangirls lining up already to stare at…"

The screams drown Gabe out for a moment, and we wait for them to subside so he can continue. "They're here for Teague." An amused smile spreads across my face and I raise an eyebrow.

"I'll handle it." A laugh bubbles up in my throat the longer Gabe stands there, obviously uncomfortable. "Can you please take Riggs and stock the snack bar? If they're as bad as I imagine, we're going to need lots of food and alcohol. Please," I add.

Gabe nods aggressively before sliding out of the office once more. In unison, Ondina and I snort our laughter. I throw my head back before attempting to compose myself but seeing Ondina doing the same has me losing it all over again. After a solid five minutes of laughing, I gather myself enough to leave the office.

The moment I open the door, I am met with a massive line of women. They're all standing with their faces toward the window, necks craning, attempting to catch a peak of Teague training. The best course of action would be to send them away. I don't like the best course of action though. I walk to the front of the punching bag, hoping to catch Teague's attention. As if he can sense my presence, his eyes shoot to me immediately. Barely a moment passes before he pulls out one of his headphones and pulls me in to plant a kiss on my forehead. As if on cue, the screaming begins again.

I laugh. "What was that for?"

"Just cuz." I feel the stubble of his chin move as he smiles against my head.

"You've got a fan club," I say as I pull away and look into his eyes. I could lose myself in his gaze. I want to commit everything about him to memory.

Just in case.

"I have no idea why. I'm nobody." He's serious. He truly believes that.

"Right," I tease. "A nobody. All of those people out there would disagree." An alarm goes off on my phone reminding me of the limited time we have. "I suggest you go shower. More people will be arriving, and I want to keep my headliner safe. Speaking of headliners, do you know where Hal is?" More screaming from the crowd causes me to scrunch my nose in discomfort.

"He's in the back. Walked in maybe ten minutes ago. I honestly think the screaming was more for him." His hand comes to my face. "How are you feeling, B?" I feel the heat rush through me and straight to my face. I fidget uncomfortably until his thumb brushes my lips. In that moment, it's just us, no audience outside, no gym, just Teague's grounding presence.

"I'm… I'm feeling good. We talked with Niamh. She wants us to help with acclimating the women back into society." The corners of Teague's mouth turn up, his eyes softening.

"Good," he says, a note of darkness in his tone.

My gaze turns heavy as his thumb traces circles on my cheek. Tilting my chin up, his lips brush against mine. I release a small sigh, then realize what I'd done a moment too late. He deepens the kiss, his tongue brushing across my lips and begging for entry. I allow it, my breathing coming in heavy gasps and moans. This man literally takes my breath away. Teague tells me he loves me, infusing a sense of confidence with each kiss. I'm utterly lost in the essence of him until he pulls away. He looks at me with a darkened gaze, his breathing ragged. He places one last, tender kiss on my lips before winking at me. He not so subtly adjusts himself before stalking off towards the locker room. I stare wide eyed as Ondina starts chuckling in the corner of the room.

"Did you see all that?"

"Yup," she laughs. "Everyone did."

A blush fills my cheeks as I look towards the window and see mouths hanging open, some stunned and others looking amused. Suddenly a voice yells through the window, "He's SO in love with you, girl. GET IT!" There's that word again. *Love.*

Scattered laughter sounds around the outside of the building, then suddenly Ondina and I are laughing again. I don't believe I've laughed so much in a while. It's lovely having my joy back.

THE HOURS FLY by and before I know it, the place is filled with people. Voices sound all around me as people bond over their excitement for tonight. As far as I know, the bets have been placed and it could go either way.

By the time we finish setting up, Ondina and I have just enough time to run to the locker rooms and change. We are sporting matching shirts in support of our fighters. Mine, of course, has Rossi in large university lettering across my back. Part of me feels guilty for picking between two members of my team, but I'm chalking it up to girlfriend privileges.

The energy in the room is charged with excitement. I rise on my tiptoes hoping to spot a familiar face with no luck. We decided at the last minute to bring in a bartender to work the snack bar. With the number of people lined up outside the building tonight, we need the alcohol. Hell, *I* need the alcohol to calm my nerves for tonight.

Declan and Axel haven't shown up yet. The security guards that are placed at the front of the venue have been ordered to alert me immediately upon their arrival. The longer it takes, the more nervous I become. My team is nowhere in sight, which adds to the nerves I feel.

Over the next hour, my nerves grow increasingly worse to the point where I feel my pulse throughout my entire body. Three fights have happened already and it's now time for Teague to fight.

Cracking my knuckles, I walk to the bar and finally get that much needed drink. Nervous sweat begins to pool in my palms.

"Rum and Coke, please," I say to the bartender. He smiles before pouring my drink.

"Here ya go," he says, handing me my drink. I take it and immediately bring the cool drink to my lips. The sting of carbonation and alcohol warms my throat and body instantly. I can feel the calming effects of intoxication settling over my body, each muscle loosening slightly. I shake my head a moment before walking back into the crowd, finding a spot where I can see the octagon. Pulling out my phone, I send a quick text to Ondina, letting her know where I'm standing in the hope she'll find me eventually.

The announcer's voice booms over the loudspeaker, the crowd coming to a hush. His voice is commanding as he goes through his rehearsed lines about each fighter, listing off their stats.

The crowd goes wild at the mention of each fighter, obvious boos from those who are rooting for the opposite fighter. A small smile spreads across my face as I observe the crowd.

Hal walks into the ring first, the crowd going wild, stomping their feet and cheering. He does a cocky saunter around the octagon, with one gloved hand raised above his head. The ladies go wild, screaming as he whips his shirt off his shoulders and throws it into the crowd.

Rolling my eyes, I turn to the other side of the stage, waiting for Teague to make his appearance. As if on cue, the announcer yells Teague's name, signaling a myriad of hoots and hollers across the room. When I see him, it's as though the air has been sucked out of the room.

His chiseled chest is on full display, his dark brown locks tousled across his face. He practically jumps into the octagon and stands with one arm above his head. Walking to the corner, he spots me and winks sending a full shiver right down my spine and straight to my pussy. I fight a wave of dizziness, righting myself and standing up straighter to maintain my appearance. It's nearly impossible to hide the blush from my face, so I let a small smile remain alongside my reddened cheeks.

With a few short words from the announcer, the men assume fighting positions, arms raised, and feet spread. For a while, they dance around each other, but eventually, Teague gets in a few good punches sending Hal skittering backward.

The dizziness I felt moments before washes over me in a startling wave. I lean against the wall, trying to gather my bearings. The room is spinning at an alarming rate.

Fuck.

Fuck.

My heart pounds, my ears ringing in panic. I stumble toward the back of the room, trying to get away from people and into the back office. Not caring who I run into, I rush, feeling whatever drug in my system quickly taking hold. My breathing increases as I make it into the back hallway and collapse. My body shivers with a cool sweat, nausea roiling in my stomach. My knee hits the ground first, my body crumpling to the floor. I steady myself into a crouch, but I realize I'm fighting *hard* to remain conscious.

Head pounding, I crawl, desperate to get somewhere safe. I keep my eyes on the floor, finding it more reliable than looking in front of me. The edges of my vision tunnel, sending me deeper into darkness. I fight it for as long as I can but eventually feel myself fading. Darkness closes in on me, and the last thing I hear before I slip away are the sounds of cheering and chants of Teague's name.

27

TEAGUE

The sound of cheering is deafening. The announcer holds my hand above my head, the crowd cheering louder with each sentence. I'm not listening, though. My eyes search the crowd for Briar. Scanning the room, I can't find her face anywhere, sending a rush of panic through my body. The hairs on the back of my neck stand up when I spot Axel. Our gazes lock, a wicked grin spreading across his face. A moment later he salutes me and ducks into the crowd, his dark hair lost in the swarm of people.

I launch myself from the stage in a panic. I feel someone following me, but I don't dare look back and lose precious time.

Where is she?

Internally I scream with panic for what that fucker has planned. I refuse to let my mind get the best of me.

Think. Every moment counts.

Barreling through the crowd, I shove people out of my way. Various sounds of distaste rumble around me, but I don't care. My heart pounds in my chest, the sweat I worked up during the fight dripping down my body.

With a loud slam, I push through the back door, just in time to spy a white van speeding away from the gym parking lot. Hal rushes to my side, watching the van peel out into traffic.

I stand there, breathing heavily, as panic overtakes me.

Hal murmurs something, but I'm not listening. Before I have a moment to think, I'm running, my feet carrying me faster than I've ever run before. My feet pound against the pavement, my knees taking the impact. I vaguely register yelling at my back, but I shake my head, ignoring the voices calling my name. My vision blurs red, heat filling my face in anger.

I run at a steady pace, keeping the van in my sight. The roar of a vehicle at my back forces me to turn my head. Glancing behind me briefly, I recognize Gabe's mustang speeding to meet me.

He pulls up beside me and ushers me to get in. Huffing with anger, I slow my run to slide into the car while it's still moving. Slamming the door closed, I stare straight ahead while Gabe drives.

"What the *fuck* were you thinking, man? No weapons, nothing to protect you. How the hell are you gonna help her like that?"

I breathe deeply, letting my anger subside a bit before I speak. The muscles in my jaw twitch as I grind my teeth in anger.

"I would die to protect her," I say. "I didn't think. I just ran."

"Well, you both would have died had you caught up with them. What even happened?"

I shake my head. "I don't fucking know. She wasn't in the crowd. Axel saluted me then disappeared, so I ran." Clenching my fists, I toss my seat belt over my chest as Gabe picks up speed. He swerves through cars, but the van does the same ahead of us.

"Why the fuck is there so much traffic at fucking ten at night," I groan.

"It's LA, man," he says. Rolling my eyes I look back at the traffic behind us.

"Where are the others?"

"Hal's behind us with Ondina and Riggs. Any clue where they might be headed?" Our bodies jerk as the car swerves again, the sound of car horns blasting as we speed by.

"No."

A phone rings over the speakers of the car. Gabe looks down, his expression turning stony before answering it.

"Ondina, you're on speaker." His voice is clipped and harsh.

"They know," she pants. "They know about the raid. Niamh called and said that when they got there, the whole place was empty. Someone tipped them off." I slam my fist into the dashboard.

FUCK.

"I think this is retaliation. I don't know what they plan to do with her, but it doesn't look good."

"How far behind us are y'all?" Gabe's knuckles turn white as his grip around the steering wheel tightens.

"Not far. I can see your mustang from where we are. Why?" I hear Hal rev the engine of his Hummer and not long after, the top of the green-gray vehicle comes into view.

"What's the plan? We can't go into this blind."

"They took Briar. All I know is I want to get her back—alive."

"Teague, throw that thinking away. We need a leader and a plan, so think and get your shit together." Pursing my lips, I jerk a nod and think.

"Okay, so we don't know where they're headed. I don't know the locations of their sites, but if we can keep up with them, we can scout out where they end up and formulate a way to get in. Riggs, can you hack into their vehicle?"

"Already on it," Riggs chimes in, his voice sounding through the car speakers. "I got into their GPS system, and it looks like they're en route to an old warehouse near the Inglewood oil fields. I pulled up a map and there's a single road that leads in and out—"

"Well, that's a huge red flag," Ondina interrupts. Without seeing them, and through the silence on the other end of the line, I can tell Ondina and Riggs are in a stare off. Hal grunts and Riggs continues talking.

"Like Ondina said, it looks like a setup. It looks bad, T."

A fresh wave of panic spreads through me, a sense of hopelessness settling low in my belly.

"They're not planning on letting any of us out of there alive." It's Gabe who speaks. His voice is so low I barely register that he's spoken. Plastering on a face of indifference, I nod, slowly.

"This may be suicide, but they underestimate what we're capable of." Hal's reassuring words spark some hope in my gut.

"I've risked my life for her before. I'm not ready to let that stop today. Find us a way in there Riggs. Do whatever you have to do." My heart pounds in my chest, I can't think properly so I breathe, words spilling out of my mouth. "We need to be prepared for anything. Call in everyone, this isn't just Briar, she is our Don. Get a team surrounding the building." I speak directly to Hal now. "Hal, get a med team to the building. Call Kris. If anything goes wrong, we'll need her." Kris has helped Briar once. I can only hope she's willing to help again. The knowledge that Hal is medically trained eases my mind a bit.

The van moves through traffic, leading us further away from

society. My heart races, every fiber of my being worried for Briar. I don't know what state she's in, but it can't be good if they were able to get her into that van in the first place.

"I'm calling in reinforcements," Riggs says before ending the call.

"In the back there," Gabe points to the large duffle in his back seat. "Fresh clothes, guns, the works. It's a tight fit, but I suggest you get started. We don't know how much time we have left and I need you prepared."

So that's exactly what I do. I prepare.

29

Briar

The soft hum of a car is the first sound I hear when I wake. My body stirs lightly as I try to gather my surroundings. My head pounds uncomfortably, the swerving of the car not helping the fresh bout of nausea that rolls in my stomach. I swallow back the bile that rises in my throat, blinking furiously in the hopes of clearing my vision.

The cool, hard metal of the car's floor rubs against my face. Struggling to move, I find that my wrists are tied behind my back, my body thrown into a fetal position on the bumpy floor of what looks to be a creepy pedophile van.

Classic.

The gag in my mouth dampens as I get some moisture back into my mouth. I lift my neck slightly to adjust my face so that it's no longer pressed into the floor. When I do, I look around and see that I'm alone in the back.

My body shakes with fear, but I breathe deeply, trying to calm myself.

What happened?

My body aches and I can feel the dryness in my throat like I'd been screaming. I crush my eyes closed, hoping to regain some of my memory.

I remember the fight and starting to feel dizzy, then I remember everything fading to black before I made it to the back room. Kicking my legs out, I try to move my legs underneath me. Unsuccessful, I wiggle and realize too late what I've done. A pipe rolls across the back of the van, the voices in the front stopping.

I feel him before I see him. The needle plunges into my neck, my body going limp and colliding with the floor again. Darkness clouds my vision, but I fight it, spitting threats at my captor.

"I'll fucking kill you for this," I say. However, I don't know how much sense it makes as the whole world becomes fuzzy and my tongue feels too big for my mouth. Everything blends together, the bump of the car lulling me back into unconsciousness.

30

Briar

Cool water washes over my body and drenches my clothes. My body seizes from the temperature, each muscle tightening in response to the chill. Spitting water out of my mouth, I whip my head, forcing my wet hair out of my face just before a fresh bucket of cool water is dumped over me again.

A scream rises in my throat. Not out of fear, but out of anger and frustration.

"You fucking dickhead. You come out here and do this shit yourself instead of letting your cronies continue to drown me in cold water." I jerk in my chair, my wrists rubbed raw against the ropes. A sting of pain runs up my hands as I feel the rope rub into my wounds with my movement. I grit my teeth, not allowing myself to show my pain. Axel told me that he would force me to come to him. Is this what's happening? *Think, Briar.*

"Shut up, bitch," the man spits, some of his saliva landing on my cheek. He slaps me across my face a moment later, the sound echoing off the walls of the empty warehouse. My eyes sting with unshed tears. I grit my teeth, my breathing slowing as I beg them not to fall.

No weakness.

My flesh burns where his palm makes contact with my face. I scrunch my face in irritation.

"That's all you got?" I force a smile to my face, but my face is so numb from the cool water that it probably looks more like a grimace. My eyes won't hide a thing though. A promise of retribution and death will be written there and that's something I can't hide. Something I don't want to hide.

The man raises his hand to me again. I close my eyes, bracing for impact, but it never comes.

"Enough," a voice calls from across the room. "It's my turn to have some fun." I recognize his voice immediately.

Axel.

"I need her face to stay pretty. She's my property now, after all."

My property. What the fuck is he talking about?

"I am no one's *property,*" I spit.

"Oh but you are, darling." A feminine voice drawls from across the building. I search for the source, but I find nothing. The clack of heels on the cement floor attracts my attention. They stalk closer until a familiar face comes into view. I see red, my brain clouding with a fog of emotions–anger, fear, frustration, shock. *She's alive.*

She stops a few feet in front of me, striking a pose and jutting out her curvy hips in a way that I would assume makes her feel powerful.

My heart stops beating, my body going cold with fear. Suddenly, my heart pounds in my chest, my chest aching with each beat. I feel each beat, my fingers pulsing with fear.

"Surprised?" she mocks. Her tone taunts me. I say nothing, only continue to stare at her, unable to speak. My throat closes up in fear. *I should've known.*

"Well? Say something to your mother dearest. It's rude not to acknowledge your elders." She stamps her feet on the floor, her heel clacking with the motion.

"You are no mother of mine," I say finally. My voice is barely a whisper.

Come on. You are braver than that.

"Oh, but you're wrong. I'm blood and blood is thicker than water."

"Actually, that's wrong. The full quote is *'the blood of the covenant is thicker than the water of the womb,'* meaning that although we're blood, my bonds with found family are more important and 'thicker' than bonds by blood. So, no. You're wrong, *mother.*" I spit that last word out and it tastes like ash on my tongue. "What have you done?" There's no answer. "How are you even alive? You're supposed to be dead."

My mother gapes at me, her mouth opening and closing like a fish as she searches for a snarky retort. She settles for a furious huff. "You will respect me, you brat. And to answer your question, it's none of your business."

I roll my eyes at her and turn my gaze to Axel, who's now laughing at our exchange.

"What are you laughing at?" Fixing my gaze on Axel, I try murdering him with my eyes. Unfortunately, that method proves unsuccessful.

A wicked grin spreads across Axel's face. "She's got a mouth on her. I think I like that smart mouth of yours." He walks closer to me, his fingers brushing against my face. He leans in close, his lips brushing my ear. "Briar," he says, his voice low. "Let's play a game."

"What kind of game?" I ask, keeping my voice low.

"Pretend," he says, his voice wicked. "Trust me." My spine stiffens. *What the actual fuck is that supposed to mean?*

One of his fingers brush against my lips, begging for entry into my mouth. I open, allowing him entry, and slips something into my mouth. I move it with my tongue then bite down hard, but not hard enough to break his finger.

Axel screams, ripping his hand from my mouth. Blood drips from his hand and I spit what made it into my mouth onto the cement floor at my side, laughing at his pain.

"You'll pay for that," he screams, his eyes gleaming with mischief.

His threat hits me like a blow to the chest. I whip my head toward my mom remembering what he said earlier. "You fucking sold me?" I gag, my stomach roiling in disgust. I spit bile as my mother's vicious laughs fill my ears. *How does she even have the power to do that?*

"Oh, I did more than sell you, darling. I'm rich. And you don't exist." She walks behind me. Her hand grazes my shoulder, the touch burning through my body. I flinch away from her touch, desperate to get away. The rope digs into my skin as I move, each tug more painful than the one before.

"Give up," Axel groans. His men are now at his side, one wrapping his hand. "You're not going anywhere."

"I would rather die than be your property," I hiss. I can't distinguish what's real and what's fake. My heart pounds.

What if I'm making a mistake?

Axel ponders my statement for a moment. The room remains silent, my words floating out in the air. He glares a moment longer before something else replaces the contemplation that was there a moment ago. Tears stain my cheeks as I see determination cross Axel's face. I breathe in, quiet sobs shaking my body.

The world moves in slow motion. Axel removes his gun from his holster and aims it at me. He nods his head, his eyes locking on me.

"Very well. You're not worth much, anyway."

I crunch the pill in my mouth right as the impact of pain registers.

Looking down, I see blood soaking through my white shirt. My breathing comes in quick gasps, the pain in my chest almost too much to bear.

A loud crash at the back of the room sends a fresh wave of pain through my body. I slouch in the chair, the restraints around my chest being the only thing keeping me upright. I feel my body slipping, a cool chill spreading with the blood loss. My face softens, my fight coming to an end.

Gunshots sound around the room, bodies falling to the floor one by one. I vaguely register footsteps as people either scatter and run or fire back.

I ache to see the source, a small bout of hope warming me at the possibility of a savior, but I don't have enough strength to lift my head, my body growing increasingly heavy.

"I'm here," a soothing voice says in my ear. The restraints on my wrists and chest loosen. I slump forward, my face meeting a wall of flesh. "No. No. No. No. No. No no no." My savior's pleading grows increasingly frantic. "Stay with me," he yelps. "Stay with me."

I breathe in a shallow breath. I wish I could speak, to thank my savior. His large hands cup my face, the jade blue eyes of Teague meeting mine. Tears fall, a weak smile crossing my face.

"I love you," I say. His face breaks, his green eyes looking pained.

"I love you so much," he says. "Stay with me."

My head shakes as my body falls further into darkness. I can't stay here. The will to live is strong. I want to live, but I can feel my body dragging me deeper into the pit of darkness. I don't know what waits for me there. Blinking one last time, I take one last shallow breath.

"I love you," I breathe, allowing the darkness to consume me.

TEAGUE

S harp sobs wrack my body. I hold Briar's lifeless body in my arms, begging for another breath, another glance, anything to give me a sign of life.

The moment I heard the gunshots, I saw my life flash before my eyes. I knew—I knew what he had done in that moment.

I saw her slumped in the chair and it was all over. Shots rang out through the building, people running as we blasted through the doors. I knew I would do anything to get to her.

You're too late.

I will not give up. I will not cower, and I will not yield to this sadness.

Ondina rips her body from me, a small medical team rushing in to help.

"She's still alive," the pink haired woman says, her voice calm yet firm. "Her pulse is weak, but we need to take her now if you want any chance of saving her." I jerk a nod, unable to speak.

"Do whatever you need to do," I croak. "Please."

Her gaze is sad, but she nods before rushing off with the others. That woman looked so familiar. I blink a few times, trying to remember.

Someone firmly grips my shoulder. I whip my head, seeing Hal towering above me.

"Axel," he says. "He's gone. No sign of him. It's like he just disappeared."

Looking up at him, I growl my response. "I will find him, and he will die. That is a promise. He will pay for what happened here today."

I will stop at nothing—nothing—to find Axel. My body shakes with determination. Hal nods knowingly.

"Then let's go get the bastard."

EPILOGUE

TEAGUE

My dreams are haunted by green eyes and golden-brown hair. Each moment that passes, my heart squeezes tighter. Sweat beads on my forehead as I wrestle with the sheets to free myself from the prison. My bed doesn't feel the same without her. I'll continue to lose sleep until she's safe in my arms once more.

Everything smells of her: the sheets, the bathroom, the kitchen. This home had been a home for only a few weeks. That alone is a reminder of how quickly things can change. It's been two weeks since Briar went missing. I handed her over, not thinking of climbing in the back of that ambulance with her. She's nowhere to be seen.

Murder is on my mind. Passion drives revenge like justice drives vengeance. But for me, love is the driving force. When the person I love has been taken away from me, I promise that I will do whatever it takes to get her back. The beast is roaring under the surface, raring to drive. Maybe it's time I let him. The world is dead to me. I will destroy everything in my path until I find her. The world is a cruel place, but I can be crueler.

I was too late. If only I'd been there a second sooner, maybe this wouldn't have happened. There's no time to worry about the what-ifs. I can't change the past; I can only change the future.

My mind wanders through all the details from that night. Where the fuck was my team? Where were they when she needed them? That will be a question for later. The only thing I have to go off of is a single note left. Whether it was meant for me or not, it made the hairs on the back of my neck stand straight.

Don't trust the Dullahan.

-R

I'll trust no one. The monster was the only one present that night. He allows me bits and pieces, but never more than that. He rears again, begging to drive. Sighing, I blink, giving myself over to him. It's time for bloodshed. It's time to damn the consequences. Whatever needs to be done, he will do it.

Walking to the bathroom, I splash some water on my face at the sink.

When I look into the mirror, I only see darkness. My eyes are black, soulless, the creature within peeking through. Without a second thought, I scream into the empty room, my hands gripping the edge of the sink.

Welcome to the beautiful ruin of our tale. From the ruin comes the beauty, and I'm confident that from the ashes, she will rise, our Queen of the Crows. It is only a matter of time. With a roaring vengeance, I step away from the sink, leaving the past behind and allowing the monster to take control.

THE END

The story continues in Beautiful Ruin:
The Crimson Crows #2

ACKNOWLEDGEMENTS

You can thank every author who has broken my heart over the course of my life for that cliffy you just read. Some of those authors include but are not limited to Tate James, Scarlett St. Clair, Kate Stewart, C. Rochelle, L. L Campbell and Jessica S. Taylor. *side eyeing the last two.*

If they can do it, so can I.

But before I get into the big thanks for all the people who made this book possible, I want to make sure you're okay. Are you good? It'll be worth it, I swear.

I want to take this moment to thank everyone who made this possible. Bear with me, I got a lot of people to thank.

First and foremost, I want to thank God for giving me this passion to write. I wouldn't have been able to make it this far without Him.

To my fiancé, Stone. You have never once doubted my dream and I am forever grateful to you for that. Thank you for supporting me through it all. Thank you for holding me while I cried when something went wrong or when I didn't know what to do next. You're the best.

To my sister, my dad, Rebecca, my future mother-in-law and future father-in-law, thank you all for your support. I have gotten tons of cheers from all of you. Y'all have helped me and pushed me to keep going even when it was hard.

To Abby, I love you, my soul sister. Thanks for the late night FaceTime calls, prayers and movie watching sessions. I adore you. I can never thank you enough for your love and support.

To my aunt, thank you for not judging me when I told you my book was smutty. I love you for your open mindedness and for all of your support. From the bottom of my heart, I want to thank my girl gang, the smutty and nutty crew: Ash, Britt, Jess and Lexi. I am legit crying while I write this portion. My dream is coming true and I wouldn't have gotten this far if I hadn't met all of you lovely ladies. I fucking love all of you.

Jess, you're absolutely the best for helping me edit all the while working on your own project. I admire you. Thank you for understanding me and my brain. Your kind words and tough love is everything I could need and more throughout this process.

Ash, you're the ultimate hype woman and so incredibly amazing when the imposter syndrome kicks in. Thank you for reminding me of my value.

Britt, I appreciate your amazing support and hype while I wrote this. You've kept me grounded even with your incredibly busy schedule. You're next, boo. Love you lots!

And to Lexi, you're so incredibly talented and the trailblazer of the group. Thank you for walking so we can run LOL. No but really. Thank you for teaching me how to do all this stuff. Self-pub is so hard.

To further that, to the Smutty and Nutty group, I love you all. Thank you for the hype and support. Special shout out to Reva. Thank you for letting me use your name. I hope you love her as much as I do.

To the authors I have met along the way, thank you for offering your support and praise as I've gone through this journey. If I had never joined the street team for Scarlett St. Clair, I would have never met some of the most amazing people that I have in my life today.

To all my alpha and beta readers, I can't thank you enough. As a self-published author, you all make my world go round. I appreciate you.

Lastly, I want to thank my dad again. You deserve your own line.

My papa bear is my biggest supporter and cheerleader. Thank you for believing in me and for being the best dad a girl could ask for. This is for you!

Xx Gabbie D.

www.ingramcontent.com/pod-product-compliance
Lightning Source LLC
Chambersburg PA
CBHW070844260626
47170CB00007B/2496